BLOOD
IN THE
CUT

ALEJANDRO NODARSE

FLATIRON
BOOKS
NEW YORK

This is a work of fiction. All of the characters, organizations, and events portrayed in this novel are either products of the author's imagination or are used fictitiously.

BLOOD IN THE CUT. Copyright © 2024 by Exit One Enterprises. All rights reserved. Printed in the United States of America. For information, address Flatiron Books, 120 Broadway, New York, NY 10271.

www.flatironbooks.com

Grateful acknowledgment is made for permission to reproduce from the following:

Lyrics from "All Make Believe," words and music by PinoGrillo, a.k.a. Francisco A. Pino, copyright © 2010 by PinoGrillo. International copyright secured. All rights reserved. Reprinted by permission of PinoGrillo.

Designed by Omar Chapa

Library of Congress Cataloging-in-Publication Data

Names: Nodarse, Alejandro, author.
Title: Blood in the cut / Alejandro Nodarse.
Description: First edition. | New York : Flatiron Books, 2024.
Identifiers: LCCN 2023049313 | ISBN 9781250326515 (hardcover) | ISBN
 9781250326553 (ebook)
Subjects: LCGFT: Thrillers (Fiction) | Novels.
Classification: LCC PS3614.O36 B58 2024 | DDC 813/.6—dc23/eng/20231030
LC record available at https://lccn.loc.gov/2023049313

Our books may be purchased in bulk for promotional, educational, or business use. Please contact your local bookseller or the Macmillan Corporate and Premium Sales Department at 1-800-221-7945, extension 5442, or by email at MacmillanSpecialMarkets@macmillan.com.

First Edition: 2024

10 9 8 7 6 5 4 3 2 1

This book is dedicated to my parents,
Fabio L. Nodarse and Dr. María Margarita Nodarse,
for being my first patrons, biggest supporters, and greatest role models.
Thank you for teaching me to love books as much as the outdoors,
and for seeing in me what I was unable to see in myself.
You are better parents than I deserve.
I love you.

And to

Cristina García, mi madrina literaria and fearless leader of the
Las Dos Brujas community.
Thank you for being a literary lighthouse to countless writers seeking
harbor in the storm-filled sea that is writing. This book exists because of
your kindness, guidance, and relentless generosity.

My city's not found in a bar
It's busy under the stars.
What clubs?
We party in our backyards.

—PINOGRILLO, "ALL MAKE BELIEVE,"
BREDCRUMBS

A dead hydrangea is as intricate and lovely as one in bloom. Bleak sky is as seductive as sunshine, miniature orange trees without blossom or fruit are not defective; they are that.

—TONI MORRISON, *TAR BABY*

I

HOMECOMING

1

THE HOUSE MIDBLOCK ON FORTY-SECOND STREET

The sun was a papercut on the horizon, light welling into the sliced sky like blood. Those early-morning beams scaling the horizon cast an incandescent glow on the roof and walls. It made Ignacio Guerra realize that he had never *really* looked at the house in which he was raised. He'd driven his 1969 Camaro ZL1 into the gated carport countless times. As a kid, he'd wrestled on the patchy lawn with his brother and cousins. As a teenager, he'd snuck in and out of his bedroom's lone window (he'd snuck girls in too), and hopped the backyard fence to get to the next block.

As Iggy stood sweating in the humid dawn, his worn duffel slung over his shoulder, he wondered how much his change in perspective had to do with him maturing and how much was the result of having spent the last three years in prison. Iggy had coldcocked a police informant who'd showed up at the dead end of that very block to set him up. Iggy had *just* handed him the oxy he'd been stealing from his mother's pharmacy when the guy had given the signal and cops materialized to grab Iggy's wrists and read him his Miranda rights. A sense of betrayal surged up his chest. He broke away from the officers' grasp and delivered a textbook right hook to the informant's temple. Those three seconds irrevocably changed things.

But it wasn't until *this* moment, at twenty-three years of age, that Iggy saw the house he grew up in for what it was: a cinder block rectangle with iron bars over the windows and shingles the color of smeared shit. Only the pink hydrangeas and rosemary that Mami had planted out front offered the faintest pulse of color or life.

Iggy doubted that the house midblock on Forty-Second Street was the place he'd call home. At least not anymore. He'd give himself the time it took to finish his cigarette before deciding whether to knock on the door or walk away.

Iggy blew smoke in the direction of his father's 2002 Chevy Tahoe, a hulking forest-green gas-guzzler that was parked at an angle in the driveway. A succession of fading stickers for the Republican presidential ticket snaked along the back bumper, a spot open for whoever the 2016 candidates might be. On the patch of grass between the car and the street, the recycling bin overflowed with beer bottles.

Iggy knew what all those dead soldiers meant and considered walking away right then. He flicked his cigarette onto the street and turned his back to the house. A car was pulling into the dead end. Iggy held his breath and wondered if it was Sofie. Brake lights flashed when it reached the guardrail. It wasn't her. The driver had mistaken the end of 42nd Street as a pass-through to 107th Avenue. Iggy closed his eyes at the memory of the dead end ablaze with blue and red lights.

Seth Baker, the confidential informant who'd posed as Iggy's friend for almost a year, didn't flinch when the cops came out of the cars parked in the dead end. When Iggy coldcocked Seth, three more cops came out of the hedges and jumped on Iggy. They rode him to the ground while even more cops shouted orders from unmarked vans. Some cops pulled his arms behind his back while others pinned his face to the asphalt with the barrels of their guns. Seth eventually recovered, wiped his mouth, and stomped on Iggy's head despite the fact that Iggy's hands were cuffed behind his back. Gravel then stuck to his sweaty face as they emptied his pockets onto the street. He tasted blood. A huge bag of pills lay on the sidewalk beneath the shadow of the basketball hoop that crowned the dead end.

Iggy shuddered. He focused on the soft hum of distant traffic, a murmur like a peaceful river. Grass crunched underfoot when Iggy cut across the lawn. The sun beat down on his back as his reflection grew in the wooden door's polish. A muddled blur stood before him when he reached the door.

He knocked and stepped away. The hinges swung outward because Armando Guerra insisted upon it when they first moved in. "No one's kicking in my door at medianoche," he'd said. When no one answered, Iggy tried peeking through the windows, but the blinds were drawn.

The air smelled like petrichor. But it was more than that. Nestled in each inhale was fresh-cut grass and ozone, the sweetness of the hydrangeas and woodiness of the rosemary. Mami had planted them because they reminded her of her childhood, of how her grandfather would pluck one or the other, depending on which route brought him home, and tuck the blossom or sprig behind her ear. At least the house smelled like home.

Iggy knocked harder. When no one came to the door, he got his copy of the house key from his duffel bag along with the lighter that Mami had given him on his eighteenth birthday. He was curious to see whether or not Armando had changed the lock. He slid the key in and turned it.

"Yo! Carlos? Pops? I'm home," he said into the small crack he'd opened. Cold air rushed past his face and the sweat on his neck tingled. "Mami," he whispered, looking for a sign that it was okay to enter the house. A shiver ran across his shoulders as if he were unfurling frozen wings.

Light from the kitchen spilled onto the tile floor and over a pile of bloated garbage bags. Heels poked through a bag of women's shoes like thorns. Armando Guerra had to be home; he never got into a car that he wasn't driving.

"Pops," Iggy called out. He stepped into the silence and closed the door behind him. Another pile of bags slumped against the coffee table, where an errant sleeve reached out from the smallest sack. It seemed to be pointing to a tumbled stack of magazines that cascaded into the skirt of a round table near the door. On that table, an army of picture frames assembled in tight rows saluted Iggy. Every family rite of passage—communions, graduations, birthdays, quinces, weddings, and baptisms—was memorialized there. A frame caught his eye. His cousins, Mauricio and Pedro, posed with their father, Lito, who died of a heart attack five years ago. Beside it was a yellowed photo of Abuelo Calixto standing between Armando and Lito when they first arrived in Miami from Cuba.

Iggy studied his father's face in the picture. He hadn't seen the man in three years, but he'd caught glimpses of him every time he'd seen his own reflection. Armando hadn't once visited Iggy or even come to the phone at any point when Iggy had called home. Not even in the early days. Over time, Armando had become more monster than man in the vague, obscure spaces created by absence and memory.

Even now, as Iggy scanned other frames for his father's face, Armando Guerra's image did little besides throw shade. In every shot, he looked at the camera the same way: shoulders squared, mouth slightly parted, head tilted down, staring through thick eyebrows as if he might, at any moment, take off at a full sprint and tackle the photographer into the next life. There was never a smile on his face, only a look of restrained contempt.

The framed faces felt distant, like ghosts from some other life haunting the present. Iggy studied a prom photo of himself and Sofie: he was stoic, his chin tipped up; she smiled brightly and rested her hand on his chest. Perhaps it was Iggy, having just re-materialized, who was actually haunting them now. The thought stung. The only eyes that didn't judge were Mami's.

Iggy stepped out of his Jordans and placed the shoes neatly by the door. The house was much smaller than he remembered it. He felt the cold tile through his socks as he padded forward in silence. In the kitchen, stacked dishes rose and slid into each other like collapsed buildings. The toppled heap spilled out of the sink, where dirty Tupperware containers cluttered the count-ers. By the looks of it, the piles of photo albums, bras, books, and bags of underwear had been out long enough that Carlos and Armando had nudged boxes and bags here and there to carve out spaces to step.

A fizz and tinkle from the back porch drew Iggy's attention to the door across from him.

He listened carefully to the clink of glass on tile. As Iggy opened the door, he closed his eyes for a moment to help them adjust to the outside brightness.

Armando Guerra sat on the porch steps with his back to the door. He was framed by two brick columns made seem-ingly thinner by the width of his back. A six-pack of Presidentes sweated beside him in the sun, their green shadows glimmering on the tile. Armando Guerra did not move.

"This is fitting," Iggy said. "Here I am, calling for you, and you're just sitting there with your back to me. You're consistent, old man. I'll give you that."

Armando straightened up but did not turn around. "¿Qué haces tú aquí, eh? What do you want?"

Iggy stepped out into the humidity. It clung to his skin. "So that's what you sound like," Iggy said, taking another step. "I'd forgotten your voice. It's good to see you too, Pops. No, really, don't get up."

Armando sipped his beer and wiped the moisture from his mustache with the back of his hand. "Go away, Ignacio." His hair was thick and dark gray, as if time had turned his head into a cinder block.

"I'm surprised you recognized me," Iggy said after a moment of silence. "I could've sworn I wasn't worth a memory to you."

Armando grunted. "You get fat like your brother?"

"Three years, Pops. You ain't seen me in three years. Turn around. See for yourself. You can't ignore me now." Iggy straightened up, spreading his legs like a fighter. He cocked his head back and flexed every muscle in his body so that when Armando Guerra turned, he'd know exactly who he was dealing with.

Armando snorted but remained motionless. Muscles still danced across the base of his neck and back, even as his shoulders sagged like a wet banana leaf that curled around the beer he held to his chest.

Iggy pictured Mami draped around those shoulders, hugging Armando with a smile on her face. He'd seen her do it a thousand times. The last time that Iggy and Caridad had spoken, Iggy promised that his eventual encounter with Armando would be calm and peaceful—*at least from my end*, he'd said. Iggy wanted to live up to that, if only this once. He'd given Caridad his word that he'd be patient and try to patch things up with his father. Iggy had even rehearsed his apology with her. But now Mami wasn't around to remind him of those words and Armando was inspiring a less penitent set of phrases.

Iggy shook out his fists, sighed, and closed the gap between them. He knelt beside Armando, but the distance between them remained inhospitable. A no-man's-land.

Armando's face was dusted with salt-and-pepper stubble. It didn't make him look old, only cold. He stared out at the yard through narrow eyes, the same look Iggy had seen in Armando's pictures. Iggy followed the line of Armando's hairy arm down to the beer bottle in his fist. His knuckles were raw and bloody. His shirt was spattered red. So were his pant legs. Even his shoelaces were adorned with gore.

"Why are you covered in blood, Pops? You lose a fight with a side of beef?" Iggy had once caught his father swinging away at a hanging slab of meat, so the idea wasn't that far-fetched.

"Why you ask stupid questions?" Armando spat back without hesitating. "I'm a butcher. I don't get to come home clean."

Iggy sighed. *Yeah, you do,* Iggy thought. *Just wash your hands and change your shirt.* Despite his promise to Mami, his patience was thinning. "You didn't even call me to tell me Mami died. You couldn't get over yourself for the *one* second it would've taken to pick up the phone and tell me what happened. I had to find out from the warden himself. And you didn't even wait for me to bury her?" Iggy turned his face, wiping at his eyes. He watched a lizard crawl down the brick column to his right. "My mother is dead. You took yourself out of my life. I'm not sure I have any parents left."

"You done? You finish your little speech?" Armando sipped

his beer and returned to scanning the yard for something they both knew wasn't there.

Iggy couldn't breathe. The void left by everything he'd just put out there started filling with anger. "That's all you have to say?"

Armando leaned forward. His chin edged closer to his chest, nestling itself in the sweaty hair that curled in tight wiry loops.

Iggy moved closer to Armando. Almost too close. He pressed his fists together so that they wouldn't fly when he spoke. "You know how hard it was for me to say all that? Do you?"

Armando said nothing. The silence grew. The day swelled with it. After another long moment, Armando tilted his head and exhaled a short burst through his nose. He intensified his focus on the tree line, eyeing everything through his eyebrows.

Iggy's knee hurt; he'd knelt for too long. The old man remained stone still. Iggy had nothing left to say, but he wasn't ready to leave, not just yet. He sat on the step beside Armando and joined in the old man's silence. Iggy's kneecap tingled.

"You been to the Marlins' new stadium yet? That shit looks like a space biscuit." Cold sweat rolled down Iggy's lower back and into the waistband of his underwear. "Maybe in a while, if we're all up to it, I'll take you and Carlos to a game." Iggy scratched at his lower back. "Miami Marlins. I like it better than Florida Marlins. Where is Carlos, anyways? Oh, and the Heat play the Raptors tonight. Game six. We should watch it." Iggy realized he was talking shit to fill the silence and stopped.

Armando polished off his beer, opened a new one, and drank.

"Well? At least tell me why your clothes are so bloody."

"I'm a butcher, Ignacio."

Iggy nodded. "You lost your temper. Took shots at a hanging slab of meat, didn't you? You got pissed and beat the shit out of a side of beef."

Armando spat on the grass at Iggy's feet.

Iggy looked up from the stringy glob of saliva. If anyone had spit at Iggy's feet at ECI, he'd have turned their face into a chunky red paste. "Fine. Where's Carlos?"

"Sabe Dios what your brother is doing. He's supposed to be studying."

Iggy nodded, surprised he'd gotten a response. "Dude's gotta work hard if he wants to follow in Mami's footsteps. Pharmacy ain't an easy thing to study."

Armando sniffled and drank deeply. "He's probably wearing headphones, drawing pictures on walls like a caveman instead of studying. He thinks he's an artist. I bet that was one of the little secrets the three of you kept from me." Armando's eyes welled up. He finished off the beer, then turned to pull a fresh one from the shade of the bougainvillea. Two birds landed in the tangle of branches.

"Secrets?" Iggy repeated. "What are you talking about, Pops? No secrets there. And what does it matter what Carlos does with his free time? What does that have to do with—"

"Me and your mother fought about you all the time, you know," Armando said. "You and money. 'How can I forgive him for ruining us?' I'd ask her. 'Because he's your son,' she'd say. 'Because we're not ruined.' She spent the whole day smiling after she got a phone call from you. I never understood her. I still don't." His slate eyes made him seem more iron than old. "And now you're here and she isn't. She promised she'd leave me if I didn't let you come back home. Looks like she kept her promise."

Iggy stood to shake the numbness from his legs. The back-yard seemed peaceful then, even if it was overgrown with ne-glect. Iggy slipped his hand into his pocket and rubbed the stylized *G* engraved on the lighter. "So now what? You saying I can't stay here?"

Armando scratched the scruff on his chin and looked up at an iguana scaling the fence at the end of the yard. He opened his mouth but abandoned whatever words formed on his lips. When he found new words, they came out slowly. "This is *your* fault. All of it."

Iggy said nothing, refused to take the bait. He was proud of himself just then for not escalating when everything in him told him to stomp Armando out. He decided to trust Mami's advice. Iggy turned to Armando and leaned in. "Look, all I want to do is get back on my feet and stay out of trouble. Mami said it was cool for me to come back. She said you guys were discussing it but that she'd make it happen. I'm gonna try getting my job back at Miami Mussel, so I can pay rent if—"

Armando Guerra tore a rumbling belch, scattering the birds in the trees. It ended with a long, acrid exhale that slapped Iggy's face. Armando reached down and opened a new beer, chugging half of it in one go.

Iggy slid to the side as the wind picked up the scent of mint and basil that still grew in Caridad Guerra's garden. "Look, we need to figure out how we're going to get along without—"

"¡Silencio!" Armando turned to Iggy for the first time.

Iggy stared back.

Armando tossed his beer bottle into the yard and pulled a cigar from the breast pocket of his guayabera. He brought it to his mouth and pinched the end between his teeth. "Listen carefully," he mumbled as he patted his other pockets. "I want to sit here y fumarme este cigarro and drink my beer." He found a disposable lighter in the same pocket he'd kept the cigar. "I have to get back to work soon y me estás jodiendo." The lighter clicked and sparked but failed to create a flame.

Armando's grief and anger had ravaged his face, but what worried Iggy the most was the realization that he was staring at some future version of himself.

Iggy straightened up. He rubbed the G on his lighter again. "I'm just saying that—"

"Let's get something straight here," Armando said, shifting back to the yard. "The only reason I'm going to let you in this house is because it meant something to your mother, que en paz descanse." He made the sign of the cross and kissed his fist. "I should have promised her you'd have a place to stay, for her sake, not yours. To honor her, you can stay here. But only for a week. Y va que chifla, okay? That's all you get." The cheap lighter spat more sparks. "And be grateful for the week."

Sadness swept over Iggy and wilted his shoulders as it settled. Embarrassment crept up behind his sternum but failed to become anger. "Look, I know it's not easy—"

"Are you deaf, mi'jo?" Armando asked, his eyes fixed on the distant palm trees. "I want silence, cojones!" He leaned forward sharply to accentuate the last word. He unclenched his fists and cupped the end of the cigar. A feeble spark sprayed the dried tobacco. Watching the old man fail miserably at lighting a cigar made Iggy angrier than it should.

"You know what?" Iggy said. "I don't need this shit. Keep your week. I'm leaving now." Before Iggy could go, Armando held up his beer. His arm was almost fully extended in front of him, as if he were toasting the iguana on the fence.

"For your mother," Armando said. He lowered the beer. "One week. Stay."

Iggy turned his lighter over in his hand. Mami hadn't been wrong about much, but she was wrong about all this. Any hope that he and Armando would get along died with her. She was a woman of deep faith, and since he could find nothing else to rely on, Iggy decided to believe that the week she'd bought him would help him figure things out.

Iggy squeezed the lighter. "Está bien," he said, turning away from Armando. "A week's all I need." He reached for the door handle. "And by the way, you shouldn't have kept your back turned to someone for that long. A lot can happen behind your back."

"Yeah?" Armando mumbled through the cigar in his mouth. He still hadn't lit the thing. "What are you going to do about it? Stab me in the back again? Sneak into the pharmacy and steal your mother's pills and sell 'em?" He waved Iggy away. "The pharmacy's gone, mi'jito. And so is your mother. Save your threats for someone else."

In two steps, Iggy crossed the porch and stood over his father. With one swift movement he popped open the top of his lighter and struck the flint. Armando's eyes darted to the flash of blossoming orange flame. Iggy waited, fire licking the air between them, until Armando used the flame to light his cigar.

Iggy closed the lighter. "No threat," he said. "Just a bad idea."

2

AZÚCAR PRIETA

A cold blast of air washed over Iggy when he entered the house. He stopped just inside the door to calm himself. He didn't feel like waiting for his eyes to adjust to the darkness again, so he opened the blinds and flooded the living room with light. He had one week to use the house for showers and sleep. There wasn't a reason to linger any longer. Grief and anger had made the old man colder and more detached than usual. Worse, he was reckless. And Iggy was one more bit of bad news away from going down that same path.

"Iggy?" Carlos's voice came into the hallway just before he did.

"What up, 'Los?" Iggy said.

Carlos drifted into the foyer with his mouth open like a little kid who'd found Santa leaving presents under the tree. "You're here."

"What? No hug?"

Carlos's feet slapped the tile as he took quick steps in Iggy's direction.

"I didn't recognize you," Carlos said. He took Iggy's hand and pulled him into a hug. Carlos's glasses dug into Iggy's collarbone. He released his hug, but Iggy held his brother for a second longer. "You're taller," Carlos said. "And thicker."

Iggy stepped back and gave his brother a once-over. Carlos was freshly faded. The baggy shorts and sleeveless La Carnicería Guerra T-shirt made him look like he'd just come back from playing ball. "You look the same, bro. The old man was wrong. Said you'd gotten fat."

Carlos adjusted his frames. "The old man's wrong about a lot of things."

"You hear any of what he said to me out there? How he spoke to me like I'm a jit?"

"A little."

"You were listening in the hallway?"

"A little," Carlos said, a half-moon smile scooping up the side of his face.

Iggy reached out and hugged his brother again. This time it was Carlos who held the hug a bit longer. Iggy returned Carlos's squeeze and eyed the piles of bags over the top of Carlos's head. "Then I won't give you the play-by-play of what just went down." He let go of Carlos. Seeing him felt like a stream of happiness was washing through the smoldering pit Armando had made of Iggy's mood.

Carlos said, "You know I tried reaching you when Mami died, right? I even went down there, but they wouldn't let me see you. It wasn't till I threatened going to the news that—"

"I know. Those prison idiots told the other Ignacio Guerra that his mom had died. Once they found out they'd fucked up, they threw both of us in the hole till they sorted shit out. I had no idea what the fuck was going on the whole time. Covered it up right quick. Made me sign all sorts of shit in exchange for early release. 'Compassionate release,' they said. Which is why I'm out now and not next week."

Carlos punched Iggy in the arm. "You being here, it doesn't feel real."

"I'm glad to see you too, kid. But why's the house such a fucking mess? Y'all donating Mami's stuff?" The thought of his mother's belongings piled unceremoniously against the donation door of a Goodwill splintered something inside Iggy. He wondered where her favorite T-shirt was, the one he'd bought her at FIU's bookstore when he'd flirted with going to college, the one she only wore when cooking aromatic food like arroz con pollo since the smell clung to clothing. He dropped to his knees and dug frantically through bag after bag. He vaguely registered Carlos calling his name. He clawed into the next bag. There was a hand on his shoulder and part of him wanted to maul that hand, but the shirt was finally in his fists and he pressed it to his face and inhaled deeply.

He held that breath. Mami was in the kitchen, wearing the shirt. Iggy had a pocketful of oxy he'd taken from her pharmacy the night before. He was meeting his boy Seth, who walked every Friday from FIU down 107th Avenue all the way to the dead end at the west side of the block to buy them. Iggy and Seth had hung out and talked cars for almost a year by then—Iggy had even invited Seth over to break bread—and he looked forward to the easy money and conversation Seth brought to the dead end. Iggy was happy that day. Mami had her hair up in a ponytail and he bent down to give her a kiss. She smelled like violets and saffron. "¿Quieres café?" she'd asked. "When I get back," he'd replied.

When the air finally burst from Iggy's lungs, it came out in shattered sobs that were barely muffled by the shirt. He pulled the nearest bag of his mother's clothes to his chest. He reached out again and again, pulling bag after bag until he was lying on a pile of Caridad Guerra's clothing. His sinuses were more swollen than that time he'd tried to blow his nose after being punched under the eye. Now he pressed Mami's shirt into his eyes so hard that the starbursts he saw became a field of white.

"Iggy?" A soft pat on his back. "Hey, bro. You're okay. It's okay."

In a lull between sobs, a metallic clink rang from the back patio. Iggy recognized the sound of a beer cap rolling across the patio tiles. Armando must have finished the last of his beers. Soon the old man would come inside before heading back to work—Iggy did not want Armando Guerra to find him crying over a pile of Mami's clothes. He feared what the old man might say, but Iggy feared his own response more.

Carlos must have had the same thought. He patted Iggy's back. "Listen. We're not donating anything yet. This is just how Mami left her stuff."

Iggy steadied his breathing and asked, "Why's it all spread out here like this?"

"She was moving shit from your room back to her old bedroom since you were coming home. Me and Pops, we can't bring ourselves to touch anything. It feels wrong, like we're disturbing her."

Iggy stood and wiped his face with the bottom half of Mami's shirt. "What was she doing in my old room?"

"Sleeping. Dressing. Reading. It's been like that for a while."

"They split up?"

Carlos raised his eyebrows at Iggy, a knowing look that said, *What do you think?* "They were working on things." He spread his hands out slowly as if smoothing a tablecloth. "That's what Mami said. You *know* I never brought it up to Pops. Outside this house, it was like nothing was going on. Mami *clearly* didn't tell you shit."

Iggy shook his head. "I always hated that about her. She'd poison herself with bad news instead of sharing the truth. No one would blame her for not wanting to be with Pops." He pictured his mother gliding through the house with boxes and bags, making space for him in ways Armando was unwilling to do. It made her presence in the room larger.

Carlos walked over to the back door and locked it.

"We can't leave her stuff out here like this forever," Iggy said.

Carlos stepped away from the door. The handle clanked, followed by the thud of Armando walking into the door when it failed to open. The door thumped as Armando pounded his fists into it.

Iggy moved to the kitchen island. A blade lay bare on a thick, solid slab of walnut used less as a butcher block and more like a cutting board. He tested the edge of the knife with his thumb. It slipped right through Iggy's skin. A deep red cherry swelled from the pad of his thumb. Iggy watched the red sphere fill the cut.

Carlos shook his head. "C'mon, Iggy," he said, gesturing to the now dripping slice, "you know better than that. The knives in this house are *always* sharp."

Iggy nodded. "Sharp tongues and sharp blades." He caught a glimpse of himself in the mirror across from the kitchen. The Miami Hurricanes shirt he wore was a sweaty mess, just like his return home. Iggy checked himself out more thoroughly. He looked angry. The mirror image of the word on his chest read I MAIM. Iggy thought it was fitting, given how he felt at the moment.

"Let him in," Iggy said.

The thumping grew louder. "Ignacio! Open this fucking door!"

Iggy sucked his freshly riven thumb as he walked past Carlos. He unlocked the door and pushed it open.

Armando stumbled in, a beer bottle swinging at his side. He looked from Iggy to Carlos, then back to Iggy. He scoffed. "One week," he said to Iggy. He reached the kitchen island and traded the empty beer bottle for his keys and knife roll.

The sound of the front door slamming shut boomed through the house. Iggy and Carlos walked slowly to the door and listened intently as the Tahoe rumbled to life.

"How many did he drink out there?" Carlos asked.

"Too many."

The Tahoe shot out of the driveway in reverse and screeched down the street.

They followed the sound of Armando's angry driving outside. The potential for a catastrophe behind the wheel lured them into the heat, made them crane their necks to see if they could catch a glimpse of the green behemoth making a left on 106th. Armando was out of sight by the time they reached the front yard.

"What the hell was that?" Iggy asked. "Since when does he drive that thing like it's the Camaro?"

Carlos shook his head. "Bro, nothing Pops does makes sense anymore."

Something flapped in the wind on the far side of the gate behind Carlos. Iggy looked over the long, sleek lines pressing against the inside of the car cover, its corner flitting whenever a gust blew. "There she is," Iggy said. He made his way to the gate at the side of the house. He opened it and stepped into the shade of the carport.

Iggy pulled the cover off the 1969 Camaro ZL1 and stepped back to take it all in. Even in the shade, Azúcar Prieta glittered in all her dark, almost-purple, pearlescent glory. "Fuck I missed this car." He balled up the cover and tucked it into a corner of the carport. A kaleidoscope of memories spun through his mind: Sofie beckoning him from the back seat, her long, tan legs leading up to his favorite smile in the world; Pops in the passenger seat, sweating over the instructions of the air-conditioning system they were trying to install; Carlos in the driver's seat, pressed up close to the steering wheel while Mauro and Dro drunkenly laughed their asses off from the back seat and Iggy, also drunk, stressed from the passenger seat over having to let his brother drive; Mami in the passenger seat, wind mussing up her hair the last time he'd taken her to lunch.

"I ran the engine once a week," Carlos said. "And I *might* have taken her cruising once or twice at night when no one was around."

Iggy took a glimpse at the odometer. "Looks like more than once or twice," Iggy said.

Carlos shrugged and smiled.

Azúcar Prieta was immaculate. "Did you have the car detailed?" Iggy asked.

"Two days ago," said Carlos. "Mami wanted her ready for the party we'd planned for the day of your release."

Iggy nodded, his eyes still on the car. "She looks better than I remembered," Iggy said as he walked around the Camaro. The ZL1's V8 engine corralled over five hundred horses beneath the hood. Iggy had restored her to her original condition, except for the Cragar rims and the paint job. She was a purple so dark that she looked like outer space on four wheels. "I'm surprised Pops didn't sell her."

Just as Iggy finished speaking, a memory sliced cleanly across his mind's eye. He knew exactly why Armando hadn't sold the car. Pops had been the only one in the family to have Iggy's back when he'd decided on the custom caramelized sugar color for the Camaro. Carlos, Mauro, Abuelo, Dro—even Mami—had all said that deep, deep shade of violet-blending-into-maroon wouldn't look good on the Chevy's muscular body. But Pops loved it, especially with the pearl finish adding such depth to the paint. "Like stirring café into sugar," he'd said. "You chose the right color, Iggy. She'll look sweet as azúcar prieta." And that's exactly what Iggy had been going for, the night's sky melting into the caramelo on Mami's flan.

"I honestly thought Pops would have had to sell her, you know, to pay bills or lawyer fees," Iggy said. He opened the door and the black interior shone, pristine as the day he'd restored it. The car smelled like hot cinnamon. Iggy figured that even the air freshener that dangled from the rearview was new.

"He mentioned it once or twice," Carlos said. "But I could tell he really didn't want to."

"Where are the keys?" Iggy asked.

A smile brightened Carlos's face. "I'll be right back."

Azúcar Prieta was the reason Iggy began stealing from Mami's pharmacy. The pills he'd taken and sold paid for parts and labor. If he'd stopped once he'd restored the Camaro, things would, without a doubt, be different.

Carlos returned with the keys, Iggy's duffel bag, and a book bag of his own. He tossed Iggy the keys.

Iggy slid into the driver's seat and closed the door. He felt powerful, like he'd donned a full suit of impregnable armor. The key clicked and the engine roared to life. The window rolled down smoothly as Iggy cranked the handle. He slid his hands over the steering wheel and inhaled deeply.

Carlos slipped into the passenger seat. He pulled the belt across his lap and strapped in. "Where are we going?"

"Buckle up," Iggy said as he put Azúcar Prieta in gear.

•   •   •

Iggy drove west by default. It felt natural. Before his arrest, if Iggy wasn't driving to the butcher shop, he was heading out into the Everglades. He loved how the emerald grass spread across the wetlands into an infinite horizon. Out there, deep in the Everglades, there were no houses. No roads. No people. It was a place beyond man's control, where the only laws were those of nature.

Not long before Azúcar Prieta had become his obsession, Iggy drove a 1985 Toyota SR5 into the heart of the Everglades so often that the truck practically drove itself. He'd sold it to a man visiting from California because the guy was a huge *Back to the Future* fan and wanted to drive Marty McFly's truck. Iggy had also sold it because the price was right, and because there were plenty of people in his family who had 4x4 trucks he could borrow when he wanted to hunt boar, gator, deer, or whatever was in season. He still had all his hunting knives, rifles, and bows, as well as his tents and lanterns—all neatly stored in the small shed behind the house. And the desire to fade into the endless green grass for days at a time was still there, even more so after his run-in with Armando.

But when Iggy reached the point in the road where he could either drive off into the Everglades or head toward La Carnicería Guerra, he made a left toward the butcher shop. Led Zeppelin and wind tore in and out of Azúcar Prieta's windows as they blazed down 147th Avenue, creating a harmonious disarray inside the car. Two of the books Carlos had brought with him fluttered open in the back seat. At a red light, Iggy reached behind to close them. One was a chemistry book full of chemical formulas that looked like chain-link fences. A sketch in bold graffiti lettering filled the pages of the other. Iggy snapped them shut.

Carlos pulled something out from his bag. "Take this." He handed Iggy a cell phone. "I couldn't afford a new one. I hope that's okay."

Iggy took the phone and stared at it. The backdrop was a picture of the garden out back. "This is Mami's phone," he said.

Was Mami's phone. She'd spoken to him on this phone less than three weeks ago. "Thanks," Iggy said, slipping it into his pocket.

"Here's one more thing." Carlos held out a balled-up fist. Iggy held out his hand. A shiny stream of black beads poured into Iggy's palm.

Iggy looked from the road down at his hand and back to the street. "Where did you get this?" Iggy asked. He closed his hand around the rosary. "You should have let the old man bury it with her." Iggy rubbed the beads. He could feel Mami's prayers still coating them. His hand tingled. "It's important to bury things right."

"Mami prayed for you with that thing every night. I thought it should be yours."

Iggy slipped the rosary over his head, carefully tucking it into his shirt. It smelled like pressed roses. "Thanks," Iggy said, returning his eyes to the road.

The drivers stopped at the red light with them were twisting in their seats to catch a glimpse of Azúcar Prieta.

"So, how's Sofie?" Iggy asked, unable to control himself.

Carlos shot him a look that said, *What do you think?*

"Forget I asked," Iggy said. He rolled up his window, and Carlos did the same.

They sat there in silence for a moment.

"She's fine," Carlos said. "She stopped by when Mami died. Said she got a new job about a year ago. Some big-shot real estate guy's assistant. She makes good money *and* the company pays for her classes at FIU, so yeah, she's fine."

Iggy nodded. "Good. I'm glad to hear it."

Carlos cleared his throat, and Iggy knew his brother was desperate to change the subject. Iggy hadn't seen Sofie in three years, but in that time, he'd thought about her every day.

"I'm not gonna bother her," Iggy said. "I know she's moved

on. Can't say I blame her. And for the record, I'm gonna try to do the same thing."

Carlos nodded.

They drove past Sedano's Supermarket. A pudgy, bespectacled man in a green bucket hat and orange safety vest gathered up shopping carts at the edge of the parking lot.

"Loqui's still working at Sedano's?"

"He never misses a day," Carlos said.

El Loquito del Sedano's was a figure whom the neighborhood had rallied around for as long as Iggy could remember. His developmental disabilities were serious, but they didn't prevent him from being extremely efficient at his job. Years ago, the supermarket's managers had allowed Loqui to reorganize the locations of the shopping cart corrals for customer convenience, and other shopping plazas had copied Loqui's designs. The market made sure he had plenty of water to drink on hot days, and whenever someone celebrated a birthday party, Loqui was always presented with a slice of cake wrapped in tinfoil. He even had a standing invite to any outdoor parties he walked by on his way home from work. Iggy found comfort in that.

Iggy made a right on Miller. A white cross stood sentinel on the corner. Bouquets of flowers were piled beneath it.

"This is where it happened," Carlos said as they rolled through the intersection where Mami had died.

Iggy wanted to get out and search the area, to examine the spot where his mother took her last breath. He slowed down but kept Azúcar Prieta moving. "I gotta know," he said with a touch of hesitation, "how'd it happen? No one gave me any details about what happened to Mami."

Carlos stuck a finger under his glasses and rubbed his eye. "She was crossing the street at night and got hit by a pickup truck."

The image of Mami with her hands out in the dark as a pickup barreled toward her flitted across his mind's eye. His rage was instant. Iggy closed his eyes, as if pinching them tightly could keep the fabric of his universe from becoming unstitched.

After a long silence, Carlos said, "And just so you know, the shop's not doing well."

Iggy nodded. "I'm not surprised. If Pops's current state is any indication of how the shop's doing, we're fucked."

"Yeah, he's definitely not helping. He's taking off in the middle of the night and showing up at like six a.m. covered in blood. Does it a few times a week."

"So instead of focusing on the shop, he's day drinking, then vanishing at night?"

"Yeah, sort of. I don't know what he does, but Mami didn't like it. He stopped for a bit before Mami died, but he's picked it up again. But it's not just that. Things in the hood have changed, bro. Not enough folks come in to keep us afloat. We're just not selling like we used to. And now that the Chop Shop is about to open, things are even more tense at work."

"The Chop Shop?" Iggy said. "What the fuck is that?"

"A new place opening up down the block from us. It's a restaurant with an in-house butcher shop. It opens in about a week. We're gonna pass by it in a little bit."

Things were worse than Iggy had imagined. The fact that La Carnicería Guerra wasn't doing well was bad news, almost as bad as the Chop Shop opening up on their block. But all that paled in comparison to an aimless, angry Armando who snuck out at night to do God knows what.

Iggy turned up the radio. Led Zeppelin's "If It Keeps On Raining" reached its chorus.

3

LA CARNICERÍA GUERRA

Calixto Guerra bought the building that would become his second butcher shop because he liked the lot on which it stood. He'd inherited his first shop in Santiago de Cuba when his father died. Castro's rise to power forced Calixto to abandon it, his hometown, and his island. This overgrown patch of land here in Miami would be the lot on which he built his own business and continued his father's legacy while seeding his own.

Power lines sagged above narrow grass fields on the lot's northern and eastern borders. The land beneath them was too narrow for new buildings, so the buffers ensured no construction would encroach on Calixto's lot from those sides. The southern and western perimeters were flanked by 57th Street and 148th Avenue, respectively. Calixto Guerra was happy that his lot was an island.

The building itself was a long rectangle that squatted on the southern end of the island. Floor-to-ceiling windows allowed light into the storefront from dawn to dusk. The open area behind the building was paved and enclosed by a tall cinder block wall topped with coils of barbed wire.

To ensure that La Carnicería Guerra stood out from the

strawberry fields, body shops, and self-storage units that, at the time, surrounded his new venture, Calixto had installed a long green pole on the southwest corner. Atop the pole he'd placed a white oval lying on its side, a sign on which the shop's logo, a green Old English G, looked out over the neighborhood.

Iggy drove toward the sign now. It looked like a giant sleeping water bird.

"Slow down," Carlos said. "I want you to see this."

Iggy took his foot off the gas. Azúcar Prieta coasted past AGL Aerospace and Villalobos Real Estate on the left; Magic City Cigars, Croqueta Queens bakery, Exit One Sporting Goods, and DVAnt Ink on the right. More businesses occupied the warehouses and storefronts that faded away from the main drag.

"There," Carlos said, pointing out his window.

The structure was a new construction, built to look like a Spanish ranch house you'd find in Coral Gables. Work vans were parked haphazardly in front of the columns that held up the terra-cotta entrance. Day laborers scrambled across the cobblestone patio they were laying.

Iggy leaned across Carlos. "So this is it, huh?"

"Yep, that's it," Carlos said, "the new kid on the block."

The white stucco facade reflected so much sun that Iggy had to squint. THE CHOP SHOP had been painted in red letters across the long window facing the street.

Carlos pointed to the building. "The owner's some trust-fund white boy from Boston who did a few semesters at UM and now thinks he's Born and Raised. Believe it or not, the fucking idiot has a mural of Che Guevara on a wall near the bathrooms. He's clearly done *zero* market research. I even went down there to introduce myself and the prick told me to get my Mexican ass out of his air-conditioning and back on the roof. The genius thought

I was a roofer. Do I look like I'd last even ten minutes in this blazing sun? I ain't tough as those dudes."

Iggy studied the new building and the army of workers crawling over it like ants. "We can't let that guy get a foothold in our hood, Carlos. We're all fucked if he does."

"I know. He's the first. And if *he* gets in, there'll be more like him buying up the rest of block. I've seen enough *urban revitalization* to know how that goes," Carlos said, putting air quotes around the euphemism. "It'll be a matter of time before we're driven out of our own hood. We'll be pushed out like those poor folks in Wynwood and Little Haiti. And have you heard about that company that's buying up and gentrifying everything off exit 1 bit by bit? We have a chance to stop that from happening here." Carlos pointed out the window once more. "Those aren't even wooden beams. They're some kind of plastic."

Iggy scanned the site again. "Wait, he tore down Mami's old pharmacy?" Iggy asked.

"Ma didn't tell you?" Carlos sounded shocked. "The pharmacy building is gone."

Iggy felt a wet red heat pumping through his chest. It was a ruthless version of the euphoric tunnel vision he'd experienced when he raced Azúcar Prieta back in the day, when he'd race other drivers through the Everglades for cash. *Launching a nuke*, they called it, since the race ended at HM-69, the old Nike Hercules nuclear missile base deep inside Everglades National Park. Iggy and Azúcar Prieta were famous for being undefeated in that treacherous race. Their legend had grown so much that drivers from as far as Virginia and Baltimore had wanted to come down in their Dusters and Impalas to go toe to toe with Iggy and Azúcar Prieta.

Iggy sucked in a deep breath and held it. If he let this venom run its course—if it reached his head and hands—he *knew* he'd find himself standing over the bloodied carcass of the Chop Shop's owner, his hands covered in cuts with no recollection of what happened, and he'd end up right back in prison.

How could anyone just tear down Mami's pharmacy, a building that meant so much to this neighborhood? How could this man just show up and indiscriminately change the energy and culture of an entire well-established area, with its own sense of pride and being and history?

As Iggy fought to calm down, he realized that he himself had already done some of that destructive work three years ago. He'd unknowingly laid the groundwork for this moment. By sinking his mother's pharmacy, he'd opened the door for someone to swoop in and buy the lot. It must have come as a shock to the business owners in the area to see the building get wiped from existence, erased and replaced after so many years of service to the neighborhood. It was a sign of what awaited them all should the economy turn on them.

And if Pops and Carlos hadn't been able to put away Mami's stuff, if they couldn't even move the bags of clothes she had left behind, what must the demolition of her pharmacy have done to them?

Iggy spotted a guy in a burgundy suit sitting at the window. His hair was so red that his head looked like a road flare. With that suit and hair, if the guy stood, he'd look like the missing exclamation point from the Chop Shop's window painting.

"That him? The one dressed like a lit match?"

Carlos looked at the man more intently. "Yeah, that's him, the red devil. Conner G. Harrison."

Iggy disliked the guy immediately. "He gives me Seth Baker vibes."

"Seth Baker?" Carlos thought for a moment. "The guy who flipped and snitched?"

"Yeah, the snake who betrayed me and sold me out to the undercovers." Iggy squinted. "When did you say this place opens?"

"Too soon. About a week."

"We got this," Iggy said, still glaring. He made eye contact with the redhead.

"*Now* you see what I was trying to tell you?" Carlos asked.

"We'll *definitely* do something about this guy and his fucking restaurant."

Carlos shrugged and shook his head. Iggy understood then that his brother had accepted the loss of Mami's pharmacy as part of his reality. Carlos was clearly sad about it, but he wasn't fighting to stop *that* reality from being *his* reality. "It is what it is, Iggy. What are we gonna do?"

Iggy's rage was clouding his judgment, so he focused on speaking calmly. "I don't know just yet. But we ain't goin' out quietly. I can tell you that. I'll figure something out." He put Azúcar Prieta in gear. "We'll send the devil back to hell. You have my word."

Iggy eyed the Chop Shop's owner once more. He punched the gas and Azúcar Prieta rumbled on.

Just past an overgrown ficus, La Carnicería Guerra came into view. It gave off the same warmth and charm that he associated with Mami's pharmacy. After all, she'd worked at the shop for the past three years, so if anyplace on this block still pulsed with Mami's energy, it was La Carnicería Guerra. Iggy was filled with an unexpected joy and a sense of nostalgia that settled something in him.

"Park on the side so they don't see us pull up," Carlos said. "We'll surprise the shit out of these guys."

Iggy stepped on the parking brake. He reached out and stopped Carlos from getting out of the car. "I'm taking over your morning shifts at the shop. You focus on your classes."

Carlos furrowed his brow in confusion. "¿Que qué? Say what?"

Iggy tossed his hands up. "You're done. The matter is settled."

"I'm done what? I can't be done at the shop."

"Don't make me repeat myself. You're done working the early shift." He tapped his own chest. "That's my shift from now on."

Carlos sat up. "What? So you're staying? But wait. Pops will lose his shit if he sees you here. And you haven't worked here in years. You don't know how things work or where anything is. Not to mention—"

"What, now you're trying to stop me from helping?" He waited a beat. Carlos stammered. "Exactly. Be quiet and listen. You just said that he doesn't come in until eight or nine anyways, so we'll never see each other. Even if he *does* see me there, I could just be hanging out with Mauro or Dro or Abuelo. And it's not like it's gonna cost him anything, so what does it matter?"

"I guess that could work," Carlos said, sitting up straight as the idea sounded better. "We could use another pair of hands. I'll still have to come in every afternoon to help out. You know, place orders and shit like that. But at least this way I'll be able to do homework. And sleep. You sure you wanna do this? Get up super early and take on all this mess?"

"I did three years in a prison. I'm used to getting up early. This ain't shit compared to that," Iggy said, pointing to the shop. "I got you, little bro. You're welcome."

They slid out of the Camaro.

"Wait here," Carlos said. "I'll make sure they're all in the back. Come through in like two minutes."

Iggy peeked into La Carnicería's window. No one was behind the counter. Iggy crept to the front door and opened it slowly. He held the bell tied to the handle so that it wouldn't ring when he eased the door shut.

The shop was as cold as Iggy remembered it. The light flooded in behind him, casting his shadow onto the refrigerated case that bisected the storefront. Countless cuts of meat were arranged in neat, well-lit rows. Each row had a handwritten sign indicating the cut and the price per pound. Waves of decorative lettuce separated each row, highlighting the freshness of the meat on display. He eased the door shut. Another of Mami's handwritten signs hung on the inside of the door. *Thank You for Stopping By.* Iggy traced his finger over the words.

He didn't anticipate how happy he'd be walking back into this place. He pulled his phone out and took a few pictures of the shop so that he could preserve this moment. The air grew colder as Iggy walked around the counter. Listening carefully for faint, distant voices, he pushed past the clear vinyl strips and into the back of the shop. The door to Armando's office was closed. Iggy hadn't seen the Tahoe outside. He was so excited to be in the shop that he almost opened the door to say hi to the old man just in case he was there. If Armando was checking the security monitors, he already knew that Iggy was there. Iggy knocked and got no response.

Voices floated over from the locker room. Iggy followed them through the remaining layer of vinyl strips.

The prep room opened up before him. Goosebumps covered Iggy's arms in the freezing space. Stainless-steel counters lined the walls and dotted the main floor. Half-processed prime cuts lay on a long metal island near the carcass chiller. Meat lockers hummed on the far side of the room as if they were practicing a Gregorian chant. Iggy tiptoed past a silent band saw. He peeked through the locker room door.

The scent of cigars and cigarettes carried through the slightly cracked door that let out into the shop's back lot. Iggy sat in a chair to the left of the door, beside a box of hoodies with the shop's logo. He crossed his arms and waited.

Someone was saying something about tonight's Heat game and Udonis Haslem when Mauro came in. He wore a white hoodie like the ones beside Iggy and his face was buried in his phone. Pedro came in next and went straight to the mirror across from the door. He perked up his faux hawk by pressing it between his hands and pulling it upward.

Abuelo Calixto entered, spotted Iggy immediately, and froze. His white mustache arched as his mouth opened. "¡Ave María Purísima!" he screamed. "Mira pa'llá por tu vida."

Mauro dropped his phone, cocked his fist back, and swept Dro behind him in one smooth motion. Dro all but disappeared behind Mauro. Abuelo still had his hands on his head. Mauro's ham-size fist lingered in the air. He blinked, unsure of whether to believe what he saw.

Carlos stood in the doorway, camera out. He said, "Surprise!" and snapped a picture of his stupefied family.

The three men descended upon Iggy and smothered him in a six-armed hug. They smelled like smoke and aftershave and spoke at once. Iggy answered questions as they came: yes, he'd been released due to a mix-up with his mother's death; no, he technically wasn't going to work at the shop full-time but he was taking Carlos's morning shifts but keep that quiet; he still needed a new job even if he was working here in the morning;

no, he hadn't done fucking steroids; yes, he was home for good, but he had one week to get out of Armando's house, it's a long story—well, not really; no, he didn't want to go to a strip club later; yes, he would take his foot out of the box of hoodies in which he stood.

"We miss your mom," Abuelo Calixto said. Something in the old man, perhaps his fluffy white mustache, made the sentiment soft as it was tender.

"Me too," Iggy said.

"You should have told us you were coming," Dro said.

"Bro, I found out yesterday that I was being released."

"Well," Dro said. "We owe you a party."

"We're having one a week from today," Iggy said. "We're turning that welcome-back party y'all had planned for me into an anniversary bash for the shop."

"No es mala idea," Calixto said. "We should celebrate what we have."

"True," said Mauro. "And today's the perfect day to celebrate. We're going out tonight."

Dro reached up and slapped a hand on Iggy's shoulder. "Yeah, bro. We gotta celebrate. You're back!"

"Not tonight," Iggy said, still feeling a bit overwhelmed from everything that had happened. Standing still and saying as little as possible had always worked when he felt this way, so he crossed his arms and said, "I gotta be here early tomorrow. And every morning until the shop's steady again."

Mauro and Dro looked at each other. "You know about the Chop Shop, right?"

"Yeah," Iggy said. "So what?"

"So *what?*" Mauro repeated the question as if doing so would highlight just how dismissive it was. "That fucking gringo's gonna fold us like an old wallet. No one's gonna come to our shop once that place opens, Iggy. You know how this city is. Motherfuckers will flock to whatever's fresh and flashy. We're old news, primo. We're the good wife who's gotten old, he's the sidepiece babysitter who gets all the action."

Iggy let that marinate for a bit. "We'll see who's fucked soon enough."

"That's what I'm saying, Iggy." Mauro folded his arms across his chest. "I don't think we're ready for that."

The shop was silent for a moment.

"Look," Carlos said. "I gotta handle a few things, so I'm gonna need your truck, Mauro."

Mauro tossed the keys. They arced into Carlos's palm.

"Thanks," Carlos said. "I'll be back in a half hour." He patted Iggy's back. "We're not ready for the Chop Shop. We're not ready for anything. But we got this." He leaned into Iggy's ear. "Before you start mopping, take a peek at the books. They're in Pops's office." And with that, he left.

Abuelo Calixto, Dro, and Mauro were all staring at Iggy.

"Carlos is right. It doesn't matter if we're ready. We're here now and there's nowhere to go but forward." Iggy picked up a mop. "We ain't gonna save this place by standing around, so let's get to work."

Iggy slipped into Armando's office. It smelled like Mami. Iggy spotted a bottle of her perfume beneath the security monitors on the desk. Piles of bills claimed most of the desktop's surface. Iggy wondered how long Pops had been keeping the books. When Iggy had been stealing pills from the pharmacy, the reason he'd been able to get away with it for so long was because of Pops's horrible bookkeeping skills. Pills went missing, but cash showed up in the register. The fact that none of the paperwork added up didn't seem to bother him, if he'd even noticed it.

Iggy sifted through the piles. He tried making sense of how much meat they ordered, where it came from, and how much they sold. The bills showed that the shop had been ordering less and less meat, and the shop's bank statements showed that less and less money was being deposited into the shop's accounts. The more Iggy dug, the more he unearthed.

Iggy had imagined that, as sure as the 'Glades are green, some questionable shit had been going on, but now he was able to confirm it. There were several two-thousand-dollar deposits that had been made in the last few months, and a single ten-thousand-dollar payment came in just after Mami died. Worst of all was the fact that Armando hadn't kept any reliable records. The shop was vulnerable to any kind of financial scrutiny, something that was totally plausible at any moment thanks to the fines and legal bills and state scrutiny Iggy had brought down on the family with his pill scheme.

Iggy slumped into Armando's chair. He couldn't at all blame the old man for feeling overwhelmed at every turn. But Armando should have let Caridad run the business end of the shop, especially since he'd done a questionable job of it before. He should have let Mami run the business's finances the way she ran the family's. But there was no denying that the infusion of several thousand dollars' worth of mystery money was keeping the shop afloat.

•   •   •

Iggy was mopping the prep room floor near the locker room when Armando came into the shop through the back door. He held a Styrofoam cooler that he unceremoniously tossed on the ground at his feet. It thudded just as the wind caught the door behind him, slamming against the wall.

The shop went silent. Dro and Mauro looked at each other, then down at the meat in front of them. Iggy leaned the mop he'd just wrung out against the wall beside the door. He bent down to pick up the cooler, but Armando stepped between it and Iggy. The mud squelched beneath Armando's boots.

Iggy stood. He stepped back to survey the trail of muck his father had created, but also to make space between him and the old man. Armando followed Iggy's gaze but seemed unperturbed by what he'd done.

"Welcome back," Iggy said.

Armando snorted and stomped toward Iggy. Mud spattered the freshly mopped floor. "Let me ask you a question. Why didn't you ask me to work here? What is it, huh? You think you better than us?"

"What? Where is this coming from?" Iggy straightened up as Armando got closer; if the old man was going to square him up, Iggy wanted him to get a good look at all of him. "What do you mean? I don't understand what you're asking. You just saw me mopping. I've been here all morning. Basically just worked an entire shift. And just so you know, I'm gonna be here mornings so that Carlos can sleep and go to class. He needs to graduate if we want a future. I think you're asking me why I didn't come to you for a job here at the shop, right?"

Armando shifted his weight to his back foot as if he might turn on his heel and walk away. "Yeah, that's exactly what I mean."

Iggy was glad he'd set the mop aside. If he'd had it in his hands, he would have cracked Armando across the face. "I have three years' worth of reasons why it never crossed my mind to ask you for a job. But you want reasons? Fine. Let's start with our little encounter earlier today. That's reason enough. You wouldn't even look at me. Then you told me I had a week to get out of the house. After that, you drove to work drunk to get away from me. And just now, when you came in, you looked like you were gonna throw up when you saw me. Want *more* reasons? Do you not see me here now, working like this is my job? And just to be clear, I plan to be here every single day until this place is back on track. It's not about my *wanting* to work here so much as it is my *needing* to work here." He almost added, *Because you've abandoned everyone.*

Armando looked down at the cooler. Iggy felt relief, like stepping out of the sun after being in its heat on a cloudless day. Armando stepped close to Iggy. His hands drifted up. Iggy resisted flinching. Maybe Armando was going to try to hug him. Or grab Iggy's face. Armando's hands would feel scarred and calloused. But maybe they'd be warm. None of this felt right. Iggy wasn't going to back away from it, even as the thought of pushing Armando onto the floor entered his mind.

Armando lowered his face into his hands and sighed. He dropped them to his side and shook his head. His eyes were hard when they reached Iggy's face, harder than Iggy imagined his hands would be. His crow's-feet made clear the disgust and impatience he felt. Iggy was tired of that look.

"You want to work here or not?" Armando asked.

"What's the job pay?"

"How much you want?"

"Enough to pay rent somewhere."

"I'll give you twelve. Cash. You do mornings, then work as many hours as it takes to keep things smooth around the shop. And so long as you're working here, you can stay at the house. If you want. Your mother, que en paz descanse, would have wanted that. But you don't get to question my orders here at work."

Iggy thought about it for a moment. Did he really want to spend his days in such close quarters with Armando? No. Fuck no. He didn't want to be anywhere near the man. But Iggy had a debt to pay. He owed it to Carlos and Abuelo and Mauro and Dro and to Mami's memory to make sure that the Guerra clan survived all this. It was on Iggy to interrupt the fall of dominoes that he had set in motion over three years ago. He owed it to his father, whether the old man knew it or not. And as reckless as Armando was lately, Iggy might even have to save the old man from himself.

"Fifteen an hour. And I'll ask all the questions I need to. How else am I supposed to understand what you're thinking? And another thing: You can't fire me. If we don't agree on something, we talk it through until it's settled. If something ain't clear, we talk it out." Iggy saw the objection forming on Armando's face. "We need to act fast, Pops. You're a good butcher. So do that. Handle the meat part. Leave the rest to me. I'm gonna do whatever it takes to make sure the shop is okay."

Armando considered Iggy for a second. "No. You don't get to set terms with me."

Iggy turned to the crew and pointed to the back door. "Please give us the room," he said calmly.

The crew looked at each other and nodded. "Smoke break," Mauro said, and they went out the back door.

Iggy turned to Armando.

"Look, if we don't do something big right now, La Carnicería is fucked. Selling top-notch meat in obscurity ain't enough to keep this place alive anymore. It's 2016, Pops. We adapt or we die. Our sales are trash and we lack vision. I don't blame you for that.

I heaped too much on you and Mami's plate when I got locked up. But right down the block there's a gringo with a butcher shop who's coming for our fucking throats. Seeing the place made that crystal clear to me. If we don't do something, that white boy's gonna run us out of our own hood." Iggy stepped closer to Armando and spoke in a hushed voice.

"But that's *nothing* compared to what's gonna happen if me and you keep getting in each other's faces instead of focusing on the shop. Carlos told me about your late-night disappearing acts. I bet that whatever you're doing will get you at least three to five. I might not have all the details, but I don't need them to know that whatever you're up to ain't good. I *also* know that whatever the fuck you're slicing is barely keeping this place afloat. I know the shop's books are so cooked that the smell makes my mouth water."

Iggy leaned forward and lowered his voice. "That shit's gotta end, Pops. Whatever you're up to, bury it. I know where that road ends." Iggy held his hand out to Armando. "Let me do my thing. I'll make sure that La Carnicería Guerra outlives us all."

Armando laughed. He laughed so loudly that it reverberated through the metal bowls near the meat grinder. Dismissive, contemptuous. His teeth were bared, eyes wide with mockery.

Rage gushed into Iggy's blood. It was in his ears. His mouth watered. If anyone besides a family member were laughing at him this way, Iggy would have driven his fists and elbows into their face until their skull was empty. He didn't trust his hands to not reach for Armando's throat, so he slid them into his pockets. The disrespect burned as it washed over Iggy.

Armando wheezed like a deflating balloon. How the fuck did Mami ever put up with this man? How did anyone? There was no way he was like this with other people. He'd have been shanked to death if he were. Iggy dared not look over at the knives on the counter.

Armando gasped for breath. He wiped his eyes with the backs of his wrists. "Look at you," he said, somewhat composing himself. "You think you're a good guy? You think you're Batman? Gonna swoop in and save the shop from the bad guys? I got more news for you, mi'jo. You ain't no good guy. Good guys are a lie, like Santa Claus and God. That little speech was nice, but it don't change nothing. Your hands don't get to be clean."

An aftershock of laughter rumbled through Armando. "And you think *you're* going to teach *me* to enseñarme a resolver? I survived communism and escaped, mi'jo. You've never lived through what I've lived through." Armando scoffed. "Besides, what did you think we were doing here, mi'jo? Resolviendo is all we've done since you fucked everything up." Armando crossed his arms as if punctuating his point. "Do whatever you gotta do, señor superhero. If we're lucky, we'll still have customers in a month."

Iggy reached for the mop. The handle was smooth in his hands. He stood the mop up and let it fall against Armando's crossed arms. "Say whatever you want. I don't give a shit. But remember this: You need *me*. I don't need *you*." Iggy pointed to the door from which the crew had exited. "The only thing I *need* is to help the crew however I can. Whatever it takes. If I ever *choose* to walk away from this place, it'll be because it no longer needs me. I'll let you know when that is." Iggy walked off, leaving Armando standing alone in the puddle of mud he'd tracked into the room.

Armando called out just as Iggy reached the door: "Hey, Mr. Whatever-It-Takes, don't go too far. You work for me now, remember? Get changed. We have a delivery coming soon."

4

BUTCHERS AND HUNTERS

The late morning blossomed as slowly as a puff of cigar smoke. Iggy stood in the shade of the green awning behind the shop, colada in hand. Abuelo Calixto's half-smoked cigar smoldered on a beer-can-turned-ashtray just outside the shop's back door. The smoky scent comforted Iggy. He missed Mami. It would have been great to ask her advice on everything that was going down, to show her he was doing his best to make good on his promise to her.

It felt nice to take in the new day and thaw out after freezing all morning in the processing room. As his body warmed up, his mind drifted. Something moved in the oak branches across the lot. Iggy squinted. A blue jay landed in its nest. It dropped a bug into the waiting maw of one of its chicks and flew off. The scent of fresh bread wafted over from Croqueta Queens. The palms that lined the inside of the wall shimmied their fronds like grass skirts. Even in the shade, sweat formed on Iggy's forehead. He tilted the Styrofoam cup up to his lips. The sugary dregs of his colada flowed into his mouth.

The shop's back door clanged open. Armando appeared in the threshold. He looked past Iggy to the wrought iron gate in the eastern wall. "They're here," he said. "Time to work." He pushed a button inside the doorway and the gate rolled open.

"Who's here?" Iggy asked.

Armando pointed at Iggy. "Stay right there and don't say shit."

A white pickup groaned into the parking lot. It bled from the tailgate like a wounded animal. Faded asphalt crunched under balding tires as the truck swept across the lot and settled in the back corner beneath the shade of the hulking oak. A tarp rippled over the truck bed, partially obscuring a faded Confederate flag sticker. Several blue jays took off from the tree.

Then a newer, larger black pickup pulled into the lot. The two sets of welding tanks strapped to the bed behind the cab clanked as the truck settled into the shade beside the old one. The four large cylinders must have made it tough for the driver to use the rearview mirror, especially with the gun rack that ran the length of the rear window inside the cab.

The door of the bloody truck swung open and a mouthful of gleaming teeth stepped out. As he stood up from the driver's seat, the man glanced at Iggy. It was a sly glance, barely noticeable. In that moment, Iggy knew the old man had served time. He was sun-scorched, skin looking like weathered leather stretched over broad bones. His long, too-black hair was pulled into a ponytail. A round belly poked out from the open vest he wore. Three animal teeth hung from a cord around his neck. Iggy placed him somewhere between Armando and Abuelo Calixto's age. His eyes were blue. They scanned Armando. Then he waved.

Two men emerged from the larger truck. The driver was a massive bearded white man so pale that he seemed translucent, like a shirtless puff of smoke in overalls. He was taller than Iggy and easily three hundred pounds. He'd pulled a cowboy hat low over his eyes. Stringy hair worked its way into his beard, a bushy thing that reminded Iggy of the Spanish moss that hung from trees in the Everglades.

The other man came around the truck to stand beside the driver. He was lean, shirtless, and bronzed. The gold chain around his neck was weighed down by a San Lazaro medallion. Shoulder-length silver hair framed a thick, well-kept gray beard. His eyes bugged out of their sockets as if trying to escape his face. A long bowie knife swung at the hip of his camouflage cargo pants, which were tucked into calf-high rubber boots. All three men were sweaty, their clothes blotched with grime and patches of dried blood.

Armando walked out to meet the men. Iggy stepped into the sun to follow him. Armando shot Iggy a narrow-eyed warning glare. Iggy heeded the signal to fall back and returned to his spot beneath the awning.

Abuelo Calixto came out of the shop and Iggy grabbed his shoulder.

"What's all this?" Iggy asked.

Calixto bent down and retrieved his half-smoked cigar. "¿Eso?" he said, motioning to the men. "Un bisnecito."

"No shit. What kind of business?"

Abuelo looked at his cigar. "You know how to restart a cigar when it goes out?"

Iggy rolled his eyes. He pulled his lighter from his pocket and held it out to the old man. "Who are these guys?"

Calixto smiled. "No," he said, motioning to Iggy's hand. "Sometimes, when your cigar goes out, all you have to do is tap out the ashes and blow it back to life." Abuelo slowly puffed into the stick. Smoke blossomed from its charred end. "¿Viste eso? No cutting, no fire." He exhaled a ball of tendrils that rose like a prayer. "Same thing happens in business. That's what we're doing today. Reavivando." Abuelo Calixto walked off into the sun.

"Rekindling *what*?" Iggy asked.

The five men met under the sun in the middle of the lot. They shook hands. Abuelo Calixto and Belly exchanged words. Iggy listened to whatever snippets of conversation the breeze blew his way. Abuelo asked Belly something about a kill he'd made the other day; Abuelo wanted to know how he got so close to such careful animals.

Belly crossed his arms and looked Abuelo over as if he were wondering why Abuelo was asking. After a moment, he let his arms swing down and he brought Abuelo close, as if to let him in on a secret. "I watch them for a long time," Belly said, rubbing one of the teeth around his neck. "I just sit there and watch and watch and watch. I study their patterns, the way they think. Eventually, they feel comfortable enough to get distracted. To them the world seems like it always is because I've always been there. The only thing that changes on that day is that I'm there to hunt, not watch."

Abuelo clapped the man on his back and they both laughed.

Belly put his hand on Armando's shoulder and brought him into his conversation with Abuelo Calixto with the slick ease of a car salesman turned politician. Bug Eyes smiled and said something to Armando. Armando nodded. Whatever he was saying to Pops, he was saying it in Spanish.

Bug Eyes's posture became loose, almost jovial. He spoke quickly, his stop-and-go cadence creating a rhythm of speech familiar to Iggy. It was the one Iggy grew up with. The words at the end of each sentence dragged as Bug Eyes constructed his next thought before speaking it. Even though he might be a swamp-ass, Bug Eyes was Cuban. There was no doubt. He was way too animated to be a white boy. The San Lazaro medallion was also a dead giveaway. That and the way his English was sprinkled with the singsong of Spanish.

The Guerra men were immaculate in their crisp white guayaberas. They were sweating but smelled fresh, like citrus cologne and mild deodorant. For once, Iggy thought, Pops smells like himself. Maybe Carlos was right. Maybe Pops just needed to be shaken out of his stupor. Even Abuelo Calixto's cigar smelled good compared to the other three. The hunters reeked in the fierce sunshine.

Iggy looked past the men. Behind them, the green and red welding tanks stood sentinel in the bed of the newer truck. Each tank had a WARNING: FLAMMABLE sticker haphazardly slapped onto it.

Beyond that sat the white pickup. The black tarp over its bed fluttered. A soft red trail dripped steadily from the truck bed onto the asphalt. It formed an ever-growing pool. "I bet they've got deer under that thing," Iggy whispered.

"Could be anything," a voice replied.

Iggy turned to find Dro beside him.

Dro motioned to the truck with his chin. "But I know they just came from the Everglades."

The shop's steel door clattered shut and Mauro flanked Iggy's other side. He rummaged through his pockets. "It's always a crapshoot with Orin. We never know what he'll show up with. Dro, you remember that day they showed up with some disco chicken?"

Iggy turned to Dro, hoping for a translation. "Disco chicken?" he asked.

Dro stared at Mauro with a mixture of disbelief and disgust. "Peacock. He means peacock. They brought like five peacocks."

"Got it," Iggy said, patting Mauro on the back. "I like disco chicken better." Iggy pointed to the men. "Orin's the one with the belly?"

Dro followed Iggy's finger out to the group of men. "Yup. He might look like he's Miccosukee, but that's because he's trying to pass as Native. He's actually just a white guy who came up with a gimmick to sell hunting trips and airboat rides to tourists. It's that white people magic trick. You know, the one where they dress and act like one of us until that reality becomes inconvenient, then switch back to white when they're done. If only that trick worked in reverse."

"I thought we were white," Mauro said.

"Only in Miami," Iggy said. "When I was up north, before they transferred me to ECI, I got grouped in with all the Latinos, which made sense since I'm Cuban. But it threw some of the guards off, like they couldn't imagine that I spoke Spanish."

Mauro shrugged. Dro nodded.

Iggy motioned to the other two hunters. "So who are they?"

"The big one is Wasilewski," Dro said. "El otro es Rana."

Trapped by the wall, Armando's deep voice rumbled around the lot. Iggy couldn't make out what he said. The perpetual thought bubble of cigar smoke that crowned Abuelo Calixto's head smelled sharper now. A tangy scent joined it. Metallic. The contents of the truck bed were ripening as it bled.

"They show up a lot?" Iggy asked. The more he studied Orin, the more he was convinced that his hair was dyed black.

"Not since Tía Cari died," Mauro said. He pulled out a pack of Lucky Strike. "She fucking hated these guys. She was sure that whatever your old man was doing at night had something to do with them."

"You know about that? About Pops's nighttime extracurriculars?"

Dro nodded. Without taking his eyes off the black tarp, he said, "Sometimes your pops wouldn't even go home after a night out. He'd come in here straight from wherever he'd been, covered in mud and blood. She'd come out from behind the front counter like a shooting star, close the door to the office, and lay into him. But you know how your mom was, elegant and anti-chusmería and shit. Never raised her voice. Not once. So we can only imagine *what* she was saying." He adjusted his glasses and smiled. "Or *how* she was saying it."

"This is the first time they've been here in a while," Mauro added. "They came all the time before that. Pretty much every time they've killed something. Rabbits. Turkey. Wild hog. Even quail. One time they brought a black bear, but who the fuck's gonna eat that shit?"

"Bro, they didn't bring the bear for us to process," Dro said. "They were just showing it off. I think Orin's got it stuffed and put it in his office."

"They ever bring horses? Or panthers? You know, any questionable shit like that?" Iggy asked.

"What? Panthers?" Dro scratched his eyebrow. "Why the fuck would they bring us panthers?"

"Or horses?" Mauro asked as he lit a cigarette. He exhaled a long stream of smoke. "That shit's illegal as fuck, primo. You know how much medication and steroids get pumped into horses? Shit'll poison you."

"That don't stop people from eating them," Iggy said. He gestured to the tarp. "At least it's legal for a butcher shop to process and sell meat bagged in the Everglades."

Mauro offered Iggy a cigarette. Iggy took the Lucky. This would have made a great bargaining chip just a week ago. He tucked it behind his ear and asked, "Does that guy wrestle gators?"

No one seemed to hear him.

Out in the sun, Wasilewski had yet to say a word. Armando pointed to the pickup. The men followed him into big oak's shade. Orin pulled back the tarp. The gamey scent filled the lot. A tangle of brown legs and antlers pressed into the middle of the bed. The sharp bends and angles resembled a small mangrove forest.

"Do these guys give you a gun-nut militia vibe?" Iggy asked.

Both Mauro and Dro nodded.

"Why's Pops working with these guys?"

Both Mauro and Dro shrugged.

Dro rubbed his eyes. "What I want to know is why they have to do this at this time of day. Couldn't they bring us their kill when it's cooler?"

"That's *unpossible*," Mauro said. "Gotta bring it while it's fresh. What kind of *asquerosity* would that be, bringing in sun-baked roadkill?" He took a drag from his Lucky.

Dro stared at his brother. "Nothing you say makes any sense, Mauro. You speak your own language. You mispronounce words, then blend languages to come up with this unholy mutant vernacular. Sometimes I wonder what goes on in that big-ass head of yours."

A heavy drop of sweat beaded just under Mauro's temple, where a sideburn would be if not for the skin fade. It trickled down the side of his face, following the path of his pencil-thin beard, and came to rest in his goatee. "But you understand me, right? Thought so. You're so *fustrating.*" He turned to Iggy. "Primo, you get lost when I talk?"

Iggy shook his head. "I *feel* you."

Mauro exhaled a long plume of smoke straight up into the air. "Anyways, like I was saying before I was rudely interrupted, I bet they just ran up on them *deers* with knives out and

fuácata"—he made a stab-and-slash gesture across his chest—
"straight up Rambo'd them shits."

Out by the truck, Armando was calculating. Iggy saw it in
his folded arms, scrunched brow, and downturned lips. Iggy felt
his own brow. It, too, was scrunched.

Armando pointed at something that Abuelo Calixto was noticing too. His hands swept over the brownish-red side of the
largest buck, a six pointer that had to weigh almost as much as
Mauro. They stopped at the gash in the neck. Armando exam-
ined the other deer in the same way. Stray beams of light filtered
through the leaves, highlighting different parts of the deer.

Orin pulled Armando aside. Iggy stared intently at the two
men, as if his visual focus could somehow help him hear them
better. Orin leaned into Armando. He said something Iggy
couldn't quite make out, but Iggy read the man's lips. "Next payment due Friday, partner. I need that money. But if you need some
extra help, let me know. I can always find something for you."

Armando looked Orin in the eye, his face impassive, and
nodded. "I'll let you know."

After a round of handshakes, Wasilewski and Rana moved
toward the newer truck. They drove away. Orin and Abuelo Calixto drifted toward the middle of the lot, but Armando wan-
dered over to the bleeding white truck. He stood at attention, his
hands behind his back, and stared pensively at the deer.

"Be right back," Iggy said. He shielded his eyes and crossed
the lot. The smell from the truck bed was much more potent. He
reached the open bed of the pickup and stood beside Armando.

Armando did not react to Iggy's presence. He continued ex-
amining the deer.

Iggy caught Orin eyeing him. Iggy looked over at Armando,
whose nostrils flared at the scent of pungent, bloody fur. Iggy

tasted the grainy iron twang that hung in the sweltering air. The smell was something he hadn't realized he'd missed. Fresh, edible meat. It wasn't unpleasant, just a lot stronger than the beef he'd been around that morning.

"What's going on?" Iggy asked.

Armando was silent, as if weighing something carefully. His arms were crossed over his chest like a rock ledge. He narrowed his eyes, just like in all the pictures on Mami's photo table.

Iggy wondered if Armando had any other expression.

"What are we supposed to do with this shit?" Iggy asked.

After a moment, Armando said, "Whitetail. They left them here so we can look them over."

The deer's eyes were still open and wet. The bodies were frozen in a moment of awkward motion. Iggy placed his hand on the doe's neck as his father had done earlier. He pressed down. The fur was warm, much thicker and bristlier than it looked. Only a few hours ago, she'd been alive, running or eating grass, doing whatever living deer do. Now she was here, jammed into the bed of an old pickup, bleeding onto the asphalt of a West Kendall butcher shop miles from her home.

Iggy motioned to the deer closest to them. "That was a sloppy shot. Look, low in the neck, just above the shoulder." Iggy traced the wide exit wound with the tip of his finger. "A failed double-shoulder shot." He moved around the truck and felt the rest of the doe's spine. It was intact. "She likely ran off after being hit. That shot didn't kill her. I bet they opened her throat to finish her off. Must have had the truck nearby. Otherwise, all this blood would be on the ground somewhere. And look, the other deer have similar wounds on their necks. They could have at least bled them out in the field before bringing them here."

Armando watched Iggy carefully. Measuring him. Searching. Judging him. He followed Iggy's gaze down the trail of blood to the sticky puddle at their feet.

"This is all kinds of wrong, Pops. We ain't in deer season. And look at that careless kill. What a *terrible* shot. What kind of hunters are these guys? How many times have me and you gone hunting in the 'Glades? How many times have we made a kill that sloppy? Exactly. Never. And do you know how fucked I'd be if a cop showed up right now?"

"No more fucked than how you left us," Armando said.

"This again?" Iggy plucked the Lucky from behind his ear. "We need to get you something new to talk about. That's getting old." He lit the Lucky and slipped his lighter back into his pocket. "And speaking of getting fucked, we need to make better choices about how we spend our time and money at the shop. These deer are bad enough, but you can't be vanishing on us anymore. Promise me right now that you're gonna quit that shit."

Armando scoffed.

"I'm serious, Pops. No more secret side projects." Iggy took a drag, then offered the cigarette to Armando.

Armando glanced at Iggy, then back at the cigarette. He took the Lucky from Iggy's fingers and dropped it into the bloody puddle.

Iggy decided not to take Armando's bait. Whatever was going down out here demanded that Iggy stay present and focused. It wasn't deer season. What would Mami say about these illegal kills? What might Sofie say? He looked over at Abuelo Calixto and Orin. They spoke with their backs to him.

Armando noticed the same thing Iggy did. He turned to Iggy and spoke quietly and steadily.

"I want you to handle these deer." He pulled a wad of bills

from his pocket and counted off six one-hundred-dollar bills. He stuffed the money in the pocket of Iggy's guayabera.

He pointed to the deer. "Tell him you'll give him three hundred for all three deer. When he says no, you slowly up the price until you reach an agreement. Two hundred each is probably what he wants, which is good since it's all I'll spend on these deer." Armando inched closer to Iggy. "But don't let him know that. You want to make him feel like he's won something, like he's in charge and he just got one over on you. When you give him the cash, make sure you look him in the eye. Make eye contact when you shake his hand."

"Why don't you just pay him yourself?"

Armando leaned even closer. From this distance, he smelled like rum and deodorant. "When they get back, have them bring the truck up to the door so we can start processing the deer. ¿Me entiendes? You wanted to help the business? You wanted to be part of this? Well here you go. Get to it."

Iggy nodded. Whatever this was, it wasn't good. But Iggy snatched the money out of his guayabera and jammed it in his back pocket.

Armando walked through the gate toward the Tahoe.

Iggy followed. "Why did Orin call you *partner* back there? And what did he mean by needing a payment next Friday? What have you gotten yourself into?"

Armando turned and looked at his son. "Don't worry about me," he said as he got in the car. "Worry about your own opportunities. Worry about these deer." He shut the door in Iggy's face, reversed through the gate, and drove away.

5

GAME RECOGNIZE GAME

Abuelo Calixto returned his cigar to the beer-can-turned-ashtray by the back door of the shop and disappeared inside, leaving only a wispy trail of smoke to mark his absence.

Orin stood alone in the middle of the lot, hands behind his back, seemingly waiting for Iggy.

Iggy eyed the faux Miccosukee. He was bathed in the shade of the oak. His old white truck kept bleeding.

Iggy's hunter intuition tingled. Something felt off, as if he was walking into an ambush even though he was standing still.

Orin took a step toward Iggy. "You must be thrilled to be out of prison. I bet it still doesn't feel real, the freedom."

Iggy eyed him from where he stood.

"Nothing feels legit," Iggy said. "Not me being out, not my mother being dead, not these out-of-season kills. Nothing."

Orin flicked his eyes at the deer, then back to Iggy. "I was a guest of Florida's penitentiary system too, you know?"

"That a fact?" Iggy asked.

"I did five years in Blackwater."

No shit, Iggy thought.

Orin said, "But what I remember most is my first day out; God, it was sweet." He exhaled slowly and leaned into the memory. "I was reborn that day, you know. A new man. Rehabilitated. With new purpose."

The words felt empty to Iggy, as if Orin had delivered those lines so many times that any genuine emotion had been rehearsed out of them. And the way Orin spoke just then made it easy for Iggy to picture him sitting on a gator's back, working a crowd, explaining *how* he's doing *what* he's doing while pinning the predator's jaws to his chest with his chin, arms out to demonstrate total dominance over the beast.

Iggy scoffed. "There's no rehabilitation in prison. You just become more of whatever landed you in there."

A smile crept across Orin's face. "That so? Then what did you become more of in there?"

Iggy cracked his knuckles. "A hunter."

Orin smacked his belly and laughed. "I want to talk to you about that. It seems you and I are not so different, young Guerra."

Iggy stared ahead. "How you figure?" he asked.

"You know exactly what I'm talking about. We both know what it's like to make it out. To get through to the other side. To survive. *Really* survive." He edged closer. "We know how to take care of ourselves and our own. We know that getting out in one piece isn't an accident. We paid a price to get out intact."

I ain't intact, Iggy thought. He was looking at his hands, the thick, blocky things that they were. He brushed one off with the other, then rubbed his palms together as if dusting them off. He looked over at Orin. They held eye contact until the deer drew Orin's gaze back to them.

Orin slowly moved toward Iggy. "I'm Orin Cypress, by the way. Calixto and I go way back, you know," Orin said. He circled to Iggy's left, coming at him from a forty-five-degree angle, the way one approaches a spooked horse. He never took his eyes off the deer. Iggy recognized the tactic. It was a deliberate approach to make sure an animal you were closing in on didn't feel threatened.

Iggy shifted to face Orin, keeping him between his shoulders, directly in his sights. "You from Abuelo's Everglades farming days?"

Orin stopped walking. He now stood between Iggy and the shop. "Oh yes," he said, slipping his hands into his pockets. "When your grandfather ran the shop, way before your old man was in charge, he used to buy lots of meat from me. I used to hunt all the time back then. Made almost as much money from selling kills to your grandfather as I did leading hunting parties into the 'Glades. Calixto bought everything.

"But now," Orin said, wiping his mouth with a blood-caked hand, "the economy has fucked us all. And that vexes me, young Guerra." He stepped again to Iggy's left.

Iggy shifted once more to face him. He could tell Orin wanted him to ask why. He didn't.

"Because all men are hunters. Not all are good hunters, but all of us hunt." Orin let the words hang in the air for a second too long. "And we all need the practice," Orin said. "I still lead hunting parties out there, of course, but I need to have a butcher shop to sell my kills to."

"And that's why we're here," Iggy said. "The deer: How much you want for them?"

Orin laughed again. "Straight to business, I see. If I didn't know any better, I'd think you were running that shop!"

Iggy nodded. A turkey vulture spiraled overhead, its wings motionless against the sun as if it were being held up by the rising heat of the day. Dark, big-bellied clouds raced toward the sun. There'd be rain. "Well?" Iggy asked. "How much?"

A minivan backed up to the lot's gate. The driver was clearly lost. The van stopped, turned in the opposite direction from which it had come, and rolled away slowly, but not before Iggy noted a family of stick-figure stickers taking up half the back windshield. *That's reckless,* Iggy thought, scanning the two adults, five kids, two dogs, and a cat arranged from tallest to shortest like some OCD police lineup. *Now everyone knows how many of your family members they need to tie up when they break into your house.*

Orin cracked his knuckles. "I'll be blunt: I could use a man of your talents, Iggy."

"It's Ignacio. And what talents? I haven't even been able to buy the deer you're trying to sell me. What talent do you think I have? And what makes you think I'd let you use it?"

Orin resumed his slow, steady pacing. The prolonged, spiral path Orin was on would eventually end with the two of them face-to-face. If Iggy let it.

"As you know, there are ways to get by, and then there are *ways.*" He looked Iggy in the eye. "Your father calls it re-solviendo," Orin said, pronouncing the word perfectly. "I have resolviendo of my own to do."

Iggy shifted again to keep Orin directly in front of him.

Orin folded his hands behind his back as he paced and spoke. "I'm having issues with trespassers on the land I rent out to farmers. Poachers, mainly. They come out to the different farms at night and steal our livestock. I need manpower to put an end to all that, and not just quantity. I need quality." He stopped pacing and faced Iggy. "I'd like to offer you some full-time security work, to keep an eye on my personal ranch."

"Personal ranch, huh? You got a compound out there?"

Orin continued his slow march. "My land is zoned as agricultural land. It's a buffer zone between the county and the Everglades.

By law, I can have one house per acre on it, so long as the land is used for growing crops and livestock," he said, waving his hand to punctuate the two reasons for him being in the Everglades. "Everyone gets along. But these fucking poachers threaten everything. My land. My men. Their respect for me. Even my horses."

Iggy held out a hand. Orin stopped pacing. "You've got all these folks living on your land, some of them hunters, and not one of them can catch some poachers?"

"Exactly," Orin said. "The other day, a couple of miles from my ranch, we found a butchered horse. Someone led her from her stall and flayed the meat right off her bones to sell it. Having someone like you around would put a stop to all that." Orin white-knuckled the teeth hanging from his neck. The gold horse head on his pinky ring caught the sun.

"So, you think people are selling horse meat? People are eating these horses?" Iggy asked.

Orin resumed pacing. "They are. And they do. And if there's one thing I can't stand," Orin continued, "it's a fucking thief. They disrupt the status quo, young Guerra. They unsettle and destabilize. They arouse a sort of panicked vigilance that disquiets the men I'm responsible for. It makes them . . ." He thought for a moment and finally said, "Uncertain."

That was the first thing Orin had said that Iggy found believable.

"You're saying it's not just the missing animals and the dead horse. It's that your men are *feeling* threatened."

"That's because we are *being* threatened." Orin pressed his knuckles to his eye and rubbed it. He sniffled, then cleared his throat. "What that bastard doesn't know is that most of us in the 'Glades are broken men looking to re-create ourselves. We've made mistakes. Paid our dues. Or at least we're trying. Even me."

"You still haven't told me what you *really* want from me," Iggy said.

"There's one trespasser in particular who's responsible for the sleepless nights I've had lately," Orin said. "He goes by Pico. He's methodically picked apart farm after farm in the past six months. We've shot at him, chased him, set dogs on him. We even had him surrounded once. And got nothing. He vanished like fog in the sun."

Iggy scoffed. "He's a man. Which means he leaves tracks. Which means he can be tracked. How come you and your hunters haven't caught him yet?"

"Open your ears, Guerra. This man's not normal. I have to catch him before he reaches my ranch."

Iggy nodded. He began to slowly circle Orin. "What else do you know about Pico?"

"Pico is a demon," Orin said. "He's got no pattern, leaves no tracks. He cuts across miles of open Everglades undetected in order to ruin my life."

"I would need something useful," Iggy said, still pacing. "Has he dropped anything? Said anything? There's got to be *something* you can tell me about him."

"Actually, there is," Orin said. "He posts these videos of himself online, destroying our tools, setting animals free. Here, take a look."

Orin walked up to Iggy and pulled a phone from his pocket. He smelled worse now that Iggy was in arm's reach, like accumulated body odor and fresh perspiration. The heat was growing, spreading over the day like a moist exhale.

Orin handed Iggy the phone. The image of a horse's head in a garbage bag appeared. Iggy tapped the screen. A gloved hand pointed to a desolate eye socket.

"That," Orin said, "is the latest of this motherfucker's posts."

Iggy shielded the screen from the sun to cut the glare. He watched footage of Pico slicing open a bag full of animal parts. His face was blurred to avoid revealing his identity. All Iggy could tell for sure was that he had long brown hair. Iggy couldn't make out what Pico was saying, but he couldn't help noticing that as he stood next to the horse's severed head, he picked up a shiny object. Pico studied it for a moment—it was clearly a knife—then he tucked it into his backpack.

Iggy raised the volume, and the man said, "This is why we can't turn a blind eye to this place. More and more horses are being stolen, and they turn up out here, like this. I don't know how else to say it—there's an entire exotic meats black market out here. The people who do this think that eating horse meat makes their dicks hard. Fucking morons. I'm going to take every single one of these slaughterhouses apart one at a time if I have to. Every single one."

Iggy handed the phone back to Orin. "You running slaughterhouses out in the 'Glades?"

"We're farmers. Ranchers. Hunters. We kill what we have to. There's nothing illegal about that." Orin took the phone from Iggy, looked at the screen, and scoffed. "We found out this guy existed because he'd post videos of himself posing as someone who wanted to buy meat, recording every detail about our farms. The authorities didn't give a shit about what he found because there was nothing worth reporting. No one paid any attention to him, so he started cutting our fences, stealing our tools, setting animals free. Now those animals are showing up butchered. And he has the nerve to say that *we* mistreat our animals."

Orin held up his hand, thumb and index finger millimeters apart. "I'm this close to setting out land mines and waiting for him with a bazooka."

Iggy laughed. "Who are you, Wile E. Coyote?"

"Far from it. Pico is the one with all the fancy gadgets. He used to fly a drone to spy on us until I shot it out of the sky."

Iggy shook his head. "That was a mistake. You should have let him spy so that you could track the drone back to him."

Orin snapped his fingers. "And *that's* exactly why I need you, Ignacio. Your instinct. Your vision. I know you used to hunt. That you know the terrain. Armando mentioned that you used to spend days out in the grass, showing up to the shop long enough to drop off a kill before vanishing again. You must be dying to get back out there. That's what I'm offering you: a place out in the 'Glades." He held a hand out to Iggy. "Come work for me."

Iggy looked at Orin's hand. "Why would I do that?"

"Because I'll give you a house on my property. Rent-free. All I ask in return is that you catch Pico. That's it."

"What are you gonna do with him if you catch him?"

Orin brandished a bowie knife from the small of his back and used the tip to dig at some dirt under his fingernails. "I'm going to show him parts of the Everglades he's never seen, the murky muck."

Iggy walked over to the deer in the truck bed. "Look," he said, "let's get these deer inside. The day ain't getting any cooler and I've gotta go find a job."

"I just offered you a job. I'll pay you five hundred dollars a week. Cash. And your rent will be free."

Iggy thought about it. If he didn't think Orin was shady, he might have considered it more seriously. Iggy didn't mind shady. It'd be hypocritical if he did, but he was trying to stay on the sunny side of things to make good on his promise to Mami. As it was, Armando's dealings with Orin already put the Guerra family at risk, if, in fact, that's who Armando was working for late at night.

"Tell me something," Iggy said, focusing on Orin. "When my old man goes out at night, does he go do some sort of work with you?"

"No," Orin said flatly. His reaction gave nothing away, but Iggy's gut said otherwise.

"Does he work *for* you?"

Orin shook his head, eyes on the deer. "What your old man *does* or *doesn't* do with his own time isn't up to me. Maybe you should ask him."

He was clearly deflecting. Iggy scratched at the stubble on his face. He didn't like that Orin had chosen to play semantics with him instead of answering his questions.

Iggy stepped toward Orin. "What do you want with my old man? What do you have on him?"

"Your father," Orin said. "He owes me a considerable amount of money." He pulled his phone from his pocket and dialed.

"How much is considerable?"

"You should ask him," Orin said. Someone answered the call. "We're ready." Not once did Orin take his eyes off Iggy. "It might be best if you think carefully about my offer, seeing as how we're all entangled."

"You don't wanna play this game with me, Orin. I don't give a fuck who owes you what. And if you think I'm gonna respond to veiled threats—"

Orin held his hands out in a gesture of surrender. "I don't want things to sour between us, young Guerra. Far from it. After all, we just met."

Wasilewski and Rana pulled into the lot in the large black pickup.

Iggy watched as the new black pickup settled in beside the old bleeding truck. Carlos appeared in the shop's back door, nodding silently to see how things were going. "I'm gonna pass on your offer."

"All I ask is that you come by the ranch tomorrow. Get a lay of the land. See what you think about where Pico might show up next. Take a look at the house I'm offering you. That sort of thing. If you see it all and it still doesn't work for you, then no hard feelings. Your father's debt will remain as is, but at least you've seen what I'm offering." Orin held out his hand again. "What do you say?"

Orin's hunters got out of their truck and made their way over to their boss.

Iggy looked at Orin's hand. When he was in prison, he never shook anyone's hand. He preferred bumping fists—less germs got passed between inmates that way—but he remembered how Armando had emphasized a handshake. *Fuck that*, he thought.

Iggy held out a fist for Orin to bump, but the old man palmed Iggy's fist and awkwardly shook it.

"I'm glad we're off to a better start," Orin said. "I like getting along with all my business partners." He squeezed Iggy's fist. "As for the deer, keep them. I don't want your money. Consider them a goodwill gesture." He motioned over his shoulder. "Rana and Lew will get them inside for you." He walked over to the black truck and slid into the cab. "Let me know what time you're coming over tomorrow," he said as he pulled out. "Armando has my number. Feel free to ask him for it." Orin disappeared into traffic, but Iggy could still hear the hollow clang of the welding tanks as he rumbled off.

Rana and Lew were already backing the white truck up to the shop, so Iggy slipped in through the back door and cut into the locker room.

"Abuelo," he called to Calixto, "do you know where Pops went?"

The old man did not look up from his deck of cards. "He's working," Calixto said. He dealt a few cards from the top of the deck.

"Right. Working."

A knock at the carcass cooler's metal doors was so loud it startled Abuelo Calixto. Mauro stopped the band saw and looked around for the noise's source.

"I got it," Iggy said. He threw on an apron and walked across to the freezing receiving room. He closed the door to the prep room behind him, then opened the doors to the outside.

The jumble of deer was just outside the door. Rana and Wasilewski stood on either side of the truck bed. Iggy wasn't sure what stunk worse, Orin's offer or the hunters. He nodded at them. Without a word, Iggy dragged three hooks along the rail up to the door. He used a skinning knife to open a slice behind the doe's Achilles tendon. Rana grabbed hold of the other leg. The two of them hoisted the doe up in the air and hung her on a hook using the slit Iggy had made.

They repeated the process with the next doe.

When it came time to hang the buck, Wasilewski shouldered the animal, walked it over to the hook, and drove it through the slit in its leg. The hunters got back in their pickup and drove off, blood still dripping from the open bed.

"What happened out there?" Carlos asked. His eyes were locked on the three swinging deer.

"A lot," Iggy replied. "I need you to find out everything you can about a guy named Pico." Iggy grabbed his bag from the locker room. "Grab your bag too, 'Los. We're going for a ride."

6

QUARTER MILE OF GHOSTS, TACOS, AND BEER

Caridad Guerra sat at the bus bench by the left turn lane on Fifty-Seventh Street. She looked up at Iggy when he slowed to a halt, then pulled the little boy at her side into her bosom. She raised the newspaper she was reading. Iggy accelerated away slowly, watching her sway in the heat haze through his rearview.

In the left turn lane on Fifty-Seventh, Caridad Guerra leaned back in the passenger seat of a silver hatchback. She argued with the driver while adjusting the AC vents. Her hair was dyed an unnaturally dark, impossible-to-ignore garnet that Iggy had always known as Hialeah Red. It was hastily twisted and held behind her head with a large claw clip. The ends of her hair sprayed out of the clip like a rooster's tail, which swung wildly as she yelled at the driver. She grew louder, audible even through the glass of her window. Caridad's hands picked up speed as she gestured. There was a lull in their conversation. She looked over at Iggy. She flipped him an acrylic-tipped finger as the hatchback took off.

Carlos leaned back in his seat. His right arm dangled out the window. "What's it like to be driving again?"

Iggy searched for a response. "I dreamed of this, you know. It's weird. Familiar, but new."

"I bet," Carlos said. "But you still haven't told me where we're going."

"We're going to make sure I have a job so I can make a living when Pops and I eventually go at it. I plan on working at the shop, but I've gotta have a plan B for when shit goes south."

"*If* it goes south," Carlos said. "Don't be pessimistic."

Iggy looked over at his brother. "I'm being realistic. Pops doesn't exactly seem reliable these days. Let's say he blows a gasket and tells me to leave. I'm out on my ass again. At least this way I have another knife sharpened, just in case."

Carlos nodded but said nothing. Iggy took it as a sign of agreement.

Azúcar Prieta slowed down as they approached the light on Bird and 117th. Caridad came walking toward them in an orange safety vest. She held up yellow Gatorade in one hand and mamoncillos in the other. Iggy waved her over. Her face had too many wrinkles. The light in her eyes wasn't there. Iggy bought a bag of mamoncillos even though some of the fruit was cracked and the fleshy meat had dried out. He thanked her and turned his attention to another Caridad coming out of the gas station up ahead to his left.

"Are you okay?" Carlos asked. "You look like shit all of a sudden. And you're creeping me out."

Iggy yanked a bandana from his back pocket and wiped his face. "You ever feel like the universe is fucking with you?"

"You mean like the way it killed my mom with a pickup truck only to have my ex-con brother come home and agitate my grieving alcoholic father while I'm studying for chemistry exams and all the while my family's butcher shop is falling apart and there's nothing I can do about it?"

Iggy blinked. "Sort of. I keep seeing Mami everywhere."

"Sounds like you need café."

The light turned green. Azúcar Prieta rumbled forward.

"I forget this is all new to you," Carlos said. "What's it been? Like two days?"

"I knew something was up days ago. But I found out she was dead yesterday morning."

"Fuck," Carlos said. "Has it hit you yet, that she only exists in our memory now? It will. I have a two-week head start on you and I still haven't gotten used to it."

The traffic light ahead turned yellow. Iggy shifted into third gear and accelerated through the light.

"Keep driving like this and you're gonna get pulled over," Carlos said.

Iggy shifted gears. "They can try."

A few blocks later, Iggy entered the parking lot of a warehouse complex and pulled up to Miami Mussel. It was the lone restaurant in an area that housed nothing but art galleries and warehouses. Just east of the Palmetto Expressway, the two-story gym-turned-seafood-boil-turned-grill-slash-craft-brewery was also the largest concrete cube in the Bird Road Art District. As far as Iggy was concerned, it was the heart of BRAD. He'd worked there before his arrest, taking orders between shipping-pallets-turned-tables. He was hoping that Herbie, Miami Mussel's owner and Iggy's mentor, still had his old job for him.

In his pre-prison days, Iggy had enjoyed not having to rely on the butcher shop and the pharmacy for work, and while he spent plenty of time at both and learned how each business operated, he brought in his own money. But now that he relied on La Carnicería Guerra for a living, he was bound to the shop in a way that was all-or-nothing. Joining La Carnicería Guerra, even for a single shift, meant that he was tied to Armando and whoever Armando did business with, a fact that left Iggy unsettled. He felt like he'd tied cinder blocks to his feet before heading off on a swim. Having a second job at Miami Mussel might help assuage that anxiety.

There was no parking, so Iggy double-parked.

"I don't wanna get down from the car," Carlos said. "I'll stay here in case it needs to be moved. Plus," he said, holding up his phone, "I wanna dig for information on Pico."

Iggy nodded. "Be back in a few."

Iggy opened Miami Mussel's door and was greeted by the space's Miami-meets-minimalism aesthetic. The walls were long, tall, and white, save for the massive wooden frames in which various 305-themed graffiti murals were featured. Iggy walked in and stood at the shellacked bar that spanned the room despite a thick column that cut it in half. Iggy signaled to a guy behind the bar, who, even though he was average height, looked like a giant stalking across an expansive liquor bottle skyline. The collection of bottles stretched and staggered up and back in rows that loomed over the bartender's head.

The bartender tied back his blond-tipped rope twists, revealing a glimmering stud in each of his earlobes. Iggy reached up and squeezed his own lobes; he needed to put his studs back in.

"What's good?" asked the bartender. He placed a napkin on the bar: the restaurant's logo, a clam with muscular arms jutting from its sides, adorned the bottom corner.

Iggy shot a quick glance at the name stitched into the leather apron. "What's up, Fabrice? I'm looking for Herbie," he said, drumming on the bar.

Fabrice straightened up and leaned away from Iggy. "You ain't from around here, huh?"

"I'm Born and Raised, Fab. Please tell Herbie I'm here to see him." Iggy did not break eye contact with Fabrice. "Let him know Ignacio's here." He slid a menu off the bar and studied it. Under EXOTIC TACO TUESDAY, Iggy read the descriptions of the various taco specials, including iguana, kangaroo, shark, wombat, and emu. He looked up at Fabrice, who still stood there as if someone had pushed the pause button on his life. "How well do these shark tacos sell?" He pointed at the pictures of the animals sticking out of taco shells. "How do you guys even get this meat?"

"You're Iggy Guerra?" Fabrice asked. "Damn, I'm sorry for your loss. Your mom was a special human being. Light made flesh. *Always* hooked me up whenever I bought meat at your shop."

Iggy blinked away a few tears under the guise of a yawn. "Thanks."

"And I hate to be the one to tell you, but Herbie's dead."

The words sliced through Iggy so perfectly that he wasn't even sure he'd heard them.

"Bro. Fab. Don't fuck with me. Today's not the day."

"No lie, bruh. Ain't *nothin'* funny 'bout that."

Iggy studied Fabrice's face, hoping he'd see some sign of this being a joke, but when Fabrice's eyes began to brim with tears, he had all the confirmation he needed. Iggy's breath left him, and he turned to look out the window. "Fuck me," Iggy said, dropping into a stool. "What happened?"

"Heart attack. Last week, right there in the kitchen. He was gone by the time the paramedics got here."

"Poor Herbie," Iggy whispered. "How's Magda taking it?"

"She's better. Staying busy. Still comes in. Cries in the kitchen like the grieving wife she is whenever she's in there, but she's tough." Fabrice poured Iggy a glass of water. Iggy took a sip.

Across from him on the bar lay a flyer advertising the grand opening of CCCV Brewery. Iggy pulled it to himself.

"CCCV?" Iggy studied the flyer. "Oh, I get it," he said. "Three-O-Five in roman numerals. Triple CV."

"That's my baby. I brewed out of my mama's utility room until Herbie tried my beer. Hired me on the spot."

"When's the launch?"

"We *were* gonna launch a week from today, but now that Herbie's gone, I don't know what I'm gonna do." He turned and looked into the kitchen.

Iggy remembered that Mami had planned a party for him on the same day. If only she were here, she'd know what to do. "Still, congrats. Getting Herbie to buy into something ain't no joke."

"Don't congratulate me yet. Like I said, I ain't sure we're even launching anymore. Shit's changed; between running the restaurant *and* the brewery, I'm spread thin. Real talk. And lots of people are moving out of the neighborhood, new people moving in. Our taco specials are keeping us afloat for now, but shit's insanely tight around here. The brewery was supposed to help the restaurant make more money, but I have a feeling that we're *all* gonna be fighting for our lives from now on: me trying to run this place *and* make beer while Magda helps when her grief lets her." He looked up at Iggy. "We're fucked, aren't we?"

Iggy pretended to study the mural beside him so he could wipe the tears from his eyes. "We're all a little fucked," he replied. The city was haunted, and no matter where Iggy turned, something was being taken from him or some specter was waiting to drag the past back into his path.

Iggy reached out and touched the wall. He recognized the swath of different-colored domino tiles, each carefully painted, zigzagging back and forth to form a mosaic of Antonio Maceo standing in front of la Caridad del Cobre. The dots on the tiles were carefully painted so as to give a realistic tone to his skin and clothing. Iggy remembered seeing a sketch of this piece in one of the notebooks in Carlos's bag.

"So Carlos did this, huh?" He was aware of what Carlos could do with a fresh wall and some spray cans, but he hadn't realized that his little brother had generated a body of work. When had this happened? Iggy thought about Carlos sitting in Azúcar Prieta, and he was proud and angry at the same time. He was beginning to understand that in addition to being family, Carlos was something else altogether, a person he'd have to get to know all over again.

Iggy ran his fingers over the spray-painted dominoes and admired the can control, the careful brush lines, the sharp edges on the tiles that looked like they could be plucked from the wall and used to start a game at any time. *What else hasn't he told me?* Iggy thought. Iggy stood and held his fist out to Fabrice. "I'm sorry for your loss. And for everything being up in the air." They bumped fists. Iggy took the flyer off the counter. "If it makes you feel any better, the shop's barely scraping by."

"That sure as shit does *not* make me feel better," Fabrice said. "Neither does that Chop Shop opening up on your block. Y'all ready for when they open?"

"It's opening whether we're ready or not," Iggy said, "but I don't wanna get caught slipping."

"I feel you," Fabrice said. "Sometimes that means just not giving up."

"Sometimes the answer is right there and all we gotta do is see it."

"I hope you're right," Fabrice said. "I could use an answer or two."

"We're gonna need more than hope, homie." Iggy tapped the picture of a pilsner on the flyer. "But for now, a beer will do."

•   •   •

When Iggy returned to Azúcar Prieta almost an hour later, he found Carlos waiting for him with his phone and tablet out. "You took your sweet time," Carlos said.

Iggy slipped into the driver's seat and said, "Did you know Herbie died?"

"What? No fucking way. What happened?"

"Heart attack last week. Poor guy."

"No shit," Carlos said. "How's Magda?"

"In shock. But that dude Fab is holding it down somehow. He gives off good vibes. And he makes good beer."

"Yeah," Carlos said in an absent-minded manner that made it clear to Iggy that he was still processing Herbie's death. "Fab's passed by the shop a few times. His meat suppliers don't always have what he needs for the week." Carlos looked at the phone in his lap, unable to remember why he'd had it out in the first place. "I'm sorry about Herbie. I know you guys were tight."

"I don't know what I'm gonna do now, Carlos. Herbie was my chance at stability. No one's gonna hire a felon. How am I ever gonna set myself up now?"

Carlos eyed Iggy. "Maybe things will go well with Pops at the shop. Maybe you don't need a backup job."

Iggy just stared at his brother, brows arched, with a look that said, *Are you really that dumb?*

Eventually, Carlos held up his phone and he tapped the screen. "I got some good news. I think I know who Pico is." He handed Iggy the phone. "Check it, this is the latest post by this crazy white guy who runs through the Everglades breaking into farms, trashing them, then setting the animals free. He thinks he's Batman for horses. This post here got him in the news again."

Iggy watched the video. It was the same footage that Orin had shown him of Pico finding a horse head in the Everglades. Iggy watched as Pico picked up the head. He scrubbed forward. He watched him find a shiny object and slip it into his bag. He watched as he pulled other animal parts from various garbage bags. "If you're wondering where this meat ends up," Pico said, "check your neighbor's stomach." Iggy paused the video.

"Bet you didn't know that went on in our backyard," Carlos said.

"Abuelo Calixto used to hang with some crazy-ass guajiros back in the day. They did all sorts of weird shit out there. They eat shit like horses porque they think que les para la pinga."

"Who the fuck eats horses to get a hard-on?"

"Lots of folks eat horse. They say it tastes like beef." Iggy tapped the screen. "Worse than that happens out in the Everglades. There's a black market of nightmares out there. This guy's gonna get himself killed if he keeps messing with those swamp-asses out there."

"If they catch him, they'll crucify him. No doubt," Carlos said. "But check it, there's more. I found a lot more shit. He might blur his face, but he talks too much. Repeats the same phrases. And he posts a lot of pictures and videos too. Leaves a huge digital footprint." Carlos pulled up the research he'd done. "Here, see for yourself."

Iggy skimmed through what Carlos had dug up. Articles, property records, financial statements, various permit and license filings. They all clicked. All they needed to do was put a face to the threat.

When he'd read his fill, Iggy pointed to the screen and

handed Carlos his phone. "How did you get all these specific details? It makes sense that he's filthy rich—how else could he afford to launch a one-man war against all those farms? But if all this information is floating around online, how come those swamp-asses haven't disappeared this guy in the Everglades?" Iggy pulled out of the lot and slipped into the stream of traffic.

Carlos scoffed. "Bro, gimme some fucking credit. It's not like I found it all neatly wrapped up, ready to go with a pretty bow. I sussed it out. I dug around. Connected the dots. It's like a puzzle, only without the image on the box cover. You slowly assemble what you find, and the picture grows and becomes clearer."

"Impressive," Iggy said. "How'd you learn to do that?"

"I'm resourceful, Iggy. And I like solving puzzles. But, if I'm honest, I learned a lot from this guy in my chemistry class last year. He was trying to impress a girl in our lab group. She went away for the weekend and wouldn't say where, but posted this picture she took from her plane's window, and since he knew the airline and that the plane was flying over a coast, he cross-referenced that with the position of the sun and the flight radar and texted her the flight number and the city she was going to. She blocked him on social media and sat on the other side of the room for the rest of the semester."

"Creepy. And interesting. Stay away from that guy," Iggy said.

"He left the program," Carlos said. "Last I heard, he'd gotten locked up for cybercrimes. Or gunrunning," Carlos said.

"And good riddance," Iggy said. "You don't need to be hanging out with people of questionable moral fiber."

"Says the guy doing business with Orin Cypress. How'd that little meeting behind the shop go? Shit looked intense."

Iggy pulled up to a red light. "Orin flat-out told me that Pops owes him money. So whatever the old man's doing when he leaves the house, my guess is that he's working off some debt to Orin."

A Porsche Cayenne pulled up beside him.

"That's not good, Iggy," Carlos said. "Orin ain't someone to fuck with. He gives off that militia, gun-hoarder, doomsday-prepper vibe."

"He offered me a job. Said he wants me to work security for him. To catch Pico the next time he sneaks onto his land."

"You're not going to work for Orin, are you?"

The driver of the Porsche, a clean-cut, side-part banker type in the midst of a midlife crisis, lowered his window. "What year is that?" he asked, motioning to Azúcar Prieta.

"Who knows," Iggy said to Carlos. To the guy in the Porsche, Iggy replied, "She's a '69."

The Porsche revved its engine. "Wanna run it?" the guy screamed as he revved the engine some more.

Iggy hung his arm out the window. "You have no idea what you're asking for. Go give your wife her car back. You couldn't beat me if *you* were in a 993 and *I* had four flats and no steering wheel." Iggy turned to Carlos with a devilish smile. "This fool thinks we're in a stock '69. He has no idea what a ZL1 is."

Carlos shook his head. "I don't think you should do any of it."

Iggy couldn't tell if the look of disgust on his face was directed at the clueless Porsche-driving pretty boy or at the thought of Iggy accepting Orin's job offer.

"Definitely don't work for Orin," Carlos said. "And don't race this loser. He's in a fucking Cayenne."

The asphalt shimmered with reflected heat. There were barely any cars between this light and the next few lights.

Iggy tapped the gas. Azúcar Prieta snarled. "You can't always do the right thing."

The light turned green and Iggy punched the clutch and shifted into first in one smooth motion. They burst forward like cannon-shot. When Azúcar Prieta purred again, Iggy shifted into second. The cars and buildings around them became blurred streaks. They slipped into third gear. Azúcar Prieta's continuous growl was a life-affirming heartbeat that Iggy needed. He wove through lanes as if traffic was standing still, which, as far as he was concerned, it was.

Acceleration and adrenaline surged through them as Iggy and Azúcar Prieta danced.

Iggy didn't need to shift into fourth gear. The Cayenne was so far enough behind him that it soon became a distant memory. Iggy and Azúcar Prieta clicked as if he'd never stopped driving her. He'd learned to listen to her long ago. He knew how to ask for what he needed, and how to give what was asked. Each shift of the gears told Iggy exactly what he needed to know and brought forth a new burst of speed that separated Iggy from the world around him.

Iggy downshifted and turned in the direction of the house mid-block on Forty-Second Street, but something was off; something just didn't sound right. Iggy turned to Carlos, who he'd forgotten was in the car. "Listen," he said. "You hear that?" He downshifted. There it was again, the same faint, grinding hum.

Carlos sat motionless in the passenger seat, his head glued to the headrest. "The only thing I hear is my heart trying to escape out my ass, you maniac. Slow the fuck down!"

"Fine. But listen." Iggy downshifted again. The hum pulsed through the air once more.

Carlos leaned forward in his seat. "I don't hear anything."

"Listen," Iggy repeated. The nagging hum returned.

Carlos shrugged. "Yeah, I hear that, but it's super faint. Maybe it's that you just haven't driven Azúcar Prieta in three whole years."

Iggy glared at Carlos. He punched the gas. Azúcar Prieta leaped forward and blazed through an intersection. "But *you've* driven her," he said. "Now open your ears. Listen."

Downshift. Soft purr from gear to gear, then the hazy hum.

"Yeah, it's there." Carlos thought for a moment. "Could be a worn shaft. Maybe the shaft end spacer."

"If we're lucky." Iggy downshifted. He turned his ear to the sound. "But if the shaft is damaged, that could lead to a mess of problems." The gears in Iggy's mind turned, searching for the possible cause of this automotive heart murmur. "Might just be a bearing too."

"Look, just stop driving like a fucking demon and we'll take her to Swanson's once things calm down around us."

"Let's go right now," Iggy said, patting the dashboard as if soothing Azúcar Prieta.

"We can't. He's moving the shop to Homestead, just off exit one."

"I guess we'll wait. I don't trust anyone else," Iggy said. "Except me." He gave Carlos some side-eye. "And maybe you."

"I hope you're not blaming me for that hum," Carlos said. "I swear I only drove her to keep her in shape. We can take a look right now if you want."

"We don't have time. And I don't blame you. These things happen. Besides," Iggy said, turning left on Forty-Third Court, "it's nothing catastrophic. She'll be fine if I treat her right."

7

SQUASHING LEFTOVER BEEF

Heat rose steadily from the earth even as the afternoon's humidity lifted. Iggy and Carlos drove through Westchester with the windows down. The scent of freshly mowed lawns mingled in the air with the promise of evening rain.

Iggy reached his block. The car slowed to a crawl at the intersection of 106th and 42nd. Iggy glanced at Sofie's house. Her driveway was empty. Her windows were dark. Iggy accelerated into the turn and drove on. There was no hum to be heard from Azúcar Prieta. Iggy glanced once more through the rearview at Sofie's house. When Azúcar Prieta pulled up to the Guerra house, the Tahoe was parked in the driveway, again at an angle. Iggy backed into the carport.

The waning sun bathed the house in a golden light that made it impossible to imagine how cold it was when Iggy opened the front door. Goosebumps covered his arms. Something sizzled in the kitchen. Iggy sniffed at the air: onions and garlic sautéing in olive oil. His mouth watered. Iggy slipped out of his Jordans and nudged them neatly to the side. He made his way to the kitchen with Carlos in tow.

Armando Guerra stood at the far side of the granite island. His sleeveless, ribbed undershirt strained against his chest. He stood there, arms and shoulders shot through with veins, as he dried his hands with a rag. A blood-red slab of beef rib oozed onto a long wooden block in front of him. Armando dropped the rag and slipped his wedding ring back on.

They watched as Armando unrolled his knife kit. Light glinted off the row of blades that Armando studied. His hand paused over an empty slot and shot back to the beginning of the row like a typewriter. He scanned the knives again. "No," he whispered. He began pulling out knife after knife, double- and triple-checking the handles as they piled up on the counter. When all his knives were unsheathed, he placed his hands flat on the counter and sighed.

"What's wrong?" Carlos asked.

Armando shook his head. He let out an exasperated sigh. "I can't find my butcher knife."

Carlos spread the dozen or so blades out over the counter. "Which one?"

"*The* one," Armando said.

Carlos looked up at Iggy. He pushed his glasses back up his nose. "The bone handle with the G carved into it?"

Armando grunted.

"You lost *the* family knife?" Iggy asked.

Armando and Carlos looked up at Iggy.

"What?" Iggy asked. He shrugged. "I'm sure it'll turn up."

"Retrace your steps, Pops. Where'd you use the knife last?" Carlos asked.

Armando looked up at the ceiling. "Let me think," he said. He returned the knives to their proper slots in the roll. "I think the last time I used it was . . . a lo mejor fue . . . never mind," he said. He picked up a knife with a curved blade. "It'll come to me." Armando began swiping the blade along the length of a butcher's iron. The steel sang and grew sharper. Armando's eyes drifted down to the empty slot in his kit as if he'd forgotten that a sharp blade danced inches away from him.

Iggy pulled out his phone and searched for the video Carlos had shown him earlier, the same one Orin had played for him when he was trying to convince Iggy what a threat Pico was. He fast-forwarded to the part where Pico found a gleaming piece of metal and slipped it into his bag.

Iggy tapped Carlos and handed him the phone. He played the bit where Pico placed the polished object in his bag and watched for a reaction. Carlos's eyes widened. "Nah," he said. He handed the phone back to Iggy. "There's no way."

"If you say so," Iggy said. He slipped the phone back into his pocket. He looked over at Armando, who was staring right at him.

"Pops," Carlos said. "You're bleeding."

Armando looked down at his hands. The blade he was sharpening slowed. He put down the honing iron and tightened his grip on the knife. He held up his arm. A stream of blood crept down his left forearm. Armando turned his wrist and the veins running under his skin bulged. He studied the red trail as it snaked from the heel of his hand to his elbow.

Iggy handed Armando a paper towel. *The old man is slipping,* Iggy thought, as he watched him dab the blood on his arm.

Armando glanced at the empty slot in his knife roll, then at Iggy.

Iggy was certain that the old man remembered exactly where his knife was. At least now Iggy was starting to understand just how deep the shit Armando was in went and that Armando was barely keeping himself from going under.

Carlos rolled up Armando's knives. "So what's for dinner?"

Armando picked up the iron and resumed honing the blade. "Take a guess?" The knife clacked across the butcher's iron.

Carlos pushed up his glasses. "Eggplant Parmesan with a butternut squash puree and a side of steamed veggies."

Armando snorted. "What's the most important thing to remember when you're working with fresh meat?" He looked at Iggy. The steel and iron blurred.

"Are you asking him or me?" Iggy asked.

"Depends on the cut of meat," Carlos said.

"No, mi'jo." Armando tossed down the butcher's iron. "It's your tools. Your knives." He thrust the butt of his knife under Iggy's nose. The long blade curved up the length of his arm.

Iggy uncrossed his arms.

"Take it," Armando said.

Iggy held out his hand, and Armando slapped the handle into it.

Armando leaned forward and slowly slid the slab of meat toward Iggy. He nodded toward it like a lion nudging its cub toward a fresh kill. "Show me how this cut is prepared." He inched closer. "¡Dale! Show me."

"What the fuck is this about, Pops? Why are you being like this?" Iggy asked. He looked at Armando, at the knife, then down at the slab.

"Yeah, Pops," Carlos said. "What's up? You know he can process rib eye."

Iggy's mouth watered. The iron bite of raw meat danced in the air along with the sautéing garlic and onions. It was all tangled into every inhale. Iggy sniffed again, chasing something that slipped away. The long knife in his hand was hungry.

"Go on," Armando said. "Cut the fucking meat."

"I get it," Iggy said in a calm voice. "Since it was my idea to work at the shop, and since I'm the one who'll be butchering the beef, Pops wants to make sure I still know how to use a knife." Iggy checked the knife's blade. It was perfectly honed. "I got this," he said.

Iggy braced the slab and slowly worked the blade through the sinew. The cut was clean. A two-inch steak came off the end of the beef rib. Good amount of fat. Nice marbling. The knife steadily sliced steak after steak off until the rib eye slab was gone and eighteen steaks lay in its place.

"Is the cast-iron ready?" Iggy asked.

Armando said nothing. He pushed off from the counter and leaned back beside the sink. Armando pointed to the skillet and scratched his chest. The thick curling hair sprang back into place over his sternum.

Iggy placed three steaks on a plate. "Pat these down and hand them to Pops so he can start browning them." He turned to Armando. "You want the fat trimmed off the rest of these?"

"You didn't wash your hands," Armando said.

"The fat stays on," Iggy said as he went to the sink. He washed up. Without turning his back to Armando, he dried his hands and gave the old man another paper towel. "Press that into your cut. It's bleeding again."

Iggy handed Carlos more paper towels. "Dab the rest of those and put them away." He went over to the silverware drawer. As Carlos patted the steaks down, Iggy took a handful of forks and knives over to the dinner table.

Armando didn't take his eyes off Iggy as he set the table. Iggy could feel the old man scanning him like an X-ray. It made him self-conscious, like he was somehow setting the forks down wrong or these weren't the right place mats. Iggy double-checked each setting. Of course they were right. They'd been the same his whole life.

Armando peeled himself off the counter and slapped the granite island.

"Bueno," he said. "Time to sear some meat."

Iggy was so hungry that the sizzling steaks sounded like a soft standing ovation. At the table, he and Carlos sat across from each other. Carlos eyed the empty place setting to his right, and Iggy knew what he was thinking: he missed Mami.

Iggy studied his steak knife. He ran his fingertip over the edge of the blade, calmly surfing the miniature waves on the serrated blade. Iggy felt a heat, like someone staring.

Carlos caught Iggy's eye. He raised his eyebrows and pursed his lips as if to say, *Well, this has been fun.*

Iggy rolled his eyes. He threw in a little shrug that said, *Been through worse. It's all good.*

Carlos tilted his head. Hands turned palms up, meaning, *Yo, come on! This is, like, a lot, bro. No jodas.*

Iggy flattened his brow and widened his eyes. *Chill. He's coming.*

Armando appeared over Carlos's right shoulder. In one hand he had a plateful of steaks. In the other, two Presidentes. He set the plate down on Caridad's spot, eyeing the fork and knife Iggy had set. Iggy wondered what the old man might say about it. Armando took a swig from a beer and sat down.

Iggy and Carlos exchanged a glance. Neither face moved.

Armando leaned forward and poked at the biggest steak on the plate, trying to dig it out from beneath the other slabs of meat.

"Pops," Iggy said, breaking the silence, "I got a question I need to ask you."

Armando glared over at Iggy. He stabbed his steak, leaving his fork planted in the meat like a conquistador's flag. He took a long pull from the sweating green bottle. He glanced at Iggy, then at Carlos. "About what?"

"The shop's books. Your knife. And Orin. And this guy named Pico."

Armando thumped the bottle down, reached for the fork, and dragged the steak onto his plate.

Iggy tracked the trail of red juice that dripped from one plate onto Mami's place mat, then to Armando's plate.

Carlos reached for a steak, his fork out as if to spear it. Armando held his hand over it, then forked it himself and plopped it on Carlos's plate. The steak steamed. Carlos lifted it up and passed it across the table to Iggy.

Iggy's salivary glands ached as he reached for the plate.

"No." Armando's voice was a low boom. He glared at Carlos, pointing to the plate. "The only people who'll eat this food are the ones who respect that it got here."

Iggy leaned forward. "I respect the fact that these steaks got here. I just wanna know *how* they showed up? What, exactly, did they cost us? And I ain't necessarily talking about money. I wanna know why the shop's books couldn't tell me where the money that keeps the shop afloat is coming from?"

Armando slammed his hand down on the table. The beer bottles jumped in place, clinking against each other. They were sweating. Armando looked from Iggy to Carlos to the empty seat where Caridad used to sit.

Iggy thought the old man was about to burst into tears. Armando's grief and sorrow had bled into panic and rage, pushed him to the brink of violence. That, at least, offered him some familiarity, some sense of control. Iggy knew Armando was pissed

that Iggy knew what he knew. The old man was rattled. Threatened, even. No one stood up to Armando Guerra, and it showed.
Iggy thought at first that the old man was just beating his chest,
trying to intimidate everyone back into their place within the hi-
erarchy so that Armando would feel like he was at the top again.
But this wasn't just that. This was a pain so deep it had bottomed
out and had nowhere to go but up and out. Iggy had seen this before, a man on the edge of oblivion: the eyes brimming with tears,
the jaw clenched so tightly that molars might crack, the look of
being lost in loss, fighting not to drown. In Iggy's experience,
posturing saved a lot of bloodshed because folks had their place
and stayed in it. Armando wasn't sure of his place anymore, and
Iggy figured that it would be a mistake to think this rage was all
bluster.

Iggy ignored the plate that Carlos held out. Carlos stood and
tried to place the plate down in front of Iggy, but the slab of meat
slid off the edge. It hung in the air for a second like a bloody
comet, then hit Iggy's plate with a wet smack.

Armando shot to his feet. He reared back, fork tight in his
fist, and brought it down on the steak. The fork skewered the
meat, then bent under the force. The impact shattered the plate.

Hot meat juice sprayed over Iggy's lips and neck, peppered
his shirt, water glass, and Mami's tablecloth. Iggy licked the
greasy splatter off his lips. His eyes never left Armando's.

Bits of white ceramic stuck to the bottom of the steak when
Armando snatched it up. It clinked as he slapped the meat onto
his plate. Armando smoothed back his hair, looked down at the
steak, and sat back down. He breathed heavily.

"No," Armando said, his eyes still on the plate. "No!" The
steak was so raw that it bled when Armando cut into it. He stuffed
a red chunk in his mouth and stared down at the far end of the

table. He chewed, mouth open, until he bit down on a shard of broken plate. Armando spat the white ceramic triangle onto the table. It came to rest on the remnants of Iggy's empty plate. Iggy stared at the shard. It was bloody and spit-covered. He identified with it. They'd both been chewed up, spit out, and tumbled their way back to where they'd come from. A venomous snarl raked Armando's face like a dare. Iggy stared off over Carlos's head toward the far end of the kitchen. Armando dragged his forearm across his lips to wipe the blood from his mouth and kept eating.

Iggy leaned back in his chair. He folded his hands behind his head.

Armando gripped his fork. He leaned toward Iggy. Head tilted. Eyes narrowed. Mouth open. There was blood in the corner of his lips. There was no mistaking the look of impending violence.

Iggy and Carlos sat quietly as Armando Guerra ate two of the three steaks he'd seared. The last one sat cold on Carlos's plate.

When Armando finished eating, he pointed to Carlos's plate with his fork. "Eat it or I will."

Carlos looked at Armando, down at the steak, then up at Iggy. Iggy nodded softly.

Carlos cut the meat with slow, hesitant strokes.

Iggy knocked on the table twice and got up slowly. "I'm gonna dig through the fridge for leftovers."

Armando stood. His chair screeched along the tile.

Iggy waited.

Armando grabbed a fresh beer and walked over to the sink. He dropped the dishes onto the pan with a clatter. "No beer," Armando said to Iggy. "Don't touch my beer." He paused on his way to his bedroom. "Check the labels on the deliveries tomorrow. Some are coming from a new supplier." He stared off into space as he drank from the bottle. "And if the side is not perfect, don't sign for it. If it's not perfect, make 'em load the rack back up and take it away. Take only the best." Armando disappeared into his bedroom.

Iggy and Carlos stood motionless. They listened for Armando's movements, for any sign that he'd come back out. When it felt safe, Carlos slid his plate across the table. "Here," he said. "Get to it."

"I don't want it," Iggy said. He slid the plate back to Carlos. "But good looking out."

Iggy opened the freezer. After a minute of shifting through pizzas and frozen vegetable bags, Iggy found a small Tupperware full of yellow rice. He maneuvered the plastic container out of the freezer and cracked it open. Arroz con pollo. He'd dreamed of the stuff for years: sticky rice, juicy, lemony chicken thighs—Mami only used thighs—peas, saffron, and red peppers. His mouth watered all over again. He held the container out to Carlos. "Mami make this?" he asked.

Carlos turned in his seat, half a steak still on his plate. "Yeah," he said.

Iggy nodded. He placed the container in the microwave and set the timer for two minutes.

•   •   •

After dinner, Iggy got in bed without brushing his teeth so that he could enjoy the last meal his mother ever cooked a bit longer. He lay in bed, watching as the ceiling fan pushed cold air around the room. He hoped it would carry him off to sleep. The three-hundred-pound side of beef that would be delivered to La Carnicería Guerra floated in Iggy's mind. Blood-red and bone-white.

The cuts came apart slowly: foreshank and brisket pulled

away from the chuck; shore plate slid off from the short loin and rib; sirloin and flank jettisoned the round. The nine subprimal cuts then exploded into forty smaller cuts that La Carnicería Guerra could sell. Iggy worried that if the Chop Shop managed to take their customers, the meat he processed would sit perpetually on display in the refrigerated case. That was assuming that Armando got his shit together and didn't bring the shop down around himself and everyone else.

The ceiling fan stirred the air so that it smelled like Mami. He still tasted the arroz con pollo's saffron finish. This didn't at all feel like his old room.

•   •   •

Iggy awoke with a beam of moonlight shining directly into his eyes. It was 1:56 a.m. He was crying. His eyes burned. He'd dreamed about Mami. She was fishing stars out of a pitch-black ocean and dropping them into her apron pocket. The more stars she collected, the more faded she became. Iggy tried running up to her to tell her not to fade away, but the black water began swallowing him as he got close to her. Yet that hadn't stopped Iggy from trying to reach her. When the water had swallowed everything but his head, she lifted his face and kissed him between the eyes.

"What do I do, Mami?" he'd asked her. "Tell me! Don't leave! What do I do about Pops? And Carlos! I'm afraid, Mom. What do I do? Please don't leave me again! Please!"

She had turned his face into the water and whispered, "Despierta, mi vida," into his ear. "Wake up, Ignacio. Wake up."

Iggy still felt like he was drowning. He slid out of the moonbeam, out of his bed, and out into the night. After pacing through Mami's garden for ten minutes, Iggy sat on the unlit front steps of the house rolling a cigar between his hands. It had rained at some point while Iggy slept, and it looked like there was more to come. The air was cool and fresh, but the ground was hot. Petrichor filled his nose. It mingled with the scent of rosemary and hydrangea when the breeze blew. Iggy's face ached where his mother had touched him in his dream. He looked for the moon but found nothing but storm clouds churning in the sky.

It began to sprinkle. The soft patter soon became a downpour. Iggy didn't mind having to huddle beneath the overhang—it was nice to be just outside the downpour's reach. *When it rains*, Iggy thought. He knew he should try to go to sleep again, but after that dream, he wasn't going to get any. Might as well enjoy the rain and the relative safety of the overhang he'd huddled beneath.

The wet street was smeared with reflected light. Cars in the distance washed across Bird Road like waves, sucking and stretching sound as they came and went. Iggy wondered if he was imagining this moment, if he'd wake up in his cell staring at the support bars of the bunk above.

The cigar he'd plucked from Armando's humidor was rich. The wrapper was flawless, smooth and tight as skin. He could almost smell the sun in the tobacco. Iggy sparked his lighter. The flame kissed the cylinder's end just long enough to toast it. Iggy bit down on it and, barely holding it to the flame, puffed gently to nurture an ember. He clicked his lighter shut and puffed the cigar again. When the ember glowed evenly, Iggy coaxed the first full puff of smoke from the cigar. It caressed the inside of his mouth.

Iggy's exhale blossomed. The sinuous tendrils twirled and kinked as they rose above his head, where they clustered into a ghostly bouquet of roses. He thought of Sofie. Iggy looked down the block toward the dead end. The porch light at Sofie's house was the only one on at that end of the street.

Iggy became aware that he was moving toward her house when brakes screeched on Bird. The rain had stopped, and Iggy had stopped moving. He'd reached the mouth of the dead end without realizing it. The red door beneath the porch light waited.

What would Iggy say when he got there? She had warned him that if he kept doing whatever he was doing to make all that money—even if he *was* using it to help her and her mom because her brother was locked up—she'd never speak to him again. "I don't need another jailbird in my life," she'd said.

And now, here he was. Lost and desperate. What if he knocked and no one answered? Or worse, what if she peeked through the window, saw him, but didn't open the door? Iggy had called Sofie once from prison. He'd practiced his apology for weeks. He'd gotten as far as "Sofie?" before she'd hung up. He understood what that meant and never bothered her again.

But what if things were different now that he was back? Should he honor that unspoken agreement they'd made three years ago? The streetlamp behind the basketball hoop flickered. His cigar had gone out.

The gate squeaked when Iggy pushed it open. He couldn't bring himself to step through. The last time he'd seen Sofie, she'd been peeking through the blinds. She'd watched the cops pin him to the asphalt with the barrels of their guns. They pulled his arms behind his back. There was gravel stuck to his face. Seth Baker was kicking him.

They had emptied his pockets onto the street. A bag of pills and a rubber-banded roll of bills lay on the sidewalk beneath the basketball hoop. She'd probably put it all together by the time he'd been shoved in the back of a cop car. She'd glared at Iggy and shut the blinds.

Iggy had yet to shake the look on Sofie's face that day. He

knew that she'd never trust him again. He knew back then that
there was no doubt that he'd not only ruined his current family
but his future one as well.

Now his armpits were drenched. He smelled like a smoldering explosion. Iggy set his cigar on top of the mailbox and
walked the path up to the door.

Iggy knocked—five rapid taps, like he'd always done—and
stepped back. He sniffed himself again and wished he'd brought
cologne. Or not smoked a cigar. Why was he doing this now?
Why was he doing this at all? Iggy leaned into the dimly lit
door.

"Sofie? Hey, it's me, Iggy."

He heard nothing. Iggy looked at the hoop hunched at the
top of the dead end. The soggy net was in tatters. How long had
it been since anyone played a game there?

He leaned away from the door and tried to figure out what
he'd say if she opened it. *I'm sorry.* That would be the first thing
he'd say. *I'm so sorry.*

I know, she'd reply.

*I should have listened to you. You were right about everything.
And Mami might not be dead if I'd taken you more seriously.*

I know.

He'd push on, *I'm different now. Tell me how to make it right.
I know I shouldn't ask this of you, but I don't know what else to do.*
He'd reach out for her and stop himself. He'd lower his head
under the weight of his remorse. He'd fold his hands behind
his back.

Sofie would close the door a bit more. *How could you ask anything more of me?* Sofie would say. *You knew something like this
would happen. I told you it would. And now what? You want me to
kiss your face and tell you everything's going to be okay?* She'd shake

her head at him, and he'd bury his eyes between her beautiful little toes. She'd stare at him for a long time, then say, *You know how this ends, don't you?*

Iggy's eyes were wet when he snapped out of it. He wiped them dry. He caught a whiff of something familiar. A delicate scent, like morning dew. Jasmine and rose. Orange. Sunlight on warm skin. He checked the time on his phone: 3:06 a.m. He felt stupid for not realizing how late it was. He had to be at the shop in less than an hour.

The porch light went out. Darkness rushed into the space between Iggy and the door, and Ignacio Guerra couldn't find his breath. The world spun. He leaned into the door to stop himself from falling.

"Sofie?"

Iggy pressed his hands across from where he imagined hers were. "Can we talk?" he asked. "Please?" Was Sofie really on the other side of this door? Was she pressed up against the peephole watching him?

Iggy stepped back and turned away. Then the door opened.

Sofie stood in the doorway wearing an oversize Carnicería Guerra T-shirt that covered her shorts almost entirely. "Iggy?"

The faint glow of a lamp backlit Sofie. Her teeth were perfect in a way that only years of braces could achieve. She smelled exactly how heaven should smell, like a fresh morning in a citrus garden. Crisp and sun-kissed. He had to stop himself from reaching out to her. "I just got out," Iggy said, regaining his composure. "Compassionate release. A whole week early."

Sofie pushed through the door and wrapped her arms around Iggy's neck. He bent down to catch her and pull her in close. Tears began rolling down his cheeks. He wrapped an arm around her waist and the other across her back. He squeezed her into his chest, pressing all of her into him.

When he stood straight, her feet left the ground, but Iggy was the one who felt like he was flying. He buried his face in her clavicle, and the exhaustion and emotion of the day washed over Iggy so suddenly that he thought he might die right there in her arms. He was crying harder, his heart slammed itself against his sternum like it was a door that could be broken through in order to get to her. Iggy felt blood pulsing through his neck, echoing in his ears. He wondered if he was having a panic attack. His tears were born of both grief and elation and he'd never had to fight so hard to stay on his feet.

He took a deep breath and focused on reining in the frenzied euphoria he felt just then, the same way he'd kept his vengeful fury at bay when he'd learned that Conner G. Harrison had razed Mami's pharmacy. He wasn't sure if he could do it, or if he even wanted to, but he was aware enough that he had to try.

They hugged in silence for a long time. Iggy breathed her in, gathered her up in his lungs so that bits of her would forever be nestled in his hippocampus as a memory. He set her down and kissed the top of her head. "I'm sorry," he said.

"I know."

"I should have listened to you. You were right."

"I know."

Iggy was so overwhelmed that he spoke to her with his eyes closed. "Things are different," he said. "So different. Barely recognizable." He wiped the wetness off his face while still keeping her close. "I'm sorry I showed up here so late. I don't even know how that happened."

"Iggy, you should know that—"

"And I'm not here to ask you for anything. I just wanted to

thank you for trying to look out for me before I got popped. You were such a good girlfriend. More than a girlfriend. And I was the worst. Week-old roadkill. There was only one way for that to end. You deserved better."

She rubbed his chest. "I know." His eyes were still shut.

She wiped more tears off his face. Her hand was so soft and warm. He wished she'd never stop touching him.

"I'm so sorry about Cari," she said. "I can't even imagine what's happening to you right now. So much change all at once."

He could feel her eyes on his face. "I miss her *so* much," he said. "It's still not real. None of it has really registered. Not really."

She wiped away a few more tears. "Look, I'm glad you're back," she said. "I know your family needs you. But I have to ask, why are you talking to me with your eyes closed?"

He cracked the tiniest of smiles. "Because if I look into those beautiful brown eyes of yours, I'll melt in a way I can't afford to right now. Promises to keep, miles to go before I sleep and all that. There's so much to do *at* the shop and *for* the shop and I'm not anywhere near stable, and I don't want to look in your eyes and see what you think of me right now since I'm nowhere close to being what I want to be and I'm just so tired."

She laughed. Her laughter was symphonic, filling Iggy with the same sense of openness he felt when looking out at the ocean at sunrise.

"But I've also gotta say some shit I don't wanna say and you're not gonna like hearing," he said. "But before all that, I wanna thank you for this. I needed it. I honestly thought I'd never see you again. Which I would deserve. But I'm not here to win you back or anything like that. I won't bother you about getting back with me or whatever past we had at any point in the future. That's not what I'm about. In fact, I gotta be at the shop soon, so I gotta get going." He took a small step back. "I really just needed a friend."

Iggy opened his eyes. "And because we are friends, if nothing else, I'm trying to be real with you in a way I should have been back when we were together."

Sofie looked confused but still managed a smile. "What are you talking about, Iggy?"

He took her hands. It was starting to feel like the only way Iggy could make good on the promise he'd made Mami to fix things with Armando was to do things he'd promised himself he'd never do again.

There was no telling what Iggy might find out in the Everglades. That land was dark and deep, and it kept more secrets than it answered questions. And as much as Iggy wanted to keep Sofie at his side, he knew he might have to do some unsavory things to keep his family from crashing down around him. He knew how these things went. And if he owed Sofie anything, it was the truth.

"The shop's in trouble, Sofie. It's one of the few things left that mattered to Mami. I *can't* bring her back, but I *can* keep that place up and running. To honor her. To remember her." He let go of her hands and backed away farther. "But in order to do that, I need to keep my knives sharp."

II

THE EVERGLADES

8

G.A.R.D.

A full moon owned the sky when Iggy arrived at the shop. He was still high from his visit to Sofie, still sorting through all that he'd felt. He was elated and as dog-tired as a man could be all at once. *I'll sleep when I'm dead*, he thought. *Right now, I'll pound coffee and process meat.*

He parked Azúcar Prieta out front and stepped into the early-morning gloom. The ancient security light over the shop's front door buttered the rubber welcome mat below with its yellow glow. Iggy noticed a black Land Rover Defender in the lot across the street. It was beautiful, outfitted for overlanding—lifted for better clearance, oversize tires, a gas can over the spare tire and four more on the roof rack. It looked like a powerful, elegant tank. It was parked head in, but Iggy was sure it had a custom grille, spotlights, and a winch powerful enough to pull the Rover up a building.

Iggy paused as he searched through his keys and looked at the Rover. It was 3:56 a.m.

He slid the shop key into the front door. A soft thump echoed from the side of the building, followed by the crunch of gravel. Iggy stuffed the keys back into his pocket and slid into the shadows. Around the corner, a solitary streetlamp sputtered its weak light onto a graffitied fire hydrant. Another soft clunk rose from behind the gate—something heavy touching down on something metallic and hollow. Iggy stalked the shadows along the shop's side until he reached the gate.

A man with shoulder-length brown hair in a trucker cap held open the lid of a dumpster with one hand and scanned its contents with a flashlight in the other. Iggy watched as he pulled out a short knife, leaned into the dumpster, and made a few slashing gestures.

Motherfucker, Iggy thought. *I'm gonna have to rebag whatever he just cut open.* Iggy crept silently back to the front door and let himself into the shop. He moved quickly through to the processing room, where he pulled a long butcher knife off the wall.

The man was still waist-deep in the dumpster when Iggy opened the back door. He was on the intruder in three steps.

"What the fuck are you doing?" Iggy asked, grabbing the man's backpack. Iggy held the knife inches from his throat, then flashed the knife in front of the man's face so that he'd understand what was at stake.

The little knife clattered into the dumpster. "I'm unarmed," the man said as he steadied himself.

Iggy stepped back and let the man slide off the lip of the dumpster. His cowboy boots clacked when they hit the ground. The man straightened out his sleeveless camouflage T-shirt, dusted off his Wranglers, and straightened out his hat. He was short and slender, but muscular. No tattoos on his arms, but quite a few scratches and scars.

Iggy held the knife out. "Hands where I can see them or you'll be wearing this knife as a beak."

"Easy, easy," the man said, opening his fingers to the night. He tried to step back, but only managed to press himself up against the dumpster. Iggy watched as the man's eyes scanned the landscape behind Iggy, hoping to find a way past him and over the gate.

Iggy cut off any chance of escape.

"Who are you?" Iggy asked in a slow, clear voice. "And why are you in my dumpster?"

"I'm sorry," he said in a nasal drawl. "I was hopin' to talk to the owner of this shop. The name's Fred Crane." He held his hand out for Iggy to shake. A sharp pop filled the parking lot as Iggy caught it with the flat side of the blade.

Rage reared up behind the man's eyes. Iggy wasn't sure he'd seen it at first—it was gone now as he dropped the hand to his side, the dopey smile returning—but Iggy recognized a predator when he saw one.

"Shit," Fred said, slumping his shoulders as he wrung his hands, "no more sudden movements for me."

Iggy aimed the tip of the knife at the man's crotch, and Fred dropped his gaze.

"The owner of this shop doesn't live in a dumpster," Iggy said, twisting the knife in the air. "I'm only gonna ask once more. Who are you and why are you slicing up my bags?"

The man's eyes followed the knife and he sighed. "I'm looking for a place to buy some meat. It's a special meat, the kind I can't find at Publix." He smiled, perfect teeth glistening in the moonlight. "I was trying to decide whether or not this might be the shop for me."

"It's not," Iggy said.

"Look, I know that the Chop Shop's grand opening is coming up, and that it's not going to be good for you at all. I have a proposition for you that'll put an end to your financial troubles."

Iggy considered stomping the man outright where he stood. "Speak. Say your piece."

"I've got no love for Conner G. Harrison or that restaurant he's opening. His financial backers spend way too much lobbying to turn the Everglades into a parking lot. The way I see it, the enemy of my enemy is my friend, or at least he might be."

"You seem to know a lot about this neighborhood," Iggy said, "but not enough to know that if I catch you digging through my dumpsters, the only business you're getting comes from the tip of this knife. Now get the fuck out of here before I hang you by the balls from a meat hook."

The man shrugged. "I'll leave, but believe you me, I have something you're going to want to hear."

The neon marquee outside the Chop Shop pulsed red. Iggy hated that no matter where he stood in the shop, he could see the fucking thing. Something deep in his gut told Iggy that whoever this was, he wasn't lying. He aimed the tip of his knife at the ground.

"Give me your bag. Now."

Fred slipped the bag off his shoulders and handed it to Iggy.

Iggy knew the bag well. It was the same black Osprey bag Iggy took with him when he went hunting and camping in the Everglades. He squeezed the bag, feeling around for a gun, which he knew this man had. Whatever was in the bag wasn't a gun.

"Turn around," Iggy said. "Now."

"Let's talk about this inside," Fred said. "This ain't the place for the conversation we're about to have."

"Why do you think I'm frisking you. Turn around."

Fred did as he was told.

Iggy patted him down, blade at the ready. He found a Glock 19 in Fred's waistband and a Diamondback DB9 in his boot. Iggy put the butcher knife between his teeth and backed away from

Fred. He slid the magazine out of each handgun, ejected the chambered rounds, and tossed them both in the dumpster.

Iggy took the blade in hand and gestured to the front of the store. "I need café," he said. "Let's go."

Iggy steered supposedly Fred around the side to the front of the store. The man walked upright, chest out, as if he hadn't just been caught dumpster diving. They stepped through the open door and into the shop. A fluorescent sputtering bathed the clean white floor when Iggy hit the lights. The long refrigerated display case gleamed.

"Wait here," Iggy said as he walked around the case. The espresso maker rattled when Iggy turned it on.

Fred watched Iggy carefully from the middle of the store.

Iggy tied on an apron before flicking on the display case's lights. The bulbs hummed to life. The red meat looked as if it still had a pulse.

"This," Iggy said, spreading his arms over the display case, "is all the meat we sell." He began pointing to the different sections along the case. "Beef, pork, lamb, goat, turkey, chicken, and I even have some deer over here." Iggy leaned on the counter as Fred eyed the meat. "If there's anything you'd like us to special order, I can do that."

Fred scratched the fine stubble on his chin and nodded. He seemed to be taking snapshots of each cut with his strange green eyes.

The night was still thick in the window behind Fred. If the sun were out, Iggy felt that he could see what was going on here more clearly. He yawned and wished he were still in Sofie's arms instead of here with this pint-size cowboy who couldn't lie his way out of a wet paper bag. Iggy looked over at the espresso maker.

He tried willing the espresso out faster with his stare. "Now, is there anything in particular I can help you with?"

Fred tucked his brown locks behind his ear. "I was lucky enough to marry a fiery Cuban woman. My father-in-law, he's a real *gua-hero*," he said, the word warbling from his mouth like a saw blade flexing. "Straight from the countryside, he is. He's fond of all sorts of meat, but he has a hankerin' for the hard-to-get types in particular." He leaned in toward the counter. "I heard from a reliable source that I might be able to get a few pounds of it here for his *coom-play-años*." Fred coughed up the word as if it had been choking him.

The espresso maker gurgled, and the smell of coffee filled the room. The sugar at the bottom of the aluminum cup softened the drip of the liquid. Iggy placed both palms on the display case. The glass beneath his hands was as cold as Fred's stare.

Iggy yawned again. "Right. So first off, I'm sure your fiery wife would want to get something better for your *guajiro* father-in-law's *cumpleaños*," Iggy said, carefully pronouncing each word that the white man had butchered. "Secondly, I'm guessing you didn't find any of this rare meat in my dumpster, huh?" He leaned forward and cocked his head to the side as if listening carefully. "No? Didn't think so. Now, unless you're more specific, I can't help you. And if I can't help you, you need to get the fuck out of my shop with your bullshit." Iggy tossed the backpack at Fred, who caught it without flinching.

Fred slipped the bag onto his back, then rubbed the hand that Iggy had slapped with the knife. "Horse. I'm looking for horse meat."

Everything that Carlos had dug up on Pico flashed through Iggy's mind. "What makes you think we sell that here? No one breeds horses for eating here in the States. Besides, that's illegal, you know," he said, locking eyes with the tiny cowboy. "There's videos on the Internet about how wrong that is, you know?"

Fred's eyes darkened as a fight-or-flight response flashed behind them. "I know you sell horse meat here," Fred said, stepping forward, the doe-eyed demeanor melting. "Just sell me two pounds, you'll make eighty bucks, and I'll be out of your hair."

Iggy downed a shot of cafecito. He stared the man in the eye and said nothing.

Fred grew impatient. "Look, buddy, if you're going to—"

"What I *am* going to do, you baby bull wrangler, is ask you to get the fuck out of here and never come back. And listen to me carefully: the Everglades is as dangerous as it is beautiful."

The man's laughter sounded like a threat. "Baby bull wrangler," he said. "That's good. Here, let me show you something?" He slid one arm out of his backpack and brought it around to his front. The zipper purred. Inside the bag, he opened a compartment that Iggy had missed in his search of the bag and out came a long knife. He flipped it in the air and caught it by the blade. "Recognize this?" he asked, holding the handle up for Iggy to see.

Iggy leaned onto the counter and crossed his arms over the cold surface. "Yeah," he said, recognizing the *G* carved into the bone handle. "That's my knife."

"Do you know where your father's knife was found, Mr. Guerra?" the man asked, sounding cold and in control, exactly how Iggy imagined he normally sounded.

"Now it's Mr. Guerra all of a sudden? You know my name. Good for you. As for the knife, I have no clue where you found it." Iggy reached over the case, but Fred smiled and wedged the knife back into the bag. The backpack then spat forth a white wad, and when Fred unfurled it, the big green *G* of the shop's logo floated before Iggy on a wrinkled hoodie. "The knife was found in the Everglades beside the remains of a butchered horse," he said with a smirk. "And this sweatshirt was found in a truck that was parked in an illegal slaughterhouse a few miles from the site. Now tell me again how you don't sell horse meat."

Iggy stood and smiled. "A knife and a sweater, huh? That *does* sound suspicious. But for a guy looking to buy horse meat on the down-low, you sure go about it in an ass-backward way." He adjusted his apron, making sure the *G* was centered on his chest. "You're not interested in buying horse meat. You're checking your neighbor's stomach."

Fred's eyebrows shot up. He took a step back with a trace of panic.

"I heard that phrase in a video I saw yesterday," Iggy said, rubbing his hands. "I think you'd like it. The guy who shot it looks a lot like you, long brown hair and everything, except I'm sure it was a wig under that cap." Iggy cocked his head up and to the side and looked up as if remembering the details. "He even sounded like you."

He shook his head as if freeing himself from the memory. "Anyway, this guy sliced this bag with a horse head in it. Then he found something shiny, like a knife, and slipped it into a backpack *exactly* like yours before starting this speech about how this was a shame, how the slaughter of animals had to stop, blah, blah, blah. So I got all curious 'cause maybe this crazy white guy had a point, you know, and me and my brother—well, mostly my brother—we dug around on the Internet. It turns out that this guy has a reputation with farmers out in the Everglades. Have you heard about this guy? This guy was dressed in full-on hunting gear and covered in cameras. Even his hat was camouflaged.

You're dressed like you're heading out into the 'Glades for some hunting, so maybe you've heard of this guy.

"They call him Pico," Iggy continued. "Yeah, I know, what a stupid name. So me and my brother got curious, but we couldn't find anyone by that name. We *did* find a guy named Picoult, spelled P-I-C-O-U-L-T. Now I think this Pico and Picoult are the same guy and these swamp-asses just mispronounced the one name enough that it became a name on its own. Picoult, who owns a real estate company, also runs a nonprofit called Global Animal something-something."

"Rescue Directive," Fred said angrily. "Global Animal *Rescue Directive*. G.A.R.D. for short."

"Yeah, that's it. So you've heard about it. What's funny is that those swamp-asses haven't put two and two together and figured out where to find Pico. They haven't been able to catch him on their land, but I'm sure they've tried to find him where he lives. They know his name, but they just can't catch him. Hey, you okay there? You look like a ghost, cowboy. The color's drained from your face. You sure you don't want some coffee?"

The man backed away from Iggy and edged toward the door.

"I'll take that as a no. Anyways, the swamp-asses *hate* this guy for sticking his nose in their business, for trespassing onto their land and setting animals free, destroying tools, shit like that."

Iggy came around the counter and stood between Fred and the front door. "Now, as I'm taking in all this information, I over-hear some dudes talking about this Pico guy, about how bad they wanna catch him. Word on the street is that there's a bounty on his head, something like five stacks," Iggy lied. "Bro, you know how much money that is? But being who I am, I keep my mouth shut about all the dots I've connected."

Fred stepped back and clutched his bag as if Iggy might snatch it from him.

Iggy unlocked the front door and made his way back around the counter. He watched as some of the tension lifted off the man.

"And now here you are, digging through my garbage, asking about horse meat in that obvious wig, looking a lot like this Pico, Picoult, whatever, driving a car he probably drives—that is your Land Rover, right"—he pointed to the black SUV—"and I'm wondering if maybe, just maybe, the license plate on that Rover across the street, that one, with the plate that reads W32 SIL. I'm wondering if it belongs to Pico." Iggy shook his head, clapped his hands. "Can you imagine if those guajiros and swamp-asses got ahold of his license plate number? I bet Pico would vanish into the Everglades, but not before they flay him alive."

Pico backed into the door.

"Now, about the knife and that sweater," Iggy said. "The knife was stolen a few weeks back, so I'm glad you found it. It's an heirloom. Been in our family for generations." He poured himself another shot of coffee. "And we sell those hoodies here. Thirty-five bucks will buy you or anyone else that same hoodie." He downed the coffee. "So what I wanna know, Samuel Picoult, is if you *still* think we sell horse meat."

9

SUDDENLY AND VIOLENTLY

A storm was rolling in from the west—Iggy could see it coming from miles away out here in the Everglades, where there was nothing but greenery and sky—and though he felt more connected to the grass, the land, he also felt a connection to that storm. But not so much as Orin, who kept looking up at the roiling sky with giddy enthusiasm as he made his way to Azúcar Prieta. Iggy noticed right away that Orin's ranch hands picked up their pace as soon as their camo-clad boss had come out to meet Iggy. The coolers that were stacked on the porch of his ranch-style house made their way into the back of his pickup with a bit of reverence. It might have even been fear, since most of the men moved like children who feared being scolded.

"I'm surprised to see you here, Ignacio," Orin said when Iggy slid out of Azúcar Prieta. "You didn't even call to ask for directions. Welcome to Cypress Ranch."

"What kind of hunter would I be if I couldn't track you down on my own?" Iggy asked. He opened the trunk and grabbed the hat and backpack he'd prepared for this occasion after finishing his shift at the butcher shop. He'd called Carlos and Armando to tell them about his encounter with Pico when he'd found the house empty, so he decided to take Orin up on his offer of a ranch tour and see what he'd say about his nemesis's appearance at La Carnicería Guerra.

Orin's face darkened like the sky. "How *did* you find me?"

Iggy adjusted the backpack's straps and tugged the hose from the two-liter hydration bladder tucked into a special compartment in the pack. "What, you think I'm going to give my secrets away for free?"

"Humor me," Orin said. A ranch hand looked over and leaned away as soon as he heard the shift in Orin's tone. He hustled off.

"Here's what I'll tell you," Iggy said. "Folks at the Sawgrass Saloon showed me the way. Even told me to look for this specific dirt road tucked away just past that tiny Tamiami Ranger Station. From there, it took me two seconds to sneak up to the gladesmen patrolling the first gate and get them to radio you."

Orin scoffed. His men continued giving him a wide berth.

Iggy closed Azúcar Prieta's trunk. "But without that help, this place would have been damn near impossible to find. And if I got searched or escorted through another gate by your men, I was gonna drive away and never come back. How many people do you have guarding your roads?"

"I'm short one man," Orin said. He smiled. "I'm hoping you've come to fill that gap."

Iggy wondered if he had porcelain veneers in his mouth. "I'm here because Pico showed up at the shop this morning. Found him digging through the dumpsters. He had my father's butcher knife and a shop hoodie he said he found not too far from a horse's head. It was the same horse from the video you showed me."

Orin held Iggy's gaze as if he was debating whether to say what was on his mind. He inhaled, held in his breath, then exhaled slowly.

Iggy knew Orin had purged whatever thought had occupied his mind when his face lightened.

"The next time you find yourself in the presence of one of my enemies, I'd be grateful if you brought them to me in the trunk of that sublime machine of yours." Orin forced a smile.

His teeth were definitely veneers.

"Well," Orin said, "I'm glad you're here. Maybe now that we share a serious problem, you understand the gravity of the situation." He turned and pointed to the men standing on the ranch house's porch. "You remember Rana and Lew." He said it not as a question, but as a matter of fact. Iggy nodded to the hunters. They didn't move from the shade.

Iggy walked around Azúcar Prieta. "I figured I'd lose nothing by coming to check out what you've got going on here and to see if I can help you figure out a way to catch that dumpster-diving knife thief." He pointed to the bruised clouds shrouding the sun. "And to be clear, I'm not interested in the job, but I'll help you catch this guy. The price is that you forgive my father's debt."

Orin laughed. "Tell me, do you know how much money your father owes me?"

"None if you want my help."

Orin studied Iggy. "You've got some fucking balls on you, kid. I'll give you that."

"What I've got is a solution to your most immediate problem. I looked at a map of this area, and I wanna see your eastern perimeter. We should get going if we're gonna stay out of that storm."

"I never said I agreed to your proposition," Orin said calmly.

"You never said you didn't," Iggy replied.

"Suppose I agree to this," Orin said. "What assurances do I have that your plan will work? How do I know you'll catch him?"

"You don't," Iggy said. "But when he gets caught, I want your word you'll clear my old man's debt to you."

"Cardona," Orin called to a young man walking who'd come around the back of the ranch. The large golden Caridad del Cobre medallion hanging from Cardona's neck jingled as he hustled over. He looked down at his boots when he'd come as close as he was going to get.

The kid was young, bright, energetic, not like the other drones and broken men he'd seen since he drove past the main gate to Cypress Ranch.

Orin pointed to Azúcar Prieta. "Help Bill and Rodrigo load some of this morning's catch into that car. Then tie up the airboat at the eastern dock." He turned to Iggy. "Here's what I'll do: You help me catch Pico and I'll cut your father's debt in half. Does that work? He'll only owe me ten thousand dollars. That's the price I've put on Pico's head. If you show me how to catch him, then your old man will be ten grand less in debt to me."

Cardona turned to walk away, but Iggy stopped him. "Listen, Cardona," Iggy said. "Set the coolers on the shady side of the car and I'll load them up myself. I don't want you scratching my car by mistake." Cardona nodded and squelched off.

"We caught some bass, some mullet, and a few catfish," Orin said. "Take them back to your father for me, please. Tell him they're to celebrate how you got him off the hook." He seemed pleased with himself as he held his hand out to Iggy. "I even threw in some otter and python meat that Rana prepped."

Iggy nodded. "Not quite off the hook," he said. "But it's a start." He took Orin's hand and shook it.

Orin's smile widened.

"Why are you so happy, Orin? Did you not hear me when I said Pico was at the shop. He has Pops's knife. He wanted horse meat. I don't want that guy anywhere near the shop, not even to buy meat." Iggy eyed the storm. It seemed to walk across the Everglades like a sped-up time-lapse video of a growing banyan tree.

Orin turned and followed his gaze.

"Let's get something straight here, Orin. I'm here for my family. They need me. And we sink or swim together. But since I'm not gonna let us sink, me and you are gonna find this guy. We're gonna do this my way, and it's gonna work."

Orin nodded. "And if it doesn't work before next Friday, which—and correct me if I'm wrong—is when the Chop Shop opens up, you'll simply owe me the full twenty thousand dollars." Orin patted Iggy on the back. "No pressure."

•   •   •

They walked through the property in silence for a while, heading east. Much of the land surrounding Orin's ranch was dense, tropical hardwood hummocks that gave way to more arable land. Iggy thought he heard gunshots off in the distance but couldn't be sure.

Ramshackle buildings dotted the far edges of the land where the sky opened up. "You know, if you come work for me full-time, I'll remodel any of these houses for you."

"That's not how this is gonna work, Orin."

They walked through acres of farmland, each with a little house and various crops. Some had horses, but most had pigs and chickens. The sound Iggy thought was gunshots was getting louder and clearer.

They pushed through a dense stand of live oaks and were soon on a trail beneath a canopy that led to a clearing. An overturned wheelbarrow lay beside a conspicuous pile of palm

fronds in the center of the opening. Orin walked over and kicked
the branches to reveal dozens of knives, locks, machetes, chains,
horseshoes, and shovels.

"What is this?" Iggy asked.

"What do you think?

Iggy shrugged. "Looks like a farm tool graveyard."

"Exactly. We've been staking out this spot for days. Got trail
cameras on every path leading to this spot. Pico's done this before. He'll break in at night and free all the animals, but not
before disappearing our tools. He didn't get away with these,
though. We think something spooked him and he hid them here.
We left it hoping he'd sneak back to finish what he started, but
the bastard hasn't come back to this spot. Not yet, anyways."

"Return those tools to their owners," Iggy said. "He's not
coming back to this spot."

They walked on. Iggy heard more of what sounded like guns
firing. This time he was sure it was guns. Lots of them. The re-
ports of assault rifles were unmistakable. On the other side of the
clearing, over a dozen men were spread out, crouched or lying
down, firing at metal targets about fifty yards away. They were
dressed in cargo pants and solid tan, green, or palmetto camouflage T-shirts. They all wore baseball caps. Bullets pinged off the
human-shaped steel as empty cartridges rained down around
the men.

One of the men in dark shades and a cowboy hat knelt in
the grass reloading a box magazine for a huge sniper rifle. He
spotted Orin and held up hand, thumb, and pinky, meeting in
what looked to be the number three. Orin returned the gesture.

"What the fuck is this? Who are these guys?"

A bolt of lightning lit the overcast sky. The men looked up.
A few moments later, some of them startled when the deafening

thunder rolled over them all. They rose from the grass and began packing up their guns and ammo. Iggy saw that many of them had full-sleeve tattoos. There were a few DON'T TREAD ON ME and American flag patches on their caps.

The clouds flashed again. Orin pointed up. "That's where I found my magic, you know. I love the way people react to a sudden crack of lightning. The unease they feel at an unexpected, blinding flash. The key to controlling men like the ones who live on my land is to be like this storm. Show up suddenly and violently. These men, all they want is simplicity, privacy, a chance to live a life of farming and self-governance. That, and a roof to keep the rain off their heads. I make it rain, then offer them shelter."

"Is that why these guys are here doing shooting practice? You running a militia or something?"

Orin wiped his mouth. "The Sawgrass Soldiers? Nah. They're more of an interest group. Just exercising their rights as free Americans."

"Don't piss in my face and tell me it's raining, Orin. You know how many Sawgrass Soldiers I was locked up with? I *know* what they are." He pointed over at the men. "Those guys ran most of the drugs at Everglades Correctional. I bet you my old man's twenty thousand dollars that half those guys right there are cops, corrections officers, or felons."

Orin shook his head. "What they are is training. Preparing." He pointed to the sky. "You never know when the world's going to come down around you. The last thing you want is to be unprepared when shit hits the fan."

"So how many cops or COs you got there?" Iggy asked.

Orin looked over at the men as they piled into pickup trucks. American flags fluttered on poles from the back of each truck. "Only four. You'd have lost that bet."

They walked farther. The land alternated from impenetrable thickets to wide-open areas back to the dense greenery. Thunder rumbled from the east. Soon, they left the trees and shade behind and stalked into the open wetlands on the periphery of Orin's land. Iggy slid his rolled-up sleeves down his arm. Sawgrass grabbed at his pants, and his boots splashed in the progressively deepening water. He pulled his cap down to the top of his sunglasses.

After a while, Orin said, "I'm glad you dressed for the occasion. Somehow, I'm not surprised. I bet you have a change of clothes in your trunk so as not to muck up your car's interior."

Iggy kept his smile to himself. "Damned right I do," Iggy replied. "I'd shower every time before getting in that car if I could."

Orin eventually stopped walking at the edge of a hummock moat. The watery depression encircled the island of trees at their back. A solution hole had formed near a group of full-grown cypresses. Thanks to his polarized lenses, Iggy could see where the weak organic acids had dissolved enough of the limestone to form a mini cave beneath the surface.

"So this, my greatest treasure, is also my biggest vulnerability," Orin said, waving toward the great yawning expanse of wetland before them. "There are miles and miles of open Everglades that Pico somehow manages to traverse completely unnoticed. It's like trying to find a needle in a haystack."

"No, it's not," Iggy said. "You're looking for Pico in the Everglades, which is much harder."

Orin rested his hands on his hips and scanned the horizon. "I see what you're saying. And you're right. Not only does he stay hidden, but he evades everything I put in his path. I've used drones, dogs, traps, barbed wire, and cameras."

Orin ticked each obstacle off on his fingers. "We've chased

him, tracked him after we chased him, shot at him, sent Sawgrass Soldiers on patrol to try to catch him, set up ambushes, and even put a bounty on his head. And all I've got to show for it is another video on the Internet. Instead of helping me stop the poachers, he's out here destroying our farms. I've even found trail cameras hidden all over the place. They don't belong to any of us, so they must be his. He's been spying on us on our own land."

"Why not just call the cops, Orin?"

"Would you call the cops to your own house?" Orin waited for an answer. "Of course not. Besides, you know that MDPD won't come out to our no-man's-land even if someone did call, so I have no choice but to handle him myself. And I plan on handling him. He says we're running illegal slaughterhouses out here, but we are farmers. We raise livestock, butcher it for eating. Sure, we sell some of what we raise. That's part of how we make money. What does he expect, that we raise animals and open a petting zoo?"

Iggy knelt. He slipped out of his backpack and set it on his knee long enough to pull out his binoculars. He scanned the horizon. The length of the grass was wide-ranging: knee-deep in some places, waist-high in others. Ibis traced arabesques among the miles of windswept verdancy, their feathery bodies bobbing and flashing like whitecaps on a roiling sea. "How long you been hunting out here?"

It was silent for a bit. "Let's see," Orin said. "I opened the Sawgrass Saloon about twentysomething years ago, and officially started E.C.H.O., what, three years after that? I caught all the gators in both my gator pits."

Iggy brought forth the memory of the pit he'd seen tucked deep behind the Sawgrass Saloon. There must have been fifteen large gators in there.

"You have another pit?"

Orin said nothing. He shielded his eyes with a hand and continued looking out into the vast green distance.

Iggy focused the binoculars on a stand of dwarf cypresses off in the distance. "So you're saying you've hunted *that* area for a long time," he asked. "Makes sense that you know it like the scars on your body. But there are a lot of wet miles between the saloon and where we are now. It's definitely quicker to take an airboat from the E.C.H.O. and this ranch. What I'm asking is: How often do you hunt out *here*, by your ranch?"

Iggy could hear Orin's pacing to his right. "Not often enough. What's your point?"

There were a smattering of black mangrove islands between the first cypress stand and the nearest one. And in addition to the handful of sable palms and thick patches of sawgrass, a hardwood hummock on the south east of the property—mostly oak and hackberry—encroached on a southwestern hummock of gumbo-limbo and mahogany trees to form a constellation of cover and potential hiding places.

"That *is* my point," Iggy said. "If I wanted to sneak onto a swath of land as big as this one, and factoring in everything you've thrown at Pico, it'd be most doable from this direction." He pointed to the vastness ahead of them. "He probably drives down the Tamiami Trail as far as he dares, stashes his ride, then slips into the grass smooth as a gator. I bet he comes from this side most often, from the northeast. Maybe even the east if he doesn't mind stalking long distances."

Orin grunted. "Yeah, he comes through here more often than not."

Iggy stood. "That's how I'd do it. You avoid the road. More importantly, you make use of the land, just like the folks who've lived out here for hundreds of years. Come to think of it, I can name twenty people between here and the Rez who've got generational knowledge on their side. I'm just a dude who loves being out here and figuring out how animals think. I'm sure they'd be better at this than I am."

Orin scoffed. "None of them have skin in the game like you do," he said, never taking his eyes off the approaching storm.

Bursts of electricity flickered silently inside the incoming clouds, then a jagged white branch of lightning split apart the horizon. A cool breeze rushed through the sawgrass toward them.

Orin's voice appeared right behind Iggy. "So how would you *catch* him?"

Iggy reached in his pack for his rifle scope. "Depends. Based on what I'm seeing out here, this guy comes prepared for a long trek. And for recording what he finds. GPS, cameras, and surveillance gear, all-weather boots and gear, camouflage, plenty of food—nuts, jerky, protein bars, that sort of shit. I'm sure he brings water, but eventually uses iodine tablets or a LifeStraw when his bladder runs dry." Iggy looked up at the clouds and pulled a mouthful of water from his hydration hose. "Maybe even collects rain."

He handed Orin the scope. He pointed at the first stand of dwarf cypresses that had caught his attention. "And he ain't gonna be dressed in cowboy boots and jeans like he was when I saw him. He'll be rocking better gear than I'm wearing now. Like, more thorough camo. More detailed. Probably a 3D, textured, long grass ghillie suit. Something that makes him invisible and keeps him dry. Or at least dries up quickly."

"What am I looking at?" a frustrated Orin asked.

"The distance between those dwarf cypresses way out there and the mangrove island closest to them, then from the mangrove to the next cypress stand out there in the south."

Orin knelt and looked through the scope. He adjusted the reticle.

"Zoom in tight on the far-side cypresses and mangroves."

The wind was crisp. Iggy slipped the hood of his shirt over his head, pulled his neck gaiter over his mouth and nose. "Now that I think of it, he's probably armed to the teeth. If I was doing what he's doing, I'd have a long-range rifle with a suppressor—I found two handguns on him when I frisked him, so I can only imagine what he's packing out here—at least two handguns. Probably knives stashed all over his body. Maybe even a sawed-off, twelve-gauge pump in case he gets cornered and has nothing to lose. You seen that *Predator* movie? The one with Schwarzenegger and those other dudes lost in the jungle? Pico is the Predator. You'd better do some critical thinking if you wanna pull a Dutch Schaefer and hunt the Predator."

Orin scoffed. "Doesn't Arnold outsmart that jawless freak?"

"You're missing the point, Orin. When the Predator gets caught, he set off a bomb in his arm and blows himself up to take out Arnold. He's ready for all contingencies."

The scope clicked softly as Orin surveyed the area. "Sounds like you have a crush."

Iggy looked down at Orin. "This land here's a savage, merciless wilderness inhabited by apex predators and heavily guarded by armed men, yet Pico has come and gone as if he's shopping at Publix at noon on a Tuesday. What I feel toward him is respect."

Orin looked up at Iggy. "What does that say about me?"

"That you'd better form a crush if you wanna catch him." Iggy pointed out over the water. "Look for that far stand of trees now."

Orin held out the scope. "Can't see them. The rain's too heavy."

"Exactly. He's moving into cover unnoticed. And there's hiding places within that cover. And if he comes with a storm, the rain adds an entire new level of cover for him to hide in. That dwarf cypress stand out there looks like this one right here," he said, pointing to his left. "Are your lenses polarized?"

Orin plucked the shades off his face and looked them over.

Iggy tossed his own shades to the old man. "Put 'em on and look at the base of the nearest tree. Look under the surface of the water. See that big solution hole under the water? And the one twenty yards away on dry land? He can sit inside those things and you wouldn't even know he was there. Here, let me get my shades."

Orin returned Iggy's sunglasses.

"Now look at that black mangrove island halfway between the cypress and that hardwood hummock out there. No, not that one, that's white mangrove. Look for the ones with the pencil-looking shoots that the tree uses to breathe. It's like a quarter mile away. There. See it? That's a good place to post up if there's mosquitos. If he's careful, he could start a really small fire and burn leaves and those pencil-looking shoots to keep the bloodsuckers away. The smoke would be a dead giveaway, but not if he keeps the fire small and under a tarp while it rains."

The storm whipped up wind and rain as it closed in on them. Iggy gestured out to the hardwoods and the middle of the grass. "From those mangrove islands, he could carefully cross over to the hummock and hide in the nurse logs or up in the trees. With all the bromeliads and vines up there, you'd never see him above you if he wore full camo." He pointed to the cypress beside them. "From there, all he'd have to do is crawl through the brush and sawgrass between here and the first few farms. If he wants to push deeper into your land, he can side skirt the houses and farmland if he stays low. After that, it's all guerilla warfare. Urban tactics. Hide-and-seek."

Orin stood and handed Iggy the scope. "I have a lot to think about," he said as he trudged off. "Come with me. I want you to see something else."

• • •

Orin grumbled the entire walk back to his ranch and kept grumbling as he led Iggy southwest through the rest of the property. They passed a few empty stables and corrals and a covered slip where a pontoon was docked beside two airboats. On another slip floated a flats fishing boat with fishing rods sticking out the side like errant ear hair. Orin screamed at two of his men for not putting away the rods before the storm got there.

They turned away from the water and walked for about a quarter mile.

"Don't you have some ATVs we can ride?" Iggy asked.

Orin said nothing and kept walking.

Iggy smelled the pigs long before he set eyes on them. The stink of stagnant shit and piss was one Iggy was familiar with.

Orin seemed to barely tolerate it. "Why hasn't this pen been mucked? Why haven't these hogs been fed?" He plucked the radio from his belt and yelled into it. Someone responded and said they'd be there in a minute. Orin took a deep breath, exhaled, then walked on.

"Humberto," he called out as they entered the shade of the pole barn. A wiry man emerged from behind a column with a bucket of slop in each hand and a plume of smoke rising from the cigar in his mouth. Pig feet shuffled on the packed earth as the old man set the buckets down. The mass of swine grunted and swarmed around the trough.

"Yes," Humberto said in a thick accent, tipping back the brim of his hat to wipe his face with his forearm. He glanced at Orin, down at his boots, then up at Iggy before nodding as a greeting.

Orin moved toward Humberto. "How long have you been living out here, working for me?"

Humberto backed away from Orin against the pigpen. He set the bucket down. "Two months."

The press of pigs grew thicker around the trough, and Humberto's eyes shot at them.

"So you *are* aware that the first task to be completed each day is feeding these hogs, yes?" Orin took another slow step to close the gap between him and Humberto. "What was so important that it kept you from doing your job?"

Humberto glanced over his shoulder. "Nothing," he said.

Orin picked up a bucket and tossed it into the trough behind Humberto. "The Everglades are full of danger, Humberto. This place could become your grave if you're not careful. Lightning strikes, mosquitos, snakes, gators—even the grass can hurt you." He picked up the other bucket. "You know what's the best way to stay safe out here?"

Humberto said something, but Iggy couldn't hear it over the frenzied squeals of the pigs.

Orin thrust the second slop bucket into Humberto's chest, rattling the fence at his back. A fat sow with a missing ear tugged on Humberto's shirt through a gap in the fence. Humberto turned. His hat fell off and plopped into the trough.

"You stay safe by staying focused," Orin said as the hogs tore the hat to shreds. He gestured to the bucket Humberto held, and the Cuban poured the contents into the trough. A chorus of slurping joined the squealing hogs that pushed the trough against the fence.

Humberto placed the bucket at his feet and stood still. The animals ate inches from his back, devouring chicken bones and ears of corn like curly-tailed garbage disposals. When Orin plucked the cigar from his mouth, Humberto flinched, spilling ash on his shirt.

"Pigs eat anything, Humberto. Anything," Orin said. He dropped the cigar into the trough and both men watched as a one-eared sow swallowed it whole, the embers singeing her tongue.

"It's important that we feed them on time. Otherwise, they get desperate and eat anything that falls into their pen. You get what I'm saying?"

Humberto nodded.

Orin brushed some ash from Humberto's shirt. "Don't ever be late to feeding these pigs or cleaning their pen."

Orin walked off and motioned for Iggy to follow him. "I can understand your concerns, your *hesitations*, over certain aspects of the way your father and I conduct business, but I can assure you I take care of my partners the way I take care of my animals. I need someone to sell my kills to, and your father needs inexpensive, high-quality meat. Think about it: by helping me, you'd be helping your family."

Iggy looked off to the horizon. "Why don't you butcher the kills yourself? I'm sure you know how to field dress a kill, how to butcher it. You'd make a lot more money that way?"

Lightning flashed on the horizon. It was beginning to sprinkle. Orin lit a cigarette. "Are you trying to talk me out of doing business with the shop? And here I was, thinking you were a good businessman." He exhaled a long stream of mentholated smoke. "Who would I sell that meat to? The men out here, who raise and eat their own livestock? Besides, your old man is so fast and so efficient. There's no waste when he wields his blades." Thunder rumbled over Orin's ranch. A rooster crowed in response.

"I'm not coming to work for you, Orin. But I can work *with* you. If you make clean, legal kills, we will definitely buy them from you."

Orin looked at Iggy, then out at the storm. Lightning struck close enough that the deafening thunder roared over them instantly. Orin looked back at Iggy, then walked off.

Iggy followed Orin along a barbed wire fence, past a corrugated steel shed that housed some chicken coops and rooster pens.

Orin pointed to the coops. "Let's make sure there's fresh hay in the coops. And that my gamecocks have fresh water."

They moved through the coops, opening the nesting boxes one by one to find eggs covered in chicken shit. Orin opened the last pen and found a dead rooster in a heap of its own filth, ants writhing over the carcass like static on a TV screen. He stood and pinched the bridge of his nose and exhaled. "Humberto!" he roared. The steel around him hummed.

Iggy pointed to the sky. "It's ugly enough out there, Orin. Take it easy on the old man. He's gonna get soaked. Besides, he's still shitting himself after that sow ate his hat and cigar."

The old Cuban came into the shed slowly, a new hat on his head.

"What's going on here, Humberto?" Orin asked, pointing at the rooster. Iggy saw that the ranchers tending to other animals pretended to work as they watched Orin in the periphery of their vision. Orin grabbed the ant-covered rooster and held it up to Humberto's face.

"I never want to see this again, you understand?"

Humberto nodded.

"Do your fucking job!"

With the rooster still in hand, Orin turned to Iggy. "This way." Ants swarmed over Orin's hand, but he didn't seem to notice. Or care. He closed the gate and they walked down a narrow path that curved through a cypress stand and ended at a tangle of mangrove. The wind was blowing so hard that it was spraying them with water. Iggy pulled his hood up again. A small opening in the gnarled roots led to a gator pool. Iggy watched the ants biting Orin's fist.

The rain fell with greater force, hammering the palm frond roof above their heads.

"Beautiful, aren't they?" Orin leaned over the fence and pointed out two gators carving silent *S*'s in the water below. From any other perspective, they would have been invisible, their stealthy instincts honed by millennia of practice, bodies designed to be predatory prodigy. They could hide anywhere, and therefore could ambush from anywhere. But from where Iggy and Orin stood, there was nowhere for them to hide. Live oaks held their branches over half of the pool, providing shade for any of the thirty gators at the edge of the property, but it was the ones out in the open that drew Iggy's focus. Even as the rain started coming down in sheets, they sat so still that they may as well have been carved out of stone. Until Orin arrived.

The old hunter reared back and threw the dead bird into the shallows beside them. He lit himself a new cigarette and watched as thousands of pounds of teeth, tails, and scales sprang to life. The gators hissed and thrashed in the deafening rain.

Orin smoked the entire cigarette in silence, deep in thought, not once taking his eyes off the mayhem.

Once the water in the pit grew calm again, Orin lit another cigarette and offered Iggy a smoke. Iggy took it and tucked it behind his ear. Another lightning bolt crackled across the sky. It was a thunderous strike that made the air tingle as if it were alive.

Orin grabbed the radio from his belt. "Lew, Rana, this is Orin. Do you copy?"

The radio crackled. "This is Rana. We copy. Over."

"Pico's probably been listening in on a scanner," Iggy said. "He can probably hear all your chatter. Every single word."

Orin threw his cigarette into the gator pond with an exasperated growl. He spoke slowly into his handheld. "Guerra's made some good observations. Meet me on my porch in twenty."

10

THE CHOP SHOP

The water was a ribbon of sunlight fluttering beside Iggy. As he raced to the butcher shop, the near-overflowing canal that ran parallel to the Tamiami Trail mirrored every shift and swerve that Azúcar Prieta made. The drive eastward across the Everglades was smooth, but the turmoil brewing in Iggy's mind dragged his attention away from the fact that the sky was clearing up.

Iggy's worries and fears clashed against the uncertainty they created. All he could think about was the savage thrashing of the gators that Orin had provoked with a dead rooster. The primal growls, the way they sizzled the surface of the water. Their tails exploding, sending jagged columns of water into the air. The way the claws and teeth piled onto each other, bodies writhing as if the water had suddenly been electrified.

By the time Iggy reached the shop, he'd calmed the gator pit that was his mind by clamping down on each problem one at a time and death-rolling it to pieces, just as the two gators who'd dismantled the rooster had. Pico, Orin, the Chop Shop, Armando's unexplained absences, the shop's lack of patronage—Iggy had begun the process of ripping each one apart, chunk by chunk, into ragged, digestible bits.

What came from that process, messy as it was, made sense to Iggy. His theory was simple: Orin was stealing horses, killing them, and selling their meat. It might explain why Armando was disappearing at night with his knives and turning up sweaty and covered in blood the next morning—he was butchering the horses for Orin, who didn't want Pico finding more evidence of his horse meat operation. Pico had somehow connected these dots and was onto them both. If Pico got what he wanted, Armando and Orin would be in a world of shit. Iggy might not have had all the proof he'd liked, but he was sure that was what was going on.

The guayabera that Iggy had changed into before leaving Orin's ranch made him feel clean, organized even. He slipped into the shop through the back. Mauro and Dro worked calmly in the prep room, and as he entered the front, he found Carlos wrapping up meat that customers had ordered.

Iggy left the coolers full of fish in the prep room, then entered Armando's office. An empty bottle of rum was laid flat on the desk. He dropped it into the trash and watched through the shop's security monitors as the owner of the Chop Shop, red hair and another burgundy suit, paused at La Carnicería Guerra's front door to adjust his jacket. Because of the heat, even his face was red. He was younger than he'd seemed when Iggy had last seen him.

Iggy tried to remember exactly when that was—was it one or two days ago?—but the last week of his life was a smudged, slurred blur, and even his sense of time was grief-stricken.

The doorbells jingled when Conner G. Harrison finished checking out his reflection and decided to step inside. Iggy couldn't fathom why the owner of the Chop Shop would be in his shop, or why he was staring at the bells tied to the door handle. Iggy opened the office door, listened, and watched the monitors.

"It's hot out there, ain't it, Connie?" Carlos stood behind the display case, a tray of freshly processed meat in hand.

Conner looked up. He was met with glasses and a perfect smile. He frowned. "It's Conner."

"Right, right. *Con-nah*. Hazme un favor, *Con-nah*. Close the door."

Conner undid the button of his Bogosse jacket, slid his hand through the inside of his coat, and slipped it into his pocket as if he were a model who'd reached the end of the catwalk. He stepped inside. The door jingled shut behind him.

Carlos slid the case open and began neatly arranging the meat. "Now, what can I get for you, *Con-nah*? And just so you know, we're all out of sausage, but aside from that, we got all the meat you can handle. And nice neon sign you got for your place, by the way. Real classy."

Conner tilted his head like a confused puppy. "How do you know who I am?"

"We met a while ago. I went over to introduce myself and you told me to get my Mexican ass back on the roof. Remember?"

Conner looked confused. He blinked.

"Besides, you think you're going to move into this hood without people finding out everything about you? C'mon, Conner. You gotta know better than that."

Conner nervously picked at his jacket's button. "I'm sorry, I didn't catch your name."

"It's Carlos." He set the tray down on the counter. "So what's up, Conner. You gonna buy something?"

Conner smiled. "Yeah, how much for that Camaro out there?"

"It's not for sale," Iggy said as he pushed through the vinyl curtain. He joined Carlos behind the display case with his own tray of meat.

"You're Iggy Guerra," Conner said.

Iggy began placing the meat in the case.

Carlos nodded toward Conner. "¿Qué te parece este tipo?"

"Así que este es el dueño del restaurante nuevo."

"Me dan ganas de entrarle a piñazos."

"Ponte en línea." Iggy looked up at Conner, gave him a once-over. He could tell Conner was uncomfortable, like he was being twisted around like a soon-to-be-solved Rubik's Cube.

"Pero ¿qué querrá nuestro neighbor nuevo?" Iggy said. "Hoy no estoy pa' sorpresitas."

"¿Por qué no le preguntamos, a ver qué dice el fósforo este?"

"That's a dope Camaro," Conner said abruptly. "If you ever want to sell it, please come to me first."

Iggy and Carlos finished their display by propping up hand-written signs with the price per pound on the steak at the front of the case.

"You said that already," Iggy said. "What's good?"

"He's here 'cause he wants to learn how to run a butcher shop," Carlos said.

Conner scratched his eyebrow. "I just wanted to come in and formally introduce myself to you guys. That, and to invite you to my shop's grand opening next week. I'm Conner G. Harrison." He held his hand out over the high counter at an awkward angle.

"I'm Ignacio." Iggy shook Conner's hand. Conner squeezed Iggy's hand as best he could. This didn't surprise Iggy. Most insecure men thought a crushing handshake established dominance.

"Hi, Iggy. It's good to finally meet you."

"It's Ignacio."

"OK, as you like." Conner looked at his hand. Ignacio hadn't released it.

"Yeah, that's what I like. So what's up, Conner G.?"

"Like I said, I wanted to be neighborly and come say hi."

"You already did that."

Conner tried pulling his hand out of Iggy's, but Iggy held it firm. "I'm not sure if I've insulted you. I'm sorry if I have; it wasn't my intention."

"Today's not the day, Conner. What are you doing here?" Iggy asked.

"I've just answered your question."

Iggy finally released Conner's hand. "No, why are you on this block?"

Conner scratched his eyebrow again. He coughed into his fist. Iggy wondered if he'd faked the cough to buy himself a moment to figure out a response.

"I came over here to introduce myself. To invite you to a party. To show you some respect since I'm the new guy on the block. There's no reason for you to treat me like shit. I haven't done anything to you."

Iggy looked over at Carlos. He arched his eyebrows in mock surprise.

"Mira pa'llá," Iggy said.

"Parece que le pica algo al gringuito en llamas."

"A ver si se lo rasco."

Iggy came around the counter. Taped to the front door was a sign that said *Thank You for Stopping By!* written in Mami's handwriting. It pulled Iggy out of his indignation long enough for him to realize that rage was not what he felt. Not exactly.

"You might think you haven't done anything, Conner, and that's the problem right there. I wouldn't exactly call this visit respectful. Nothing you've done has been respectful." He stepped closer to Conner. "You move onto our block and open, of all things, a butcher shop, after knocking down what used to be my mother's pharmacy. Then my brother goes over to introduce himself to you and you tell him to get his Mexican ass back on the roof. And now you come over here acting like we're boys when what you should be doing is hiding your face in shame inside your new shop. Who do you think you are, coming over here like it's all good?"

"I'm trying to be civil. You're willfully misinterpreting my actions and taking them personal. They're not. It's just business."

"Personally."

Conner stepped back. "Excuse me?"

"Personally, Conner. Not personal. Personally. And yeah, I'm taking this personally. You're fucking with this neighborhood. With our livelihoods. And not out of necessity. You're doing it 'cause you can."

Conner stepped farther away. The look on his face made it clear to Iggy that the white boy was still unsure of what the problem was.

"I'm a businessman," Conner said as if it were the most obvious thing in the world. "I saw a gap in the market, and I jumped on it."

"A gap. You saw a gap? In the butcher shop market. Really, Conner? You saw a gap in the butcher shop market. In this neighborhood. The same neighborhood that's had a butcher shop in it since 1980?"

"I own a restaurant. Only a portion of it is a butcher shop."

"In this neighborhood."

"There aren't any restaurants in this neighborhood."

"Really? What's that over there?" Iggy asked. He pointed to the cafeteria on the corner across the street. A bunch of mechanics and warehouse workers stood around a ventanita eating croquetas and sipping Cuban coffee from tiny white cups.

Conner followed Iggy's finger. "That's not a restaurant."

"It's a restaurant, Conner. Folks eat there every day."

"It's a fucking dump. It needs to be cleaned. And updated."

"That's your problem right there, Conner. You swoop in here like you're entitled to dictate what's good and what ain't."

Conner dug his hands into his pockets. "I am *not* entitled. I *earned* everything I have. My money has nothing to do with this. There aren't any real businesses in this area. I'm here to serve this community. You should be thankful, actually. I'm good for you and your property value."

"Oh, shit. My bad. You're a philanthropist. I get it now. You're here to serve the community. And apparently, you're an expert on real estate, the city of Miami, and everything that deals with our culture, history, and who we are. I think I get it now." Iggy's hand was in his own pocket. "Out of curiosity, how long have you lived down here? A year? Two?"

Conner shrugged. "You don't deserve to stay open if you can't stand a little competition." He looked around the shop, studying it as if he were seeing it for the first time, which, in fact, he was. "Judging by the looks of this place, you don't deserve to be here at all." He stepped toward Iggy. "I wonder what the health department would say about this dump."

"Fuck yourself, Connie." Carlos spat over the counter. "Mauro! Get out here and listen to this white boy talking about—"

Iggy held a hand out. Carlos stopped coming around the counter.

"Do you hear yourself?" Iggy asked. "You're here in our shop in a three-piece suit, in summer, threatening our business with the authorities. All because you can. You're making my point for me."

"This suit is called formal wear. It's what's worn when doing business. And I didn't make things this way, OK? That's just how business gets done."

"My guayabera *is* formal wear, Conner. You'd know that if you knew *anything* about anything. That's not how business gets done out around here. The streets talk, Conner. Word of mouth carries weight."

"The streets? Word of mouth? What are you even talking about, you Cube? I'm sick of this condescending bullshit. Skip to the part where you tell me to check my privilege already."

Iggy took a deep breath and exhaled slowly. This guy was testing his patience, something Iggy had already run out of.

Conner turned in place, scanning the shop. "I notice there's no Black Lives Matter sign in here. No rainbow flag either. I figured there'd be at least one of those somewhere around here with all that *wokeness* coming out of your mouth. How much does the government give in handouts to failing butcher shops?"

"Handouts?" Iggy laughed. He turned to Carlos, who was also laughing. "Handouts?" he repeated as he began laughing in earnest. This kid was so used to handouts that he thought everyone got them. Conner couldn't fathom that the only assistance Iggy ever got was what he gave himself—the reason God helped those who helped themselves was so he wouldn't have to do any work.

"Handouts," Iggy said when his laughter subsided. "This coming from the poster boy for entitled trust-fund babies. Just so you know: we don't do handouts, even when they're offered."

Conner buttoned his coat. "Just so *you* know: this shithole slop shop won't be here in a year. In case you haven't noticed, no one wants to buy gross meat from a bunch of ex-con Scarfaces." He smiled. "You losers are finished. *Com-pren-day?* You have my word."

The door jingled as Iggy held it open. "Your word is worth its weight in gold, Connie. Now get the fuck out of my shop before that shithole of a mouth gets you in trouble."

"*Your* shop? Wow. You *just* got out of prison and you're suddenly a business owner? That's impressive. Did you steal this business from your parents, just like you did that pharmacy?" He let that hang in the air for a moment. "Yeah, I know all about you, *Iggy*. You can't hide from the Internet." Conner pressed his hand to the display case. It squeaked as he dragged it across the cold surface. A long, greasy smear remained on the glass.

Iggy was still smiling. He held the door open as if he were trying to chase out a cat that had snuck into the shop. "¡Dale, culo cagao! Salpica. Out you go."

Conner casually walked over to Iggy. "No. You get out." He drove a finger into Iggy's chest. "And take this place with you. I'm OK right where I am. In fact, I'm so comfortable here that I could stand in this spot until your mother shows up." He looked up at Iggy, stared into his eyes. He watched Iggy's smile fade as his words slammed into him. "I thought she'd be here. Guess she got stuck in traffic."

Iggy pulled the door shut. He turned the lock so slowly it barely clicked. Iggy moved toward Conner silently, numb to everything but the mention of his mother. He stopped inches from Conner. He bent forward, cupping his ear. "What did you just say? There's no way you just said what I think you said. I *know* I misheard you just now."

Conner slid his hands into his pockets. "I didn't stutter."

The breath shot out of Conner as he hit the floor and slid. He came to a stop when his head hit the floorboards on the other side of the room. He tried scrambling to his feet, but Iggy was on him before he even sat up. Conner's body left the ground and the seams of his suit crackled like lightning.

Iggy dangled Conner on the end of his fists like a fish on a spear.

Conner kicked Iggy as hard as he could. Iggy shook Conner so violently his head snapped back.

"Kick me again," Iggy said. "I dare you."

Conner held his hands up in submission. Iggy walked him over to the door.

Mauro pushed through the vinyl strips but stopped behind the counter.

Carlos came around the counter and unlocked the door. "You might wanna apologize before I open this door, Conner. If Iggy shot puts you out of here before you've squashed this, you'll spend the rest of your life looking over your shoulder, wondering *when*, not *if*, one of us is gonna run up on you."

Iggy lowered Conner to his eye level. "That's no way to live, Conner."

Mauro walked around the counter. "I say you throw his ass outta here right now. See how far into the street you can chuck him. See if you can hit a passing car."

Iggy jostled Conner. "This kid weighs about a buck fifty at most. I can reach the sidewalk from here."

"Please," Conner whispered.

Iggy lowered Conner and set him on his feet in front of the door. He tightened the grip he had on Conner's jacket. The door clacked as Carlos undid the lock. Iggy pulled Conner close. "So how we doing this? You walking out? Or you flying business class?"

"I'm sorr—" Iggy jerked Conner mid-sentence. Conner gripped Iggy's wrists.

"You stuttered, Conner. I didn't catch what you were saying. Try that one more time, only say it like you fucking mean it."

"I'm sorry. I shouldn't—I shouldn't have said that about your mom."

"You shouldn't have fucking *thought* it." Iggy pulled Conner onto the tips of his toes.

Conner nodded. "I know. I'm sorry."

Iggy let go of his jacket. He brushed Conner's shoulders and sleeves.

Conner tried to close the jacket, but the button was gone. Conner scanned the floor and found the burgundy button at Iggy's feet. He knelt, reached for the button, but Iggy stepped on it. "That's mine."

Conner did not take his eyes off Iggy as he rose.

Iggy stepped forward, pressing Conner against the door. He leaned in so Conner had to look straight up to be eye to eye with Iggy. "If you ever set foot in this butcher shop again, I'll crack your spine like a glow stick."

The bells jingled as Conner backed out the door. He stopped to look at the sign on the door. "Enjoy this dump while you can," Conner said as he turned the sign on the door from OPEN to CLOSED.

•   •   •

The Guerra men huddled around the security monitors in Armando Guerra's empty office. They replayed Conner's encounter with Iggy over and over. Abuelo Calixto yipped when he first saw the way Iggy manhandled Conner. They watched the moment with awe and perverse pleasure: Conner poking Iggy in the chest, Iggy mopping the floor with Conner, then dangling him in the air like a used bath towel on a hook. They even added commentary, as if they were narrating a sporting event.

Mauro turned to Iggy. "You think you could've held him with one hand? Looks like you could've. It would have made a better shot if you'd held him out with one hand."

"Bro, look how fast he shoots up in the air," Dro said. "I can't believe I missed this!" He ran the footage in slow motion. "Look. Right here." He paused the video. "You can actually pinpoint the instant when his soul leaves his body." Conner's head was tossed back. His arms were open as if he were ascending into heaven mid-rapture. Dro unpaused the video. Conner's head snapped forward. His body went limp for a moment.

Iggy leaned against the corner. Mauro and Dro might have been impressed with Iggy's strength, and Abuelo Calixto might have been proud that Iggy had stood up for Mami and the shop, but none of them understood what was at stake here. "Turn that shit off," he said. "We got work to do."

"We have to erase it," Carlos added. "This *never* happened."

"For reals?" Dro asked. "You're not gonna post this?"

"I'd play this shit on a loop if it was me," Mauro said. "I might even put this on a shirt for you."

"We have enough problems as it is," Iggy said. "Turn that shit off."

Carlos reached over and turned off the monitor. "Think about it: Iggy *just* got out of prison and he's already in some shit." He turned to Iggy. "I'm not blaming you, bro. I think you did a great job controlling yourself. Better than I would have."

Iggy nodded from his corner. "Gracias."

"But now we need to make sure we watch out for this pasty gringo."

Mauro and Dro turned to Iggy. Their dismissive expressions frustrated him.

"Carlos is right," Iggy said. "We don't need any more problems, especially not with that white boy. Erase this from your brains. You heard? Brain erase. We keep our hands clean from now on. Especially me. I can't be giving anyone a reason to come at me 'cause I ain't ever going back to prison again. Never."

The room was silent. And cold. Mauro and Dro were suddenly very interested in their phones. Abuelo filled out his lotto slip.

"Bueno," Iggy said eventually. "A trabajar. ¡Dale!"

When everyone was gone, Carlos asked Iggy to move.

Iggy stood and let Carlos sit at the computer. Carlos sifted through the computer and erased the entire month's footage from the security files. "Close the door," he said to Iggy. Carlos picked up the phone. He called the security company. After a ten-minute conversation with a customer service rep, La Carnicería Guerra no longer had a security storage plan.

"Why'd you do all that?" Iggy asked.

"Just in case. The cameras still work, but they don't record shit on the servers anymore. If that milky stick of dynamite lawyers up and comes looking for the footage, there won't be any for him to find. It'll look shady as fuck, but he won't be able to use the footage against us."

"Good looking out," Iggy said. He threw his arm around Carlos. "Now let's get to work."

An afternoon shipment of meat meant Iggy had plenty of processing to do, and if he didn't want to be there all night, he had to get started now, without touching his lunch.

"Where is all this meat coming from?" Dro asked. "There's enough here to last until *after* the apocalypse. There's so much fucking meat in here that you can see it from space."

"I ordered it," Iggy said. "Every pound."

An hour later, adrenaline still surged through Iggy's veins.

It was thirty-seven degrees in the prep room, but Iggy didn't feel the cold. He kept seeing Conner's freckled face as he left the shop: red brows scrunched over eyes as hateful as they were blue; thin lips snarling over perfect canines; a weak chin sprinkled with red stubble that would never be a beard. The idea that someone so weak, so cowardly, had even thought of stepping up to Iggy like that enraged him. They weren't even from the same species as far as Iggy was concerned. But despite all that, Conner was a real threat.

Eventually, the adrenaline faded and the cold caught up with Iggy. He slipped into a hoodie. He breathed more easily by the time he'd laid out the work that needed doing: he would chop, slice, and grind through the rest of the day. He couldn't let Armando's absence slow them down. And there was no way he was going to sit back and let the Chop Shop drive La Carnicería Guerra out of business. If the shop needed him to stay after his shift to help out, he'd be there. When deliveries came, he'd handle them. The front counter needed a body to weigh, wrap, and sell meat? He'd do it. Someone clogged the toilet with a monster shit? Iggy would plunge and mop. He no longer needed to find another job. For the moment, he'd found his calling.

Iggy needed La Carnicería Guerra as much as it needed him. And it felt good to be needed. As long as Conner G. Harrison existed in his neighborhood, Iggy would do whatever he needed to do to keep La Carnicería Guerra open and thriving. Anything.

11

SAWGRASS MIDNIGHT

Iggy hoped to fall asleep the moment his head hit the pillow. The day he'd just endured was as stressful as any day from his first week in prison. But after what he'd seen at Orin's ranch, even after his encounter with Conner, despite having processed enough meat to feed an army, Iggy couldn't shut off his brain. On the drive home, Iggy saw that the Chop Shop had completed a back deck that could have been featured in *Architectural Digest*. More bills would arrive at the shop soon, the Heat had been eliminated from the playoffs, and Iggy was constipated.

To top it off, running through Iggy's mind the whole time were replays of his encounter with Pico. And even though he'd called dozens of times, the whole day had come and gone, and no one had heard from Armando. A new set of worries death-rolled across Iggy's mind, but without Armando's input, Iggy and the crew were operating at suboptimal efficiency. As far as Iggy knew, Armando had no clue that trouble was closing in on the shop from all angles. Maybe that was for the best.

Iggy accepted his exhaustion. It was better than dealing with his anxiety. He hadn't slept since he'd gotten home, and every single one of his troubles would be waiting for him the next morning.

He fell asleep at some point, but it wasn't for long. Iggy opened his eyes to find Carlos standing over him. Iggy scratched his nuts. "What the fuck are you doing?" The air was cold, but sweat coated Iggy's face, back, and arms. He was so fucking tired. He yawned.

"Dad's missing," he said.

"No shit. He'll show up at some point. Besides, I left him like fifty messages about Pico being at the shop. I said some savory shit to him, so trust me, he'll call as soon as he hears them. Go back to sleep."

"He's never done this before. Not like this. He's out there, incommunicado, doing God knows what. Something's wrong, bro, I can feel it."

"So what?"

"His car's gone. His knives are still on the counter. His phone is on his nightstand. But his wallet is gone."

"So what do you want *me* to do about that? You want me to just drive aimlessly around Miami with my fingers crossed to see if I find Pops?"

Carlos nodded.

Iggy covered his face with a pillow. "Go to bed, Carlos."

Carlos pulled the pillow off Iggy's face. "I can't. I'm scared."

"Scared of what?"

"I don't know what I'll do if he's dead too," Carlos said as tears pushed through his pinched eyelids.

Iggy slowly reached out and took his pillow back. "What makes you think he's dead?"

"I don't know. I'm just scared for him. I don't know what to do. He needs help, but I can't fucking help him!"

Iggy eyed his brother, then the clock. It flashed 11:23 p.m. "Fine. All right," Iggy said, knowing he'd get no sleep now even if he tried. "You stay here in case he calls. I'll go find him." Iggy rubbed his eyes. "You owe me, bro."

•   •   •

Ten minutes later, Iggy had pulled up to La Carnicería Guerra in search of Armando's Tahoe. When Iggy couldn't spot it from the front, he drove up to the side of the shop. Armando's car wasn't there. *All right, Pops*, Iggy thought. *Where are you?*

Fifteen minutes later, Iggy swerved across four lanes of traffic, weaving an invisible braid across Calle Ocho. The traffic light flicked from green to yellow, and his momentum eased him into the front of his lane under the red light. All four eastbound lanes were empty, and if it weren't for him and Azúcar Prieta, so would the four westbound ones. The air conditioner hissed when he rolled the windows down so that the city could creep in.

Iggy spent so much of his first year locked up thinking about his father that it felt like he was trying to telepathically will him to visit him in prison. He'd wanted advice, like how to move, stand, talk, walk, and think in a place where no one was your friend. However inadvertently, Armando's silence had taught Iggy how to do just that.

The traffic light still glowed red. Iggy laughed. He was out of prison and *still* looking for his father, and *still* unable to find him. But for Carlos's sake, he'd keep trying. Iggy attempted to conjure up a route to his father. He pictured himself hovering in place over the street, focusing his thoughts on Armando. He waited for some salient detail to curl its finger and call him over. He wasn't surprised that after a minute he couldn't come up with anything. How was he supposed to find someone who never wanted to be found? And who he wasn't sure he wanted to find?

Iggy's phone buzzed. He was startled to be looking at Mami's phone. The text from Carlos read, *It feels weird to still be texting this number . . . Just be safe. Please.* Iggy leaned back in his seat and blinked away tears; not a single one left his eyes. As he sat there with his eyes closed waiting for the rest of his tears to ebb, he searched his mind for Armando again.

Iggy pictured himself from above again, then he zoomed out, slowly at first, as dark tendrils wriggled from his fingertips, crawling along streets, in between alleys and side streets, through the windows of those sleeping, eating, or showering, up over bridges and baseball fields and stadiums, hospitals, and airports; they burst through the tinted windows parked on the city's grid, on causeways and interstates and overpasses that looked like concrete guts spilling out onto the city; they lurched over the long stretches of asphalt and residential neighborhoods, through the chain-link and wooden fences; they sifted through the leaves of oak and mango trees, slithered past casinos and hotel bars, slipped over alligators and through the cages around airboat motors until the tips of his shady fingers sank deep into the Everglades.

Iggy blinked as a car behind him honked. The light was green, and instead of going around Iggy, the driver leaned on his horn. Iggy punched the gas and Azúcar Prieta roared off into the night. He laughed at himself for thinking he had some sort of psychic bond with his old man. He figured that since Armando was in a dark place, he'd gravitate toward an equally dark place. Iggy aimed his headlights west toward the Everglades.

A low fog covered the Tamiami Trail as it tapered into a two-lane road. A wide canal shimmered on the right side of the trail like a serpent. The city faded away when Iggy crossed 177th Avenue. New housing developments encroached on the Everglades from the south side of the road, and when the last condos faded a few blocks later, there was nothing but black sky above, black water and grass to his sides, and a black horizon ahead.

Clouds swarmed over the pale sliver of moon above. Iggy could barely see it, but its glow felt heavy on his skin, hot like a chemical reaction dancing all over his body. He smelled it, just like he smelled the water around him in that moment, when no one who mattered to anyone was out and about. It was wet in his nose, but not like approaching rain. It was the smell of earth exhaling, of the moon returning puddles to the clouds. Iggy breathed in deep, taking it all in as the last beacon of civilization glimmered ahead. Eight huge spotlights swirled in the sky, summoning anyone who wanted to try their luck and change their futures.

Iggy passed the gun range to his right and the Four Corners rose up from night. Beyond that, the Miccosukee Casino and Resort sprayed light all over the intersection on which it stood. Iggy eased into the right lane and flipped the turn signal, but he wasn't feeling it. The place was too bright. Too much going on. He thought about Orin. The old hunter had insisted Iggy pass by his bar, the Sawgrass Saloon, for a beer. *That place might be more Pops's speed*, Iggy thought. Maybe Armando really was at the end of this dark, dense river of grass.

Mile after mile of asphalt was absorbed by the night. The canal continued to slither alongside Azúcar Prieta. Each of the half dozen airboat operations that Iggy passed was as dark as it was silent. The Miccosukee Indian Village came and went, the concrete buffers of its parking lot jutting out like knocked-over tombstones. Miles of mangroves, cypresses, and pines crowded the road like outstretched hands.

A break appeared on the south side of the road and Iggy slowed down. He would have blown right past it if not for the gold light that flickered through the mangroves' gnarled branches like a low-lying star.

The narrow gravel path curved, then opened onto a large rocky lot about a hundred yards off the road. The trail hugged a squat building like a moat, keeping the mangroves and pines at bay. A gold neon sign hummed above the front porch, washing over the Sawgrass Saloon's parking lot like a fading sunset. A smaller sign, just as invisible from the road, read EVERGLADES CAMPING AND HUNTING OUTFITTERS.

Soft laughter drew Iggy's attention to the porch, where two cigarettes glowed in the dark like gator eyes. He hadn't seen the two figures when he'd first pulled in, but they were there nonetheless, materializing from the shadows as his eyes adjusted to the darkness. A whisper passed between them, and a pop of country music escaped into the night as the slim silhouettes slipped back in through the door.

Iggy parked Azúcar Prieta, crunched across the gravel lot, and climbed the steps to the porch. He did not hesitate in pushing through the Sawgrass Saloon's door. The air inside was musty but cool, heavy with cigarette smoke and stale beer. The space was dark, with a few dim bulbs glowing like fading fireflies above the worn-out pool tables. Iggy finished scanning the room. Armando Guerra was not there.

The dense, still smoke that hung low in the air made it difficult for Iggy to make out distant faces, so he walked past a pool table with a neglected felt top; under a row of alligator, boar, and bear heads—each one missing a canine—mounted side by side on the wall; past pictures of various hunting groups, a jukebox and dartboard, old reels and fishing rods nailed on the far wall, and a collection of license plates clustered by the bar's bathroom.

Twangy country music crackled from the jukebox loud enough

to fill the gaps between voices, the clack of billiard balls, and the thump of beer bottles on various surfaces. A few shorts and flip-flops dotted the mostly sleeveless-topped, jeans-clad, and cowboy-boot-wearing crowd.

Iggy checked the darkened corners. He imagined that was on purpose, so that folks could do whatever they liked unnoticed, to watch and be watched. Orin was at a poker table outside on the back porch with Rana and Lew at his side, but no Armando. A flyer for E.C.H.O. was taped to a wall near a dark, roped-off corridor that more likely than not led to Orin's office. Iggy wanted to see the office, and not *just* out of morbid curiosity. If any evidence could shed light on the connection between Orin and the unexplained deposits Iggy had seen in the shop's books, that's where it would be.

Iggy nodded at the bartender, a wispy blonde who polished beer mugs with a .45 ACP tucked into her waistband for all to see. Her sharp blue eyes lingered on Iggy. He pressed his thumb to his pinky and flashed her the same three-fingered salute Orin and the Sawgrass Soldier had exchanged out on the 'Glades. She nodded. She turned her attention to an outstretched arm holding a fistful of bills and Iggy turned the corner.

He followed the corridor and knocked on the door to the Everglades Camping and Hunting Outfitters' office. No one answered, so he pushed through and locked the door behind him.

The room smelled like an ashtray. Piles of yellowed Camel Crush butts overflowed from various cups and food-flecked take-out containers. The large emerald rug beneath the desk in the middle of the room was worn, but still made Iggy feel like he was standing on grass. Rich wood paneling covered the walls, adding to the feeling that Iggy was somehow outside. Stuffed raccoons and possums looked down at him from their perches on the wall, and several birds spread their wings as if trying to flee. In the back corner, a bear with a safe built into its chest towered over the bookcase and gun safe that flanked it. Behind the desk, a window looked out at a tangle of mangroves and the pitch-black Everglades. The bars over the window did not make Iggy feel safe.

Another window across from the stuffed-bear safe had a view of the shadowy side of the parking lot. This end of the building was cut off from the Saloon's back porch, so the commotion of the bar didn't affect the pines and mangroves outside Orin's office.

Through the safety bars, Iggy spotted two SUVs parked facing the mangroves. Beyond them, beneath a makeshift carport attached to the building, the black pickup truck that Lew and Rana drove was parked combat-ready, a tactical decision that ensured the truck was facing the lot's exit, prepared to drive off into the night at a moment's notice. He knew it was theirs because the welding tanks he'd seen earlier were still strapped to the back of the cab. The carport was surrounded by metal rods and tubes that Iggy imagined were part of whatever welding project the two hunters were working on.

Iggy returned to Orin's desk and rifled through the papers stacked on its edges. Purchase orders for beer, soda, and chips were crumpled beside a survey map of Orin's land. Iggy studied the circles that had been drawn around the places Iggy had pointed out to Orin when he was showing the old hunter where he'd look for Pico. He traced a line back to where the ranch stood. The main house, pole barns, pigsty, and even the gator pit were all there, represented by tiny squares and rectangles. It was clear to Iggy that Orin had paid close attention when they had scouted the potential routes Pico was using to trespass on Orin's land.

Iggy noticed three small structures isolated in the middle

southwesternmost part of the map. No roads or marked trails led from Orin's ranch to the lone buildings. And based on the area's elevation and depth of the water table, they were likely surrounded by ferociously dense brush and buried beneath a thick canopy. Iggy used his phone to take a picture of the whole map, then he zoomed in and took a picture of the three lonely squares, using the ranch as a reference point for distance and location.

As he put his phone back in his pocket, Iggy noticed a small notebook sticking out from beneath a stack of unopened mail. He opened it and found a handwritten column of names on dozens of pages. Beside each name was a phone number and some other number. Many of the names were repeated in subsequent pages. The earliest entries on the first two dozen pages had been crossed out, but there were plenty more recent names that weren't. As Iggy read, he recognized the names of a few restaurants. He wondered if this could be a list of Orin's horse meat clients.

Something caught Iggy's eye on one of the latest pages. On the top right-hand corner, he read Armando's name. Beside it, *20K* had been circled, and an arrow pointed to *10K?* in Orin's bold handwriting. It became apparent to Iggy that this was where Orin did his bookkeeping, so he pulled his phone out and took a picture of each page. When he'd finished, he flipped back to the end of the book and found dozens of addresses. The most recent entries were jotted down hastily. Iggy wondered what the correlation between the names, numbers, and addresses was, if any.

He texted the pictures to Carlos along with a message that read, *Can't talk now, but what do you make of this? How are these things connected?* Fearing that any response from Carlos would make his phone chirp, he made sure his phone was on Do Not Disturb mode and slipped it back into his pocket.

The rapid thump of hurried footsteps outside the door

grabbed Iggy's attention. He heard a voice say, "I saw him right by the bathroom and then he was gone."

Iggy must have made more of an impression on the bartender than he'd imagined. They were looking for him, but it was clear that they weren't sure where he'd gone.

Iggy rushed to the gun safe beside the bear. He tried the handle, but it was locked. Iggy knew better than to try guessing the combination. He had no time to waste, so he ran over to the desk and dug through the drawers. There had to be a knife or something to defend himself with. It dawned on Iggy that if Orin caught him rummaging through his office, he'd need a lot more than a knife to escape.

The knob on Orin's office door turned. The dead bolt stopped whoever was outside from barging in.

"Hey," the bartender said, "you remember this door being locked?"

"I don't know," replied a man's voice. "No one goes into Orin's office. Everyone knows to stay the fuck out of there."

Iggy had just finished closing the desk drawer when his gaze drifted to the wall above the door. Iggy recognized the ArmaLite AR-30 sniper rifle by its long barrel, bolt, and bipod. He quietly made his way to the door. He knew it was a heavy rifle, so he made sure to take it off the wall carefully so as not to make a sound. He cradled it like a baby and skulked back behind the desk.

Iggy detached the box magazine and counted five rounds. These bullets, however, were not designed for hunting animals. These were .338 Lapua API rounds and each one was as long as Iggy's middle finger. The silver tip meant the round was incendiary and designed to pierce armor. If Iggy let off one of these rounds at whoever was outside the office door, he'd eviscerate and immolate them in one fell swoop. But Iggy wasn't going to shoot his way out of the office with a twelve-pound, bolt-action sniper rifle and five bullets. Instead, he pulled out his phone and called Orin.

As the phone rang, Iggy edged to the side window and opened it just enough to fit the rifle's barrel out through the bars and rest the bipod on the sill.

"To what do I owe this pleasure, young Guerra?"

Iggy adjusted the scope. "Hey, Orin," he said calmly. "I just pulled up to the Sawgrass. Where you at? I'm looking for my old man?"

Behind him, Iggy heard the bartender say, "This door shouldn't be locked," the bartender said. "Break it down."

Orin said, "He was here a while ago, but I'm not sure where he is now. Listen, I'm out on the back deck. Get out here. Let's have a beer."

Someone laid into the door. It crackled, wood straining at the force of the blow, but it held. "Are you out of your mind," said a new voice. "We're not smashing down Orin's door. That guy's probably not even in there!"

Iggy leaned into the scope and took aim. "Okay, Orin. I'm heading over. But listen, I wanted to ask you about—"

Iggy hit the mute button on his phone, centered the oxygen and acetylene tanks strapped to the pickup, and pulled the trigger. The bullet severed the valves and regulators of the tanks, essentially decapitating them. The incendiary, armor-piercing round did exactly what it was designed to do, igniting its targets on impact. And since the targets were highly flammable welding tanks, a deafening, blinding flash of fire tore through the night. Pieces of blazing wood were still in the air when Iggy unmuted the phone.

"Holy shit, Orin! What the *fuck* just happened?" Orin hung up. Iggy closed the window. He slid the bolt back, pulled out the bullet casing, and emptied the box magazine. If Orin found four rounds in the gun instead of five, he might piece together what happened. But if he found none, he might question himself and wonder whether it had been loaded in the first place.

Iggy pocketed the remaining API rounds, returned the rifle to its place above the door, and listened to the commotion outside the office.

Just as he'd hoped, the group at the door had raced off to see what was going on outside. And now that he'd established a reason for having been at the Sawgrass Saloon, he needed to get out. And fast.

Iggy stepped out of the office, closed the door behind him, and joined the stream of people flowing toward the fireball behind the E.C.H.O. building. But instead of making his way to the incandescent mangroves and roasted cars, Iggy got into Azúcar Prieta and drove away from the glowing dive bar.

12

UNHORSED

The stars flitted around the moon like insects on a bare bulb. Iggy kept his eye on it as he drove, accelerating as if he'd eventually catch up to it. A stream of police cruisers from the Miccosukee reservation raced toward the Sawgrass Saloon with their lights ablaze.

Iggy didn't know where else to look for Armando, but after driving east for a while, he wasn't that far away from the shop. He decided to stop there. He was thirsty, so if nothing else, he'd grab a glass of water, then call Carlos and let him know that Armando was still in the breeze.

Iggy pulled up to the rear lot. He was through the shop's gate and at the back door just as the moon was devoured by clouds. He slid his key into the lock, listening to the pins click over the teeth, and opened the door.

"Hello," a voice called from the darkness. It was a threat, not a welcome.

Iggy froze, not just because he didn't recognize the voice, but because there should not have been a voice in the shop at this time. Iggy's shoulders rose as he stepped through the door, more as a response to the understated warning than the freezing air. Whatever was crawling over his skin couldn't get to him, he thought. It can't get through the sweat. He flicked the switch and the lights in the back room flickered on.

"Close the fucking door," the voice said. Armando stood in the entrance to the main freezer, a butcher knife in each hand. The door thunked behind Iggy, and he threw the lock shut without taking his eyes off Armando.

"You're not supposed to be here," Armando said, gripping each knife as if he were wringing the life from it.

"Where the fuck have you been?" Iggy spat. "We've been looking for you."

"Why are you here, Ignacio? You shouldn't be here."

"I was looking for you. What's going on here, Pops?" The apron over his father's chest was clean and long, stopping just short of his rubber boots, which squeaked softly as he shifted his weight from foot to foot.

Armando eyed Iggy in a way that he'd only seen a few times before but knew well—it made Iggy look around for something to brandish. Finding nothing within arm's reach, he made his way to the fridge, knowing there'd be something in there to fill his empty hands.

"Why are you really here?" Armando asked.

Iggy took the glass pitcher out of the fridge. He filled a cup and drank from it, the pitcher up against his chest. He downed the glass, eyes never leaving his father.

"Leave," Armando said, taking a squeaking step forward. "Go back home. No quiero verte hasta mañana."

"Why?"

"¡Dale! Get out of here!"

The graying scruff on Armando's face made him look more like something out of a low-budget horror movie than a legitimate butcher. But the steel in his hands was no prop.

"I thought we agreed that there'd be no more secret side projects," Iggy said.

"Go home, Ignacio."

Iggy filled the cup once more, glad for the heft the glass put in his hand. The pitcher clinked against the rosary around his neck, and Iggy felt the sweat on his body tighten against his skin. Grief, he thought. Or curiosity. "Straight up, I came in here to grab a drink. But finding you like this isn't a coincidence. The universe brought me here so I could see this with my own eyes."

Armando's look did not lighten as he stepped under the lamps in the middle of the room. The shadows that hid his eyes only made the old man's silence sharper.

"Fuck, Pops. What are you doing here at this hour? At least tell me what you're up to. I could use the distraction."

"None of this is a distraction, mi'jo. This is not something to entertain you so you can pass the time. Leave now."

Iggy studied Armando. The old man was dead serious, and the look he shot Iggy was colder than the room in which they stood.

"I'm already here. I don't even know what the fuck you're doing, but I know it's not good. And since Pico's been snooping around the shop, I'm guessing whatever it is needs to get done fast. I'll grab a hoodie and an apron and give you a hand so that we don't both end up in jail."

Armando Guerra grunted, then returned to silence. "You have no idea what you're asking for, Ignacio."

"It doesn't matter. Let's get this over with, whatever it is?"

"You asked for it. Ponte un apron and come with me." And with that, he disappeared into the main freezer. "And turn off the lights out there!"

Iggy grabbed an apron off the hook by the door and followed his father.

The main freezer was much colder than the back room, something Iggy still hadn't become accustomed to. A bank of lights shone down onto the hanging sides of beef on the far corner of the long room. Iggy stepped toward the light. He tied off his apron as his eyes adjusted to the dark. A line of knives glistened on the counter.

"Here," Armando said, and he handed Iggy a butcher knife, handle first. Iggy took the blade. Armando flipped on the rest of the lights.

On the freezer's floor, next to the drain, lay a horse. It was sprawled on its side, legs stiff in death. Its tongue was a dry pink thing long enough to reach past a jumble of yellow teeth and touch the floor.

Iggy looked into the mare's eye, open and empty, and he wished he'd taken off his sweaty shirt. "Pops, how could you do this?"

"I didn't kill it."

"How can you have this poor thing in here, especially after having Pico in our dumpsters looking for horse meat? Are you out of your motherfucking mind?" Iggy had known that Armando was butchering horses the moment Pico had shown him Armando's knife. And if that wasn't bad enough, now Armando was butchering horses inside their shop. Iggy was so thoroughly disappointed that he couldn't look Armando in the eye. "This isn't who we are, old man. This isn't who we wanna be."

"We'll be done in half an hour. Start at the chest, under the sternum. Cut toward me. You remember how to do this?"

"I've never butchered a horse before, Armando."

"Horse, pig, deer, panther, bear—it's all the same, mi'jo."

Iggy shivered. He wasn't sure if it was because he was wearing a wet shirt in a meat locker or because he'd accepted the reality of his father was standing over a dead horse. Iggy crossed his arms over his chest.

Armando disappeared through the door at the far end and returned with a hoodie. "Ponte eso," he said, tossing it into Iggy's chest. "¡Dale! Let's get this over with."

Iggy undid the top of his apron, slipped the hoodie on, and tied the apron on again.

The mare was huge, a beautifully muscled thing that should have been on some racetrack instead of a butcher shop's cold floor.

"Where'd this horse come from?"

"She was sent from heaven so that I could pay our bills. Now help me."

Iggy knelt beside the head. The fingers of his left hand moved through the stiff, thick mane until they felt something warm. His hand came away with blood. Iggy tightened the grip he had on the knife in his other hand. He slid his fingers along the coarse thicket again until they sank into a hole he hadn't seen. The opening swallowed his index finger entirely. "Someone shot this horse, Pops. Someone shot this horse in the side of the head and now it's in our shop." Iggy stood.

"This is how we're getting by, mi'jo. This is how we're re-solviendo. Thanks to you, we have enough fines, bills, and lawyer fees to last two lifetimes. This is how we've survived."

"Did Mami know about this?"

Armando regarded Iggy with a venomous glare. "Claro que sí, mi'jo," he said in a low voice that harbored a touch of shame. "Your mother found out right away. We fought about it all the time. I stopped for a little while, but when she died, I had no choice." He exhaled slowly through his nose. The hiss did nothing to soften his form. Armando adjusted the blades in his hands, almost as if he were looking down at his own reflection in the steel. He pointed to the mare with a blade.

"Start at the top and cut your way toward me." He knelt between the mare's back legs. Armando looked savage, as if he'd brought the animal down on his own and was about to sink his canines into its flesh.

Iggy pushed his sleeves back past his elbows. He knelt. The blade clacked as Iggy mindlessly slipped it between the horse's teeth. There's no way this was right, no way this made sense. "We gotta get this out of the shop."

"We will. In pieces."

There was no point in arguing with Armando Guerra. Iggy had said he'd help, and that's what he was going to do. He sighed in resignation. "But why's this horse here, Pops?"

Armando pointed to the mare with the tip of his knife and shot Iggy a glance that would broker no argument. "Cut!" He sank his blade into the horse. "Cut toward me. Now."

"You're doing this here 'cause of Pico. Because he's snooping on Orin's farms, right?"

Armando let out an exasperated sigh. "I owe Orin money, Iggy. He fronted me the money for butchering five horses, now I have to pay up. But since Pico found the bones and guts from the last one I did on the ranch, I have to process the horses here now. This is how we keep making money without getting caught. Once I'm done with the first five, he'll give me another five."

"You launder illegal meat?"

"You wanted to know what I'm doing? Here it is. Now help."

"How the fuck could you be mad at me for what I did when here you are doing the same shit?"

Armando said nothing.

Iggy pressed on. "You know Pico has an eye on us. This is

exactly what he's looking for. He thinks you're selling it out of the shop. That crazy gringo knows something's going on."

Armando shrugged. "Let's get this over with, mi'jo. Pico isn't my concern. He won't be anyone's concern soon enough."

Iggy moved beside the horse. "He's your concern as long as he's breathing. He could sink the shop faster than the Chop Shop. And he's got your knife, the one you lost. And this," Iggy said, gesturing at the horse, "you can't just throw any of this away in the dumpsters, if that's what you were thinking. He knows the difference between horse bones and steer bones." Iggy pointed the tip of the blade at the mare's teeth. "Pico knows his shit." He grabbed the tongue and jammed it back into the open mouth. "Damn it, Pops, how could you do this? If Mami didn't want you doing this, then why are you doing it?"

"Mira, Ignacio, you are part of this now, whether you like it or not. Help me now or vete pa'l carajo and don't come back. *This* is what it is right now. You wanted to help? Well here you go. Focus on controlling *this*. Capitalize on *this* opportunity." Armando spat. "Handle *this* problem."

Iggy slipped the butcher knife into the hair at the sternum. He smoothed the skin with his left hand and cut too quickly. The blade jumped and slipped into his left palm as softly as an X-ray. Iggy felt it bump into something firm beneath the meat of his hand and he shot to his feet. By the time the knife was done clattering on the concrete, blood had filled the cut. It was a clean, straight line that stretched diagonally from the base of his index finger across his palm, to the heel of his palm opposite his thumb. Iggy made a fist around the wound. Moments later, he clutched a handful of blood. It welled up, then snaked across his wrist, down to the tip of Iggy's elbow. There, the stream of warm blood swelled into a berry that ripened and fell at Iggy's feet, pattering softly into the horse's open mouth.

"Ignacio!" Armando yelled.

Iggy's entire arm felt cold. He looked away from his red arm and toward the sound of his father's voice.

Armando held his knife out, the blade red with its own harvest, and it wasn't until he got to his feet that Iggy understood that Armando was pointing to something. Iggy turned, scrolled his gaze over the sink's shining faucet, and back to Armando, not exactly sure what he was supposed to do.

Armando was on him in two steps. "Get to the sink!" he yelled, clamping his hands down on Iggy's shoulders.

Iggy caught sight of his fist. Blood coated his thumbnail, creeping into his cuticle and the tiny creases in his fingerprint. He became acutely aware of his wound, of the way it made him vulnerable, disadvantaged, exposed. The sight of his own blood enraged him.

Armando squeezed Iggy's shoulder. Iggy instinctively brushed Armando's hand off him and, with one foot back and his good hand cocked in a fist, he held his red fist out to his father.

"Stop!" Iggy screamed. He opened his injured hand and the gash wept fresh blood. He held it there like a raw stop sign. Armando stood motionless. It took all the restraint Iggy could muster to not start throwing punches.

Armando raised his hands, palms open, as if he were being held at gunpoint. "Ignacio, I—"

"Back the fuck up!" Iggy's voice reverberated off the stainless-steel paneling and concrete floors. "Don't fucking touch me."

"You're hurt. And bleeding," Armando said, lowering his hands. "That's going to need stitches."

Iggy's shock faded as quickly as it had set in. When it clicked in his head that he was safe, that he was no longer in immediate danger, he reined in his anger. He looked down at his hand, then at the horse.

"Whatever," he said to his father. "I'm good. Let's get this horse out of here."

Armando backed away. He turned to the horse and rested the tip of his knife on its exposed genitals. "Wrap that hand and help me gut this," he said, regaining his composure. He made a quick incision around the mare's anus, carefully separating it from the surrounding skin and tissue. His movements were subtle and precise. He maneuvered the tip carefully, making sure not to poke inward toward the colon and bladder.

An opening grew slowly, separating the skin until the brown balloon knot of the anus was free. Armando slowly pulled it out of the body a bit before repositioning himself on the horse's chest. He looked up at Iggy. "You okay to give me a hand?"

"A hand's all I got."

Armando plunged the knife into the mare's sternum, near the bottom of where the brisket would be. It slid through the soft skin, a steel shark fin slicing through waves of hair and skin. Before long, the incision was a mouth that opened just above the layers of muscle and tissue. When the muscle wall was exposed from sternum to anus, Armando flipped the knife over, blade side up so that the edge was cutting away from the body, and made a delicate incision into the muscle wall. He slid his finger into the cut. He pulled the muscle and skin up, away from the paunch. The blade took small bites from the cut's edge without risking a poke at the stomach. He did this until the mare's insides were exposed to the shop's fluorescent light.

"Wash your hands and grab a new sweater from my locker.

There's towels in there too. ¡Dale! Dry your face and bring me one of those big garbage bags."

Iggy looked down at his chest. Red strings sprayed across the cotton apron. He walked to the nearest sink and ran water over his fist until the blood on his arm had spiraled down the drain. He took the bandana from his back pocket and wrapped his hand, using his teeth and free hand to tie off a tight knot. All the while, he watched Armando, elbow-deep in the horse's torso.

"Please bring me a bag," Armando Guerra repeated.

Iggy grabbed a bag from a box on the counter and handed it to Armando.

Armando looked at the bag, and then at Iggy. He shook his head and maneuvered his hand under and through the horse's chest cavity. He worked his way past her heart and lungs and up into her throat.

Iggy knelt next to Armando. The mare's insides smelled a lot like the insides of a deer or boar, warm and musty like the iron in its blood. He opened the bag as Armando squeezed the mare's esophagus. Armando slid his blade up just above the spot where he'd pinched the throat, and with a flick of the wrist, he cut through the esophagus. He worked his knife back under the sternum and into the opening in the abdomen before pulling it out of the body.

Armando placed the knife on the horse's neck to free up his other hand. With his free hand, Armando crawled to the horse's rear and took hold of the freed-up colon. He lifted the ends of the entrails like a sagging hammock.

"Bring that over here."

Iggy slid forward. He worked open the inside of the bag, forearms and elbows making the largest opening possible, and held it out, a yawning plastic chasm between him and his father. The bandana tied around his palm was soaked through.

Armando pulled up on the esophagus, and Iggy slipped the bag beneath it. Armando placed the top end of the intestines in the bag. He grabbed his knife once more and began slicing the digestive tract free from the body, feeding it into the open garbage bag. Bloody guts streaked Iggy's arms as the entrails slid over them.

The more guts Armando fed into the bag, the more entrails slid over Iggy's arm like a fat slimy snake, the more Iggy hated Armando. This was everything Iggy needed to avoid now that he was out of prison. Instead of fresh starts and open horizons, he was here, on a butcher shop's floor, clandestinely filling a bag with warm horse guts to make sure his father didn't end up in prison. How could a man who'd held a grudge against him for three years be doing the same kind of shit that he'd criticized Iggy for doing? Iggy was convinced that desperation had made Armando do many questionable things, but doing them while Pico was out there actively looking for a reason to bring them down was plain stupid. It'd be like Iggy selling those pills to Seth Baker knowing there was an informant looking to rat him out. This worried Iggy because for all the bad things that Armando was, stupid wasn't one of them.

When the bag was full, Armando cut the entrails, pinched them off, and motioned to Iggy for a new bag. Once the second had its fill of guts, Armando tugged at its edges to make sure it swallowed everything. He tied off the bags. "There. Now double bag them."

Iggy had to stop working to wash the sticky blood from his hands and arms. Horse blood mingled with the blood from his gash. After wrapping his hand in paper towels, he worked the dead weight of the bags into another garbage bag. He scanned the hole his father had made in the horse. It was big enough for a person to crawl into.

Armando looked down at his blade and hands, thick with viscera, and went to the sink. He flicked the water on and washed his hands, careful to thoroughly clean his fingernails.

"This has to stop," Iggy said, pointing to the bag of guts at his feet. "This is the kind of shit that will ruin us."

Armando said nothing.

Iggy looked at the horse, mouth and chest open, ribs and teeth bared. "Never again, old man. You can't keep doing this." Iggy knew he'd never abandon his family because they did illegal shit. And deep down, Armando knew that as well. Iggy resented the familial pull that had brought him to his father's side, especially since it hadn't brought Armando to his side when he'd been locked up.

"We needed this money. But this is the last one I'll do here until Orin handles Pico." Armando grabbed a fresh towel off a neatly folded pile on the counter and held it out to Iggy. "We're survivors, mi'jo. Nosotros resolvemos, you understand?"

Iggy took the towel and pressed it to his wound. "This isn't resolviendo, Pops. This is tempting fate."

Armando regarded his son, then turned to the horse, giving Iggy his back once more. "Go to the emergency room, mi'jo. Get that hand stitched up."

"You gonna pay for it? I got no insurance and no money. I'll fill it with Neosporin and use some butterfly closures."

"Then go home, Ignacio," he said, picking up his knife. "I'll take care of this."

Iggy flexed his hand. "That's the point. You can't. Not by yourself. My fingers all work, so I'm not going anywhere." Iggy reached for the knife and accidentally dropped the towel he'd pressed into the cut. It landed on the pool of blood at his feet. As it soaked up blood, Iggy couldn't tell if it was his blood or the horse's saturating the white cotton.

13

They didn't make it in time.

Iggy had been sound asleep when Carlos barged into his room to tell him that Pops was being arrested at the shop. By the time Azúcar Prieta slid to a stop behind Armando's Tahoe, Pops had been cuffed, dragged out, and taken to Turner Guilford Knight Correctional Center. He knew exactly where Armando was heading. Iggy knew TGK well. The thought of his father trapped in that meat grinder did not provide the welcome shock he once imagined it would.

Mauro and Dro were waiting for Carlos and Iggy when they pulled up. A small crowd of neighboring business owners and their clientele gathered on the corner across the street. While Carlos walked over to talk to the people, Mauro showed Iggy the footage he'd recorded on his phone. Pops was already cuffed by the time Mauro had gotten his phone out, and a cop was perp-walking Pops out through the front of the store, guiding him by the bicep like a child misbehaving at church.

Carlos stood with his fingers interlaced over his head as he spoke to Iggy. "Mr. Wong across the street was in there when it happened. The cops just barged in, walked straight to the back, and started screaming for Pops to show himself. They pulled their guns on him when they found him in a bloody apron with a cleaver in his hand. He just stood there and said to them, 'These are tools, not weapons. *You* put down *your* weapons.'"

"What did they arrest him for? What's the charge?" Iggy asked.

"Illegal commercialization of wildlife," Dro said. He showed Iggy a text on his phone. It was to Pops's lawyer.

"He'll be texting you soon. I already sent Lowell all the paperwork," Dro said. "Forwarded it right when the cops left."

Iggy scanned the growing crowd. He flexed his aching hand, which was now a permanent fist. The cut was still raw, but at least it no longer bled profusely through the bandaging. Armando might have ignored Iggy when he'd been arrested, but he and Mami spent a fortune on getting Iggy the best lawyer they could, so the moment Christopher Lowell's name was mentioned, Iggy understood just how expensive things were going to get.

"Good looking out, Dro," Iggy said as he wrapped his cousin up in a hug.

"What do we do now?" Mauro asked.

"We rally," Iggy said. "Everyone inside." He spread his arms wide open like a mother goose and ushered his diminished flock into the shop. He locked the door behind him and fired up la cafetera.

According to Dro, the cops had searched the entire shop, shivering in the cold the entire time. They had a warrant—Pops had left it on his desk—and they took some meat from the freezer with them. They searched the dumpster behind the shop and took all the bags they found in it. Abuelo followed the cops to the jail and planned on bailing Armando out as soon as he could.

"How much do we have for bail money?" Carlos asked. "We can't leave Pops in there." He said this casually, as if he'd been in this situation a hundred times before. But the way his eyes darted from face to face made it clear that he was working to hide his fear.

Iggy couldn't blame him. He was doing the same work to stay calm and focused. "It's not just bail I'm worried about," Iggy said. "It's all the legal bills that come after that. And all the other bills we've already got."

"We'll figure it out," Mauro said. "We always do."

Iggy thought about his late-night butchering session with Armando and the trip he'd taken out to the Everglades to dispose of the evidence. He remembered that Pico had Armando's knife, and how Pico might use it as evidence to slice them all without getting anywhere near them. Pico must have turned it in, along with whatever other evidence he might have collected against Armando, and now here they were, suffering another cut. This latest wound hurt more than the others. Conner, the Chop Shop, the shop's slow descent—even Pico's raid of the shop—it was all somehow tolerable. But having Armando torn away and disappeared like that steeped Iggy in a quiet sadness that made it hard to breathe. Even worse, Pico was out there somewhere while Pops sat in a jail cell as they all scrambled to stop from coming apart at the seams. Iggy wasn't ready to lose both parents. It just wasn't going to happen.

"How can this be happening again?" Carlos asked.

"We got sloppy. That's how."

• • •

An hour later the soft springs squeaked as the remaining men of the Guerra clan settled themselves on Mami's couch. The space was decorated with comfortable furniture designed to make anyone who sat there feel like they were a special guest. Iggy half expected Mami to come out of the kitchen with a tray loaded with tiny cups, ready to offer everyone cafecitos. But it was too hot outside, and Mami was dead.

Mauro, Pedro, and Abuelo Calixto chatted in low voices. The couch squawked every time any of them shifted. Carlos hovered at the entrance, staring at his shoes. Iggy looked down at his feet too. Mami would not have approved of anyone wearing shoes on the carpet, so he walked over to the front door and slipped off his Jordans. Carlos did the same.

"Yo!" Iggy called to the crew. "Shoes off! Let's go! You'd never be wearing them shoes in here if Ma were around."

Abuelo Calixto turned to Pedro, who was pinned between him and Mauro. "¿Qué dijo?"

"Abuelo," Iggy said, gesturing toward the door. "¡Dale! Shoes off!"

Abuelo Calixto turned to Iggy, pushing his glasses up his nose. "Hábleme en español, mi'jo!"

"Que te quites los zapatos. Y no te hagas el bobo. I know you understand me. All of you. Take them shoes off!"

Iggy organized the shoes by the door. He waited for everyone to settle down again. Carlos sat on the love seat beside the couch. He then dragged the coffee table that would have formed a barrier between him and the rest of his family off to the side.

"Look, unless we all want to end up on the streets, we have a lot of work to do. I don't know if any of you realizes this, but we need Pops out if we're gonna stay employed. He's the best butcher of all of us. People trust him. But we can't help him unless we start making some serious money, and fast. And if we're gonna get him out and stay employed long-term, we need to do damage control, get Pops out, and get ourselves ready for the Chop Shop's grand opening."

"Can't you just launch a few nukes?" Mauro asked. "There's gotta be someone you can take out into the Everglades to fleece."

Carlos turned away from a photograph of Mami in her wedding dress leaning into Pops's bow-tied neck. "Do we know what they took from the dumpster? And who pays attention to anonymous calls anymore?"

"I know for a fact that whatever was in those dumpsters wasn't ours." The remains of the horse Iggy and Armando processed were at the bottom of a canal miles from the Tamiami Trail, and Iggy was so grateful he'd followed his instincts and taken the guts and bones from the dumpster where Armando had tossed them. "It's on the police to prove that Pops put them there, but that's not our concern right now. Lowell said that shit won't stick in court. They're trying to make other animal abuse shit stick, and that's what we need Lowell and his lawyers for, to defend Pops from that bullshit. Our biggest problem right now is coming up with the bail money."

"So what do you want us to do?" Dro asked. "Unless you want us to sell our asses on Eighth Street, we're never gonna come up with that money."

"We need like, what, twenty grand?" Mauro asked.

"That's if we don't mind this shit getting dragged out for months and letting Pops do a year or two," Iggy replied. "To make sure Pops gets out quickly and doesn't go to prison, we need at least twice that much." He held out his bandaged hand. "For now, this is what we need: Abuelo, I need you to make lots of sausages," Iggy said in Spanish. "Just make sure that you've got more than you've ever made."

"Estoy retirado, mi'jo," Abuelo Calixto said, adding, "Retired!" in English for emphasis.

"We can't afford this shit now, Abuelo. You're back in the game."

He walked over to Armando's humidor and fished out the longest, fattest cigar in the cedar box. The familiar nicotine tang and earthy leaf calmed him. "This is better than any of that shit you smoke," he said, handing it to Abuelo Calixto. "Take care of the sausages and you can smoke one of these a day. Plus, you get to boss these two around all day," he said, gesturing to Mauro and Dro.

Mauro and Dro shook their heads in disbelief, their faces souring at the prospect of having Abuelo Calixto micromanage their days.

"We need you," Iggy said, holding out the cigar ring to his grandfather.

The old man took the label, placed it in one of his guayabera's chest pockets, and nodded. "Está bien," he said, eyeing Mauro and Dro.

"Good. Now you two," Iggy said, turning his attention to Mauro and Dro. "I have a special job for you. I need you two to keep processing all the meat that shows up. Start processing right when you get in and don't stop until it's closing time."

"Iggy bro," Mauro said, "where's that meat even coming from? It's, like, a lot of meat. It's gonna take a long time to move all that."

"Yeah, I've been wondering that myself," Dro said. "How are we gonna save the shop when we've sunk ourselves into more debt by ordering a fuck-load of meat that's gonna sit in the coolers forever?"

Iggy shook his head. "Y'all ain't focused at all. I need you paying attention to the here and now. Each of us has a role to fill. Our butcher shop needs its blades sharp and active. You two are the main blades, and processing meat is what y'all are best at. Without you two, this place would have fallen apart a long time ago. I've been incarcerated. Carlos is at school. Pops is in jail, drowning in anguish and bad decisions. Abuelo is . . . well, he's Abuelo. My point is," Iggy said, walking up to Dro and Mauro, "that you guys have been the *Guerra* in La Carnicería Guerra for a long time. If you keep doing that a while longer, I *know* we'll make it out of this."

Once the crew left, Carlos pulled out his iPad and handed it to Iggy.

Iggy stared at the screen. There were images of horses. "What's all this?" he asked.

"I dug around for a bit when you sent me all those pictures and phone numbers. There seems to be a link between Orin and that crooked horse track down in Homestead."

"The one that gets shut down every other week for fixing races and doping horses?"

"Yeah, that one. And it turns out that the addresses are all places from which a horse has been reported stolen. The rest of it, the names and numbers, I don't know what to make of that except that a lot of those people live out in the Everglades."

"No fucking way," Iggy said, studying the image of a horse with the word MISSING stamped beneath its head. Now there was no doubt that Iggy was right about the connection between Orin, Armando, and Pico. The three of them were chasing one another through the Everglades, and Iggy needed to make sure that Armando was the one who made it out.

"Did you hear about the explosion at the E.C.H.O. offices last night?" Carlos asked. "The news said that half the building—the offices, not the bar—blew up in some gas accident last night. It's a miracle no one was hurt. You don't know anything about that, do you?"

14

CUBE CARNAGE

Iggy drove to work the next morning having slept so little that his eyes burned. He'd been up all night worrying about Pops being imprisoned and what he was going to do to get him out. Azúcar Prieta's headlights split the 3:46 a.m. darkness and lit up the front of La Carnicería Guerra.

Crude white swastikas dripped down the windows. The phrase FUCK CUBES defaced the storefront in huge red letters. Beside it was a poorly painted cube. The phrase appeared three more times on the side wall along with a huge, cartoonish dick attached to a freakishly malformed ball sack. A long, spotty line cut across the face of the shop and down the side wall as if someone had run alongside it spraying paint. Whoever had ruined the shop hadn't painted a single swastika correctly. Iggy wondered if the person who did this had ever held a spray can before.

In the two minutes that he'd been soaking in all the carnage, Iggy had gone from shock to anger, then to embarrassment for the poor fool who thought that this was supposed to be intimidating, then back to anger, and finally, to understanding and acceptance. The shop had been violated and that was now Iggy's reality. He *knew* Conner had done this. Iggy had yoked him up and Conner had gotten humiliated. Iggy expected retaliation, and here it was.

He stepped out of Azúcar Prieta and into the humid air. Two thoughts crossed his mind: *Fuck Conner Harrison* and *I gotta fix this*.

Iggy walked the perimeter of the building. No windows were broken. The gate was intact. The back of the shop was fine, save for the errant, waist-high paint lines and misshapen swastikas and penises.

Iggy returned to the car. He turned off the engine. Killed the lights. There was nothing to be done about the shop right now, not with deliveries coming in soon. He'd worry about it later, once he'd finished his work and the rest of the crew showed up.

The spray paint was barely dry as Iggy walked past it. "What kind of insult is *Cube*?" he wondered as he unlocked the shop door.

At this hour, La Carnicería Guerra belonged to Iggy. He stood just inside the front door, looking through the graffitied glass. He made coffee and sipped it. The cafecito was hot and sweet. It calmed him despite the caffeine.

The hand-drawn sign on the inside of the door had caught his attention. With the tip of his index finger, Iggy carefully traced the letters his mother had written. *Thank You for Stopping By*. He sipped his cafecito, yawned, and traced the sign again. It felt good to be this close to Mami. She'd held this very poster board in her hands, touched some of the same places he was touching. Iggy wondered if the fingerprints on it were hers. They had to be. What must this place have felt like when Mami walked through it? It couldn't have been this cold.

Iggy decided that this would be the last time he traced the sign, at least for today. It could be the final step of his morning routine: come into the shop, don a hoodie, start a colada, set up a work area, then trace the sign while sipping cafecito.

Abuelo, Mauro, and Dro had done such a good job of leaving the place set up that there wasn't much for Iggy to do until the deliveries arrived. He'd already honed his knives and set up a workstation in the frigid silence of the processing room.

Iggy yawned. Sleep had been hard to come by. Between the dream he kept having about Mami and her apronful of stars and Pops's incarceration, it was a miracle he'd slept at all. Iggy turned on the sound system and cranked the volume. The delivery truck would be here soon, so all that was left to do was choose a play-list to blast through the speakers while he worked.

The meat trucks backed into La Carnicería Guerra's loading area at 4:13 a.m.

Iggy pushed open the doors to the carcass cooler, a room just off the main processing floor.

He greeted the deliverymen with his hood up, gloved hands, and a frozen scowl. His breath steamed in the frozen air.

"Yo, what happened to your shop?" said Laz, the younger of the two men. "Y'all get pranked or something?"

Iggy shrugged. "Someone had too much time on their hands."

"You *do* know they spray-painted Nazi symbols and beefy dicks all over your shop," Laz replied. Willy, the other delivery-man, grunted in agreement.

Iggy yawned. "It's just paint. Besides, we needed fresh paint anyways. My brother doesn't know it yet, but he's gonna be painting murals to cover up all that shit, so you know, it all works out. Carlos gets to spray-paint some frescos and the shop gets an upgrade. Win-win."

"Nazi cocks," Willy finally said. "That's such a bitch-ass thing to do."

Iggy felt himself getting angry all over again, so he asked about the other places they delivered meat to in order to change the subject. They chatted about Herbie Pulgar and how sad his death had been.

"Miami Mussel might not make it to next year," said Willy. Laz nodded.

"Fab knows what he's doing," Iggy said.

"I think so too," Laz said, "but Magda cut their meat orders like in half, bro. She's trying to save money. They're barely buying anything."

This worried Iggy. Herbie Pulgar might be gone, but Iggy's loyalty to him wasn't. Magda couldn't be left to fend for herself, neither could Fabrice. They were all that was left of Iggy's former boss and mentor. Maybe there was something Iggy could do to save them both at once.

"It looks like you guys are ordering all the meat that Miami Mussel can't," Laz said. "I gotta ask, what are you guys doing with all this meat? I've never visited this shop so many times in a week. Y'all stocking up for the apocalypse?"

Iggy nodded. "Something like that." He asked if they knew the meat supplier for the new place down the block.

"The Chop Shop?" Laz asked. "Whoever's running that place has no fucking clue what they're doing."

Iggy made him a fresh colada. Extra espumita.

After thoroughly caffeinating himself, Iggy checked the labels on the boxes as he'd done with every order that had come into the shop. He made sure everything was accounted for. Laz and Willy stacked the boxes in the receiving area on the side wall of the cooler. That work was for the crew. Iggy's main concern was the half steer.

They hooked the beef carcass to the overhead railing by its

hindquarters. Iggy walked around it. The steer had already been skinned, gutted, and decapitated at the slaughterhouse. Now, it swayed gently. Iggy inspected the muscle. He ran his finger over the coating of snowy membrane and layers of fat. It was cold but not frozen. Fresh. Beautiful, really. Smooth white bones arched the length of a concave rib cage like exposed cathedral trusses. He would take the temple apart not with apocalyptic rage but with calm stainless-steel coldness.

Iggy scrawled *IG* on the clipboards, clapped Laz and Willy on the back, and said, "Dale con everything." Once they'd driven off, he double-checked that all the doors were locked. He cranked the volume on the speakers. Pitbull's signature yip filled the prep room. Wrong energy. Iggy needed something steadier and more contemplative. He skipped the song. Biggie's "Suicidal Thoughts" came on. He pulled the hood up on his sweater.

In the locker room, Iggy slid into his chain-mail apron. He tied a cloth apron over that.

Back at his workstation, Iggy put on a chain-mail glove over his injured hand, a latex glove over that. He wouldn't be able to cut as efficiently as he normally would, but he needed to cut nonetheless. If only he'd worn this glove when he was butchering that horse with Armando. He double-checked the knives he'd laid out. All sharp. All eager.

Iggy guided the just-delivered half steer along a track on the ceiling, crossing the refrigerated room as if he were walking with a three-hundred-pound balloon in tow. He paused where the carcass cooler's track ended and the processing floor's track began.

Iggy turned the eight-foot-long carcass so that he was facing the ribs. He looked it over. Eight feet. Iggy counted up five ribs from the bottom and made a cut above the fifth rib. He made sure to poke it all the way through to the other side. That's where he'd later separate the short rib and plate from the chuck.

The next cut Iggy made was between the twelfth and thirteenth rib. The knife slid between the ribs and sliced all the way up to, but not through, the flank. Iggy stopped sawing just short of the far side ribs. He then turned the knife and cut toward himself, slowing down as he reached the vertebrae. The halves opened up like a mouth.

The cut was so clean and controlled that Iggy smiled. Mami would have appreciated that cut. She always appreciated a job well done. But she was in the ground now, no longer able to appreciate anything. Iggy brushed tears from his eyes and grabbed a handsaw. He worked it though the spine. Flecks of bone flew as Iggy sawed. The motion became smooth, like throwing a solid jab over and over. Bone cracked as the saw went through for the last time. The large chunk of meat dangled by the ribs from the section that Iggy hadn't cut through earlier. It caught the weight of the front quarter. The cut in Iggy's hand ached, but he kept going.

The stainless-steel cart that Iggy wheeled beneath the front quarter shone like a mirror. Once it supported the weight of the meat, he cut it free from the hindquarters. The cart squeaked as Iggy wheeled it to a hook on the track that went out to the processing floor. Iggy lifted the slab of beef to slide the hook between the ribs. It felt heavier than 150 pounds, but it weighed less than Conner when Iggy had hoisted him up in the air.

Iggy braced the hindquarters with one arm and freed it from its hook using a long pole. He dropped the pole and caught the beef in a bear hug. Iggy then walked it over to another hook on the lower track and stuck it on. He opened the door to the processing floor. The spray paint that danced along the windows brought the image of the vandalized shop to Iggy's mind. He needed to stop dwelling on all the bad shit that had recently happened and start doing something to change things.

The foreshank followed him along the track and out to his workstation. Iggy found the cut he'd made earlier between the fifth and sixth ribs. His knife slipped in again and followed the cut through to the vertebrae. Another mouth opened up between the chuck and ribs. The handsaw made quick work of the spine.

A new song bumped through the speakers. Boom-bap drums echoed through the large room, working their way into Iggy's bones as effectively as his saw cut through beef vertebrae. He bobbed his head to the beat. Iggy plopped the chuck onto his counter. Behind him, the rib swung on its hook. Retro-funk synths warbled in over the top of the beat. Should he fire up the old Butcher Boy and be done with the ribs, or put his knives to work on the chuck? No matter where Iggy started, a long morning of hard work awaited him. That was a comforting thought.

He took a deep breath in through his nose, held it, then exhaled through his mouth. He wasn't going to stress about any of that right now. It wouldn't get this meat processed any faster. Iggy moved to the band saw. The music was loud. The vibe was chill. Iggy bobbed his head and felt himself falling into a groove. It didn't feel like there was much going for him, but he had an empty space, good music, and lots of meat to process. He knew the importance of letting himself fall into his work, of emptying his mind and getting shit done. Iggy looked forward to being in control of his environment for a few hours, of not fretting and feeling overwhelmed by his situation.

By the time his troubles began circling again, Iggy was in a flow state. With his hands moving as they were, his mind was free to pick them apart one at a time, as if they were a rack of ribs in need of processing. Iggy slowly sliced apart his worries to the rhythm of his knives. Bones and concerns were methodically small-chunked; meat and fears were cleaved into manageable portions.

Three hours later, when Iggy had finished his shift, he was tired but felt good, as if his vision were clear and he were better able to handle everything that he needed to do. His hand hurt so much that even the painkillers he'd taken might as well have been breath mints. But Iggy felt accomplished. He'd finished his work earlier than he'd expected, and that felt great. At his locker, Iggy peeled the sweaty T-shirt off his back. Mami's rosary dangled around his neck. He'd had the dream again last night. The image of Mami pocketing stars grew bright in his memory. He tried not to interpret the sensation as sadness.

"Small victories," Iggy said aloud.

He told himself that Mami's star collecting was an exercise in small victories, like the one he'd just practiced. One thing at a time. Little by little, bit by bit. Iggy slipped into a crisp Carnicería Guerra guayabera. All small victories would be dedicated to Mami. Maybe even Pops.

The sun warmed the front of the shop with its golden early-morning light.

Iggy finished the coffee he'd left earlier and got another colada going. When the crew came in, they'd have some cafecito waiting for them so that they wouldn't have to deal with the desecrated storefront without caffeine. That definitely counted as a small victory.

While the coffee brewed, Iggy scrolled through his social media apps to see what had been going on in the city. After a bit of scrolling, he wondered what La Carnicería Guerra's website was like. He searched and found nothing. He dug some more. The shop had no social media accounts of any kind. How was it possible that a shop struggling to make sales had no online presence?

One by one, Iggy set up social media accounts for the shop on every platform he could think of. Next, he made it so that a post to one platform would be published on all the others. He understood this shop. He knew where the magic and good vibes were nestled within its walls. Ideas for shots and camera angles scrolled through his head. All he needed now was to share his vision of the shop with the city.

Caffeine and inspiration struck Iggy. The first post was the picture of the shop from the outside that he'd taken the other day, before it'd been defaced, while he waited for Carlos to corral everyone in the locker room. In the picture, light poured into the windows, brightening up the white walls and tiles. The long rows of meat in the display case glowed even from a distance. Azúcar Prieta was off to the side. Her purple body was in sharp contrast with the shop's once-white exterior. Iggy wasn't sure which was more beautiful, the shop bathed in light or his car reflecting the sun. He went outside. He took a picture of the shop from the same spot, making sure to capture the extent of the damage. He posted the images together. The caption read: *We're open. We're unfazed. We can't be stopped.*

Iggy entered the shop and snapped more images. He posted photos of the space, including the shop's old-school equipment and Mami's handwritten signs. Most important, Iggy flooded his accounts with snapshots of the meat: freshly processed brisket and arm roast; aged short rib; curated charcuterie plates. Pâtés, confit, sausage links, and rashers of bacon each got their moment in the digital limelight, along with a short description and price of each item.

Iggy was seated at a table by the window and watched as

the crew's cars screeched to a stop as they pulled up to the shop. Abuelo nearly slammed his pickup into Dro's Acura, and Mauro's FJ Cruiser almost plowed into them both. They all did the same thing Iggy had done: sat and stared through their windshields.

Iggy pushed through the front door into the morning air. It was nice to be out of the cold.

Mauro was the first one to snap out of it. "That mother*fucker!*"

Iggy heard his reaction clearly, even though the windows were rolled up.

Dro parked in front of the shop. Abuelo followed.

"What the fuck is this horseshit?" Dro asked, gesturing with a backhanded wave.

"Let's get over to his spot and do some remodeling," Mauro said, raising the Louisville Slugger he always kept in the car into the air as if it were a broadsword.

Iggy waved him off. "Chill with that," he said. "Put that shit away and get these cars into the back lot. I want you out of these customer parking spots. Now!"

"No seas un resingado," Abuelo said. "How are you so calm? How have you not found that piece-of-shit gringo and finished what you started the other day?"

Iggy stared right at him with a silence that brokered no compromise.

Abuelo looked at Mauro and Dro. The three of them looked at one another, at the shop, at Iggy, and then back at one another.

Mauro dropped the bat into the passenger seat. "Okay then, primo. What's the plan?"

Iggy pulled a dark-green bandana with the shop's logo from his back pocket and dabbed the sweat that had quickly formed on his brow. "I'll call the cops in a bit and report it. Then I'll call the news media. Thanks to Conner, we'll have free press for a few days. We've got shop's anniversary coming up, so this Friday, we're throwing an anniversary bash. We'll get together with everyone in the hood and celebrate life. The way I see it, Conner's given us a gift."

"And you're sure it was Conner?" Dro asked. He pushed his glasses back up the bridge of his nose.

Iggy tucked the bandana away. "What's more likely: That random people did this, or that Conner's retaliating? Either way, we carry on like it's business as usual. We act like this ain't a big deal 'cause it isn't."

Dro looked at Mauro for a long moment. They both got back in their cars.

Iggy flipped the sign Mami had made to OPEN.

The moment they reached Iggy at the front of the shop, Abuelo Calixto, Mauro, and Dro huddled around him. Dro put his hand on Iggy's shoulder. "Okay, so we're going to ignore all those dicks and shit sprayed all over the shop?"

Iggy nodded. "Yeah, we are."

Dro leaned forward and lightly poked Iggy's chest. "Okay then. Can we at least talk some more about how you yoked up that gringo for talking shit?"

They mobbed Iggy with hugs and kisses like he'd just reached home plate after hitting a home run. "Don't poke him in the chest," Mauro joked. "He'll launch you through the stratosphere."

Iggy held a finger to his lips. He whispered, "Shhhhhhhut the fuck up."

"Look, I get it," Dro said. "You don't want to talk about the drama in your life. And that's fine. But let's not pretend that this fucking guy *didn't* wreck the shop."

Iggy looked Dro over, then did the same to Abuelo and

Mauro. He pointed to the espresso maker. "Les hice café," Iggy said. "Drink some coffee before I get to it."

"I smelled it all the way from the back," Mauro said, pouring himself a shot.

Dro stared at his phone. "Iggy, did you make these social media accounts for the shop?"

"Yeah," Iggy said.

"Your old man's gonna be pissed," Dro said. "We asked him about this years ago. He told us to sit on our thumbs and squeeze our cheeks tight. That's a direct quote."

"This is how we're doing shit now. We're going all out."

"Is that the new follow request I just got?" Mauro asked.

"Yeah," Iggy said. "Posting on socials is the *least* we can do to help the shop."

Abuelo Calixto cleared his throat. He held up his phone and pointed to an online post. "Look! I just made a digital flyer advertising La Carnicería Guerra's Anniversary Bash. That's what we're calling it. Go on, repost it to your accounts. Get the word out."

Iggy, Mauro, and Dro looked at one another. They turned to Abuelo. The old man scrolled through photo after photo on his screen, double-tapping each one. Iggy's phone buzzed. He had dozens of new notifications. Abuelo tapped his phone. Another notification.

"Since when are you on social media?" Iggy asked.

"I'm mostly on los dating apps," Abuelo Calixto said, still looking at his phone. "Pero a veces these other ones have things I like. You like my flyer? I did good, right? I *love* parties." Calixto looked up at his grandsons when he became aware of how quiet the shop was. "What?" he asked. "¿Qué les pasa a ustedes?"

"Look at you go, old man," Mauro said. He clapped Abuelo on the back.

"I had no idea that old people even knew how to use their phones for shit like that," Dro said to no one in particular. "What other weirdness are you hiding from us, Abuelo?"

Abuelo Calixto smirked. "You're uninvited to my party on Friday," he said to Dro. "And the rest of you better watch yourselves, or you're next."

"Listen," Iggy said, "be sure to tell everyone you know about this Friday. Repost my posts. Get everyone you know to follow us online and to show up in person. Now gimme a second. I've gotta call Carlos and let him know he's got a whole lot of painting to do. And fast."

Iggy went to his locker and hung up his apron and hoodie. He grabbed his bag and took one last look at the processing floor before heading out the back door. As he walked to his car, he hoped that his work spoke for itself. He wanted the quality of his cuts that morning to express his interest and concern for the family. Iggy prayed that the crew saw his work and thought, *This guy cares.* Mostly, he wanted his effort to say, *Thank you for welcoming me home and I'm sorry for the way I fucked up, but I'm here now and I won't let y'all down again.*

Work was the language the Guerra family understood. Sweat equity was *the* equity. Iggy wondered what Pops would say about all his work if he weren't locked up. Would he approve of any of this? Iggy knew, deep in his heart, that the old man would find something wrong with everything he'd done. But the more Iggy thought about it, the clearer it became that he didn't care.

15

PUBLIC RELATIONS

Conner Harrison walked up to La Carnicería Guerra flanked by two police officers as Iggy finished his phone call with Carlos while standing at the front door of the shop. "You're all set then? Okay, I gotta go. ¡Dale!"

There were folks milling about the front of the shop, taking in the vandalism. If they expected a show like the one they'd heard took place between Iggy and Conner, they were in for a disappointment.

Conner wore the same burgundy suit he had on two days before. The cops raked the length of Azúcar Prieta's body as they walked by her. Conner's eyes never left Iggy's face.

Iggy stepped into the afternoon heat and, even though he knew this was an ambush, smiled as he approached the trio. "What's up, gentlemen?" Iggy asked.

"That's him," Conner said. "The Cube who assaulted me."

Iggy paused. He turned to the officers. "Either of you ever heard that word used as an insult before? Cube? Like what's that even mean?" The cops looked at each other and said nothing. "You know the first time I came across that?" Azúcar Prieta's keys jingled as Iggy walked over to the side of the building. He pointed to the wall. "Here. Spray-painted on the shop last night. That is the first time I've ever come across that word used like that." Iggy returned to the front of the shop. "But it looks like we'll talk about that later." He pointed to the younger of the two cops, a baby face with a shaved head and too-tight uniform shirt. Iggy eyed both cops' nameplates. Scott and Pérez. "Officer Scott," he said to the baby face, "it's cafecito time. What do you say we take this party into the air-conditioning and I'll make us a colada while we talk?" Iggy pulled the door open. The cops eyed Conner, then walked inside. "After you, glow stick," Iggy said to Conner, tamping down the urge to make good on what he'd told Conner would happen if he ever set foot in La Carnicería Guerra again.

Conner remained still. "Officers, don't leave me alone with him. It's not safe."

"Then why'd you insist on coming over here with us?" asked Pérez, the older officer. "Stay outside if it makes you feel better."

Conner said nothing. He skirted by Iggy and stood between the two officers.

The band saw's low hum crept into the storefront from the prep room. No one was behind the counter when Iggy got back there, so he peeked through the vinyl curtains to see where everyone was. Mauro worked the Butcher Boy and Abuelo was grinding sausage on the other side of the room.

"Yo!" Iggy screamed into the room. Dro looked up, but Mauro's earplugs ensured that he heard nothing. Dro waved his arms like a concertgoer looking to get a friend's attention in the crowd until Mauro saw him and powered down the saw and turned to Iggy.

"Y'all want some more cafecito?" Iggy asked.

"Fuck yes," Mauro said, eyeing the cops. He made eye contact with Iggy and tilted his chin up, as if to ask, *You want me out there with you?* Iggy tapped his chest twice, a gesture interpreted as, *I got this.*

Dro caught Iggy's gesture and spun his finger through the air as if to say, *Run that shit*, in reference to the cafecito question.

The saw roared back to life as Iggy reentered the storefront. He stepped behind the counter and fired up the espresso maker. "What do y'all want?"

"We'd like to ask you about an altercation between you and Mr. Harrison here," Officer Pérez said. He flipped through a notebook and skimmed some notes. Officer Scott was giving Conner a once-over. Conner still stared at Iggy.

"I'm not sure there was any altercation at all, officers," Iggy said.

"You threw me on the floor," Conner growled. The espresso maker hissed. "You ruined my suit." Iggy poured the coffee into la batidora and stirred sugar into the foamy liquid.

"A suit that, for some reason, you're still wearing," Iggy said. He set two ribbed cups on the counter and poured two shots of espresso. The officers sipped their coffee straightaway. Iggy set out another two cups and poured coffee into them. He stuck his head into the back. He yelled, "Cafecito!" and Mauro and Dro came into the front.

"What's going on?" Dro asked. He sipped the coffee and scanned the room again.

"Something about an assault," Iggy said.

"A what?" Mauro said. He knocked back his shot and Iggy poured him another.

"We need a statement from you as to what went down here the other day," Scott said.

"Let me save us all some time, officers," Iggy said. "This asshole came in here and acted like a fool. I asked him to leave, and when he insisted on acting a fool, I escorted him out and asked him never to come back here again." Iggy turned to Conner. "Yet here he is, *still* acting a fool."

"Can you show us your security footage from that afternoon?" Pérez asked.

"Follow me," Iggy said. He held the clear vinyl open for Pérez. Before going into the back, he turned to Mauro and said, "Stay here with the officer and our neighbor."

Officer Pérez stood in the office, his thumbs hitched in his belt.

"We don't record any footage," Iggy said in a low voice. "We have cameras up so that we can keep an eye on the place, but nothing gets recorded. The server space for that shit's too expensive. I'm telling you this in confidence because we don't want anyone to know that. If we recorded any footage, I'd have proof that Dipshit out there vandalized the shop. Or at least we'd know who he paid to do it."

Pérez jotted down everything Iggy said. He leaned over the monitors, carefully studying the various screens. "I don't know what happened here, but that kid is pissed." He stood up and faced Iggy. "So you think he sent people over here to vandalize your shop?"

Iggy shrugged. "Whoever it was seems to think *Cube* is some kind of insult."

"So if I question your boys out there, they'll corroborate your story?"

"It's that carrot's word against ours."

Pérez made a few more notes. "That works for me," he said. "Saves us lots of paperwork. But do yourself a favor," he said as he turned to the door. "Don't do anything stupid. Don't give Mr.

Harrison any reason to call us again." He paused, thumbs back on his belt. "He's not all there, and you don't want to get locked up again. We understand each other?"

"Perfectly," Iggy said.

Pérez shook his head. "I hope so."

Iggy left the office and pushed through the vinyl to the front. Pérez followed closely behind.

Mauro and Dro stood outside with Officer Scott, studying the shop's vandalized exterior.

Pérez brushed by Iggy on his way to the front door. He held it open and said, "Stay the fuck away from each other." He nodded to Conner. "Let's go."

Conner looked at Iggy and spit on the floor. "Enjoy the free publicity," he said as he walked outside.

As Conner stomped away, Pérez followed him with his eyes. He watched Conner reach the sidewalk and take off toward the Chop Shop. He turned to Iggy. "Remember what I said."

The door jingled shut.

The shop was so cold it caught Iggy by surprise. He jogged through it. When he reached the storeroom, he grabbed a hoodie and slipped it on. He began packing vacuum-sealed deer meat into a small Styrofoam cooler.

"What'd the cop say?" Mauro stood at the storeroom's door.

Dro appeared behind him. "We straight?"

Iggy went back to loading up the cooler. "I owe that bitch-ass, strawberry-milk-looking motherfucker the beatdown of his life."

"Fuck it," Mauro said. "Let's ride." He walked out the door.

"He doesn't mean that literally," Dro yelled to Mauro. He leaned toward Iggy and whispered, "You don't mean that literally, do you?"

"Not at the moment," Iggy replied. "But to answer your original question, yeah, we're straight. We just need to lay low and keep working. Y'all process that extra meat that came in?"

"You know it," Dro said. "I don't know why you ordered all that meat, but if it blows up in our faces, at least we'll have lots of food until we find new jobs. I just hope you know what you're doing," Dro said, and brushed past Mauro and out to the prep room.

"So what are you up to now?" Mauro asked.

"I need more meat," Iggy said.

"What?" Mauro said, half surprised and half exasperated. "We don't need more meat."

"Everglades meat. Let's hope Orin feels like hunting." He motioned to the crowds outside with his bandaged hand. "But right now, I'm gonna do exactly what Conner suggested and make the most of all those cameras out there. Remind me to thank him for that."

16

LOCAL, SOCIAL MEDIA

Iggy's statement to the reporters was short. After showing them around the outside of the shop, answering loaded questions about whether or not he forgave the culprits ("Forgiveness is divine," he'd said, "and I am not a god."), and plugging the shop's anniversary bash at least half a dozen times, Iggy was sick of the heat. He wanted to head inside and sit quietly in the cold air.

He turned to the crowd. He ignored the cluster of microphones and cameras from three local networks, four radio stations, and a few national affiliates, opting instead to speak to the gathering of his fellow business owners and patrons. "Look, whoever did this was acting out of fear. He's a rat bastard and a coward. But I feel for him. That's no way to live. His soul's damaged. If he's listening, I'd like to invite him to our anniversary bash this Friday." Here, he looked at the cameras. "'Round here, we're all about family and we take care of each other. This ain't us."

When Iggy paused, the traffic on Miller sounded more like rushing water than cars. "My mother loved our community. She devoted her life to it. Invested in it. If she were here, I know seeing the shop like this would hurt her. But I also know that she would double down on her effort to serve everyone who lives out here, and that's exactly what we're gonna do. We're open today, tomorrow, and we ain't going anywhere. And this Friday, we're celebrating that with all of you. We're having all sorts of specials and giveaways. Stop by and see us."

Iggy thanked everyone and went inside. He walked past the front counter, through the prep room, past a silent band saw, and into the locker room. Carlos was at his locker, on his phone, hiding from the cameras. "How'd it go out there?" he asked. "You charm the cameras with that smile of yours?"

"You know it," Iggy said. "The best part is that Conner thinks he hurt us." Iggy wiped his face with his bandana. "We couldn't have afforded that kind of exposure if we wanted to."

Outside, reporters gathered beneath the blue sky to get more footage of the desecrated butcher shop. From where the cameras were set up, the meat displayed in the shop's refrigerated display counters would be appearing in the living rooms of the entire city just before dinnertime. A breeze stirred the palms along the avenue. The traffic on Miller surged and stopped, surged and stopped, as if pumped through the streets by some huge, unseen heart.

"Yo, we need a hand in there. Your little media plan is working," Mauro said. A line had gathered outside the shop's front and wrapped around the side of the building.

Iggy turned to enter the prep room, but a cherry red Jeep Wrangler pulled up to the front. The top and doors had been removed, as if the owner had come back from a day at the beach. But Iggy knew that the owner of that car had just come from work, because Sofie got out of the Jeep in business slacks and a button-down shirt. Iggy stood just outside the front door to greet her.

"Look at you, all professional and shit," Iggy said, unable to restrain his smile. He had tried, and immediately failed, to play it cool. "You look like they call you Ms. Villar at work, or is it just Sofie?"

She laughed, and Iggy's knees felt as wobbly as metal springs. "I work at a real estate firm. It's just Sofie." She looked up at the shop and her mood shifted. "I can't believe someone would do this," she said. "Especially to this shop. I saw your post and came right over. My boss asked me to buy a pound of everything you have. He knows that I'm friends with you guys, and I told him that you sell a lot of different things, but he insisted. He said he wanted to show support."

Iggy was thrilled at the idea of spending time with Sofie. "That's gonna take a little time, but that's okay. I'll get you a hoodie and I'll give you a tour of everything we have. Sound good?"

She nodded.

Behind the counter, the crew watched Iggy and Sofie with adolescent glee.

•   •   •

Iggy's heart was still fluttering an hour after Sofie left. He had no idea if there was anything going on between them, but he loved how he felt in her presence, like the sun was shining on him without making him sweat or get sunburned. Once she'd left with a Jeep-full of meat, Iggy and Carlos had spent the last hour planning the shop's new murals and selling out of spicy sausages. Iggy had just restocked the flank steaks when a 1960s Chevelle rumbled into the parking lot. "Carlos, what year you think that is? A '66?"

Carlos looked up from the steaks he was weighing. "It's a '65. And that's Fab."

"Fab from Miami Mussel?" Iggy came around the counter. "He's a Chevy boy too? No shit. And it's a '66."

"Yeah. You should see the interior of that thing. The leather on the seats is as soft as a cloud."

The Chevelle pulled into an open parking spot by the front of the shop.

Iggy trashed his gloves and wove his way through customers on his way out. By the time Fabrice had settled in the rectangular shadow of the shop's sign, Iggy was at the driver's side door.

"Yo, what year is that?" Iggy asked as Fabrice rose up out of the open door.

Fabrice dropped back into the driver's seat. "Damn, bro, where the fuck did you come from?" Fabrice had his hand over his heart. "You scared the shit out of me!"

"My bad," Iggy said.

Fabrice pinned back his dreads by sliding his sunglasses to the top of his head and looked up at Iggy.

"It's a '66, right?" Iggy said, holding out his hand. Fabrice got out of the car and shook it.

"Yeah," Fabrice said, looking Iggy over. "A Z16."

Iggy crossed his arms to take the car in. "She's beautiful. Where'd you find her?"

Fabrice smoothed out his shirt. "Ears to the streets. She needs a few things I'm working on, but she's intact."

The red two-door needed paint touch-ups here and there, but from what Iggy could tell, the interior was as nice as Carlos had suggested. All in all, it was a thing of beauty. The simple, elegant lines of the wide body demanded the attention of anyone who set eyes on it. "I didn't know you were into cars," Iggy said.

Fabrice nodded. "You drive that dark Camaro, right? Where's it at?"

Iggy gestured with his chin to a solitary parking spot on the side of the building. "She's parked out back so that no one dings her doors."

"Shit, you'd better. How much work you put into that beast?"

"Too much," Iggy said. Birds swooped down from the sky to rest on the power lines that drooped throughout the neighborhood.

Fabrice nodded toward Azúcar Prieta. "You wanna launch a nuke?"

Iggy laughed. "Even if you meant it—and as much as I'd like to take your money—I'm not up for it right now."

"Yeah, I heard about your old man," Fabrice said.

"He'll be out soon. Lawyers said the cops are just rattling cages, you know. Trying to scare whoever's been stealing and chopping all them horses that keep showing up in the Everglades."

Fabrice shrugged. "I ain't no one to judge nobody. Wouldn't be here if I did."

Iggy nodded. "I appreciate that."

Fabrice pointed at Iggy's hand. "I gotta ask though. What happened?"

"Occupational hazard."

"Speaking of occupational hazards, you guys ready for that?" Fabrice said, nodding down the block.

Iggy looked over at the marquee, a huge neon thing with the words THE CHOP SHOP glowing even in the day.

"I heard you and Whiteboy G. Harrison had a little scuffle."

"I got something for that fucker." Iggy scratched his stubble-turned-beard. "So what you doing out here?"

"I saw what happened to y'all on the news. I saw your posts and wanted to come show some love," Fabrice said. "Those are some dope pics you took. The artist's eye runs in the family."

"It comes from my mom's side."

"Also, we need some meat. Our delivery didn't come in this morning."

"We don't sell shark and wombat meat, bro. Not sure we can help."

Fabrice laughed. "Nah, just beef and chicken. Magda decided we can't afford to buy shark meat and shit like that anymore. Need less expensive shit. I told Magda that we need to keep investing in those crazy-ass tacos since they're the only thing that sells like that, but she wants to save money."

An hour later, Fabrice had stacked coolers on the counter containing twelve pounds of ground beef and ten pounds of chicken. He even promised to come back for some sausage when it was ready. Iggy wanted to think that Armando would have had a new appreciation for the butcher shop's social media presence if he knew what it had done for them.

"So listen, Fab, you know I can get my hands on all sorts of exotic meat, right? Boar, bat, otter, gator, all sorts of snakes, even wild turkey? And deer, obviously."

Fabrice scrunched his eyebrows, uncertain what to make of Iggy's question.

"So I've got this idea that I wanna pitch to you, so if you've got the time, we should talk. I got something you're gonna eat right up."

Fabrice looked at his phone. "Shit, I got some time right now if that works."

"It does," Iggy replied. "I'll be right back." He disappeared into the back and returned with another Styrofoam cooler, which thumped when it hit the counter.

Fabrice gestured to the cooler with his chin. "What's in there?"

"The future of Miami Mussel." He thought of Armando, how he'd insisted that Iggy worry about his own opportunities. And that he look people in the eye. He looked Fabrice right in the eye and smiled. He said nothing more in hopes of building curiosity.

Fabrice nodded and took the bait. "A'ight then. Let's hear it."

17

HOW THE DEVIL FINDS OUT

Once the meat for Friday's Anniversary Bash was ready, Iggy left the shop and walked the same path that Mami had the night she died. While he was happy to be done processing all that meat, Iggy was worried about money. Orin had delivered quickly; the wild boar he had dropped off that morning had been butchered. Carlos and his crew were working on the shop's new paint job. But Pops was still locked up, Pico was still out there, and Iggy was out of money. He needed to do something, and he needed to do it fast.

He watched the traffic stutter by as he got close to Mami's corner. He was glad not to be driving in it, accelerating and braking to get nowhere.

He found that walking helped clear his mind whenever he thought about how the cops had still done nothing to find Mami's killer. It helped him breathe.

Iggy walked past the white homemade cross marking the spot Mami died. The lacy shadow of the leaves and branches shifted over it like a veil. The sun lit the tips of the trees and they flashed red, like flames. Beside the leaves and discarded water bottles that collected in the gutter, a piece of cloth caught Iggy's attention. The paisley pattern reminded him of one of Mami's dresses. What was she wearing the night she died? Could this be a piece of that dress? Iggy picked up the scrap. He crossed the street and whispered a prayer for Mami.

He reached the other side and heard El Loquito del Sedano's before he saw him: the heavy breathing and metallic clatter of Loqui wrangling shopping carts was its own traffic jam in the supermarket's parking lot. El Loquito stalked carts all over the sprawling lot, the brim of his bucket hat flopping above his bulletproof glasses. The lenses magnified his eyes so that they seemed to take up half of his head. Loqui stacked carts three or four deep, then shepherded his boxy metal sheep into the shade, where he corralled them into a shopping cart pen on the north side of the lot. For as long as Iggy could remember, Loqui did this all day, every day, and as long as Loqui was happy, Iggy was glad to see *that* hadn't changed.

Iggy cut through the parking lot, watching the squat man in the safety yellow vest lumber from cart to cart. El Loquito wiped his face on his sleeve and disappeared into the bushes. Nestled in the shade and foliage behind the pens was his makeshift workstation, organized as always. The focal point was a scuffed-up plastic chair that was more beige than white from years of use. A white towel lay draped over the armrest. It was flanked by an upturned milk crate that served as an end table, on which sat a transistor radio that perpetually crackled between Spanish talk shows, Heat games, Dolphins games, and Marlins games. Under the chair, a stainless-steel thermos lay sweating against the heat and humidity—like everything else in the world.

Iggy circled the southwest corner of the lot, right across the street from where Mami died, and collected all the carts he saw. He stacked them into each other and muscled the long squeaking line toward the shade, stopping to aim the lead cart at the empty lanes in the cart pen.

A low grumble made Iggy look up, but it wasn't until the neon-yellow vest came into sight that he understood that it was coming from Loqui.

"No! No! No!" he chanted, ambling over in a slow jog that looked as if Loqui were catching himself before falling with every other step. "Son míos," he said, "I can do it!"

Iggy eased off the carts and put his hands up. They coasted to a stop at the edge of the shade.

"I know," Iggy said. "I'm not taking your carts. Only helping."

El Loquito looked him over, adjusting his glasses.

"What happened to your hand?"

Iggy's hand was bleeding through the bandage. "I sliced myself."

"Is that why you look sad?"

"I'm sad 'cause my mom died."

"Okay." Loqui leaned into the line of carts that Iggy had been pushing. It was easily four times longer than the stacks Loqui had rustled up, and they barely budged when Loqui drove his legs.

"Can I help?" Iggy asked. "You'll be done quicker if we work together."

"No, only I do this job. It's break time now. Come with me. You need water."

Eventually, El Loquito del Sedano's drove the stack of rattling carts into their corral. He stood panting in the shade. He removed his hat and glasses and wiped his face with his white towel. When he was sufficiently dry, he hung the threadbare rag back on the arm of his chair. He then opened his thermos and a trickle of water sprayed his chin. He pulled two bottles of water from a small red cooler and gave one to Iggy. The other he poured over the ice in his thermos.

"Yo, I feel new right now," Iggy said when he'd drained the bottle. "I didn't realize I was so thirsty."

Loqui looked over at Iggy as he sipped from the thermos. "You still look sad."

Iggy nodded. "Yeah, I'm still sad. But not thirsty, thanks to you."

"When did your mom die?" He asked it in such a way that Iggy wondered if Loqui had meant to ask it, as if maybe the question had escaped from Loqui's mind and tumbled out into the world. Iggy looked across the parking lot, across the street, and spotted Mami's cross.

It was tiny in the distance, but the bone-white paint Carlos had used made it shine, even in the shade. Iggy wanted to talk to Mami so badly, to place his fears in the lap of the only person he trusted, who never judged him, who wouldn't harm him when he was unarmored. He felt momentum building and instead of pressing down on it, he let himself feel it. "I don't know how to stop being sad and afraid and lost and pissed."

El Loquito weighed what Iggy had confided in him. "Talk to your dad," Loqui said, his tone grave, as if he'd offered Iggy the words to a powerful magic spell. "When my mom died, Papi and me talked about it. It's bad to lie. Not saying when you're sad is a lie."

"I'll think about it."

"But he's your dad," Loqui said, "and you both don't have a mom anymore."

"My dad's in jail. I can't see him right now."

"Talk to him," Loqui said, as if it were the most obvious thing in the world. "Say your feelings so they come out." He blinked as if waiting for Iggy to see the logic of what he'd said. The sincerity in Loqui's huge eyes rattled something in Iggy's throat. His eyes welled up.

"It's okay," El Loquito del Sedano's said, placing a gentle hand on Iggy's shoulder. The warm weight of Loqui's touch almost stopped his breath.

Iggy mopped his face with the bottom of his shirt and stood. He felt a bit drained, but somewhat better.

"Was that the saddest you've ever been?"

Iggy scanned the parking lot. It was mostly empty, and he felt like running off and escaping instead of answering this question, but El Loquito looked like he genuinely wanted to know, like this mattered to him and he'd sincerely listen. "Probably."

"Can I tell you a secret?" Loqui asked.

Iggy nodded, not trusting that a sob wouldn't slip out.

"My saddest time was not that long ago."

"I'm sorry to hear it, buddy," Iggy said.

Loqui sat in his chair and looked out over the intersection. "I was here at night. It was after work. I was sitting in my chair. The Heat played the Hornets. It was quiet. I saw a truck turn off its lights all the way over there," he said, pointing to the end of their field of vision, about a hundred yards away from the intersection.

Iggy sat up. "What did you see?"

"The truck hit the woman. She walked into the street and the truck with no lights hit her," he said, driving his fist into his palm with a smack.

Iggy flinched at the sound. "When was this?"

"At night. Under those lights." Loqui pointed to the corner and Mami's cross.

Iggy searched Loqui's giant eyes and found the stillness of

truth in them. "My mom died right there at night," Iggy said, pointing to the intersection. From Loqui's chair, there was a clear line of sight to the corner. "Tell me what you saw?"

"The truck with no lights hit the pretty woman and she went like this," he said, his fists circling each other as if he were pedaling a bike with his hands.

Iggy retched, turned, and threw up in the bushes. He hadn't eaten all day, so it was all water. Was Loqui fucking with him? And could he really be talking about Mami?

"I did the same thing when it happened, but on my shoes," Loqui said.

Iggy looked down at his Jordans. They were, mercifully, puke-free. He wiped his mouth with the back of his hand. "What color was the truck? Did you see who was driving it?"

"It was white. Shiny and white."

"And the driver? Man or woman?"

"I don't know."

"And the pretty woman? What happened to her?"

"She went high in the air and made noises when she hit the ground."

"Then what?"

"Then she didn't move. I got scared so I went home."

"Did you tell the police what you saw? About the white truck?"

"No."

Iggy squared his shoulders to El Loquito and closed in on him. "Why not?"

"Because I cried when I got home and I told my dad what I saw and he said it was okay and that I needed to calm down or the police would come get me and take me to jail and ask me questions. I didn't want to go to jail. And since this is a secret, you can't tell anyone what I said because that's how secrets work."

Iggy understood what Loqui's old man had spared him from. If the cops had found out that Loqui had witnessed Mami's murder, they'd have grilled him mercilessly and put him through the wringer to get at what he knew. Iggy knew the impact that an interrogation would have on the poor guy. It was an experience that would have taken Loqui a long while to recover from. But he needed to know what Loqui had seen.

"I need you to tell me more about the truck. It was white and shiny. What else?"

"Four doors."

"Was it a Ford, a Dodge?"

"It was white and shiny and had four doors."

"And the truck turned off its lights and was parked over there?" Iggy asked, pointing to the spot Loqui had indicated earlier.

Loqui nodded.

Iggy stood. "Wait here."

He sprinted across the street as if no car could kill him. When he reached what he thought was the spot the truck had lain in wait, he turned toward Loqui and pointed down as if to ask, *Here?*

Loqui pointed to Iggy's left, and Iggy walked a bit farther down, stopping every few steps to point his question until Loqui gave him a thumbs-up.

Iggy looked around, searching for anything that might confirm Loqui's story. Why would anyone set a trap like that? And *who* would want Mami dead? Iggy looked at the cross down the block. Was he losing his mind thinking someone purposely killed Mami—that it was planned? But why? Iggy took a knee in the grass.

A cigarette butt lay beneath some blades of grass. Iggy stood and saw another not two feet from the first. He picked them both up, held them side by side. Both were Camel Crushes—the blue camel logo was still intact—and both were smoked down to the filter. He counted three more in the grass, same brand, same condition, all within four feet of each other. He looked to see if there was a bus stop, a bench, something that would explain why someone might smoke five cigarettes in this spot.

Iggy found nothing.

He snapped a picture of the butts with his phone and pocketed the first two butts he'd found. Someone had been here, in this spot, for an extended period of time, smoking these cigarettes while waiting there, and just dropped them. No flicking them, no grinding them underfoot, just letting them fall. Almost as if they'd been sitting still, watching the intersection, waiting for someone. Five cigarettes—someone had definitely waited there for a while.

There, in the grass, were tire marks, short and sudden. He followed them to a spot about three feet from where he now stood. The tracks were blurry, wet, reshaped by rain and time, but there they were. If Loqui was right, whoever had run down Mami had waited here, smoking Camel Crushes, and punched the gas the moment they saw her approach the intersection. Iggy snapped a few photos of the faded tire marks and crossed the street back to where Loqui sat waiting.

"Thank you for telling me your story," Iggy said, holding out his hand. "I won't tell anyone."

Loqui looked at Iggy's outstretched hand. "That's how secrets work."

"I know. You can't tell anyone either. This is something only me and you know."

"Yes," El Loquito del Sedano's said, taking Iggy's hand. "It's very important because if you tell someone's secret, the devil finds out."

Iggy jogged straight back to La Carnicería Guerra. Carlos was up on a ladder working on his mural. Two members of his crew were working on their respective murals as well. Carlos had almost finished his. The pig head with two knives crossed behind it seemed to float off the wall, as did the shop's name, which swooped below the pig.

"Mom's death wasn't an accident. I've got proof she was killed." Iggy held up one of the cigarette butts, and Carlos reached down and took it in his gloved hand. Iggy told him about everything Loqui had showed him.

Carlos looked defeated when Iggy stopped talking. He sat on the ladder's top step. "Bro, Iggy, even if you're right—which I don't think you are, by the way—this doesn't change anything."

"The fuck it doesn't. Our mother was murdered, Carlos. It wasn't just some random accident. Someone rode her down."

"Iggy, I know you want to feel like you're in control of something, especially regarding Mami's death, but this ain't healthy."

"Carlos, I'm telling you, I'm not wrong. Someone was waiting for Mami and ran her over. How are you not furious right now?"

Carlos climbed down from his ladder. He put down his can of paint and returned the cigarette butt to Iggy. "When Mami first died, I couldn't understand why it had happened. I didn't sleep for a week. I was so exhausted that I realized that there wasn't a reason. It just happened. That's it. There wasn't anything more to it. I wanted there to be a reason so I could make sense of it. But that's not how this thing works, Iggy. The universe is random, cold, and uncaring, and brutal. Please, Iggy, don't go stretching out your grief any more than you need to. And don't get yourself into any trouble. The last thing we need is you getting locked up again."

"You're wrong, Carlos."

"Fine. Okay then. What are you gonna do?"

Iggy thought about it. Maybe Carlos was right. Maybe Iggy wanted to feel like he was in control of something, that he could somehow make something about Mami's death better. "I don't know."

"Let me give you some advice," Carlos said. "Focus on what's ahead, not what's in the past. You wanna do something? Do something that needs to get done for the shop."

Iggy exhaled. He was exhausted of feeling like everything was just beyond his reach. And he was hungry. Down the block, the red neon of the Chop Shop's marquee pulsed. There was something he'd been thinking about, a way to get Pops out of jail immediately as well as cover his legal costs. The pulsing red light and Carlos's advice were enough to convince Iggy that it was time to do what he'd been delaying. He got into Azúcar Prieta and pulled up beside Carlos. Iggy gestured up at the wall Carlos had been painting. "It looks great. Y'all almost done with the murals?"

"Well, Hola and 'Tomika are finished. And as you can see, I'm almost done."

"Good," Iggy said. "Now, I want you to paint a cube, you know, the geometric shape, somewhere on that wall. But make sure it can be seen from the Chop Shop. I just figured out how to make the money to set Pops free."

III

CARIDAD SOBRE TODO

18

SUGAR FREE

Iggy drove to the Chop Shop. He pulled up and made sure to park Azúcar Prieta lengthwise across the front window where Conner sat. Iggy reached the restaurant's front door and turned to look back at his car. She was godly.

The door didn't budge when Iggy pulled on it. Conner stood across from Iggy. His hand was still on the lock.

"We need to talk," Iggy said.

"No, we don't, Iggy."

"It's Ignacio. Trust me, you're gonna want to hear this."

"You embarrassed me in front of those cops," Conner said.

"You embarrassed yourself." Iggy wanted to punch through the glass door, grab Conner by the neck, and drag him through the parking lot. With all the dirty shit that he'd done to Iggy and La Carnicería Guerra *that's* what he was thinking about? But Iggy was here to make money, so he'd work with whatever he got. "It's all good, though. I'm here to even the playing field and embarrass myself."

Conner raised a skeptical eyebrow but unlocked the door all the same.

The Chop Shop's interior was sleek and elegant, but too

sterile to have any charm. Iggy sat across from Conner in the booth at the window.

Conner folded his hands on the table. "I'm listening," he said, looking confused. Or sick. Iggy wasn't sure.

"I lied to you the other day, when you first came to the shop. I want to apologize for that."

Conner looked down at the table. Iggy could see him replaying that day in his mind's eye, hoping to recall what Iggy was talking about. "Be more specific," he finally said.

"You asked me if Azúcar Prieta was for sale. I said she wasn't. That was a lie. She is."

Conner pushed away from the table. He let his hands drop to his side. "Why?" he asked.

"Because it's time for me to sell her."

Conner studied Iggy for a moment. "It's because of your father. Because he got arrested. I knew all you Cubes were shady, but I would've bet that you'd be the first one to end up in jail. Again."

Iggy shrugged. "If you're not interested, just let me know."

"Why come to me?"

"You like the car. Plus, you're right next door." Iggy swallowed hard because his pride was far bigger than a horse pill. "And yeah, I need the money to get my old man out of jail. I don't want him in there a second longer than necessary. I *know* you can buy Azúcar Prieta right now, no problem." Iggy hoped to appeal to Conner's vanity, to feed into the image of himself he wanted to project. Besides, he needed to sell his baby with as little hassle as possible. If a mechanic heard the Camaro's hum and started digging around to see what was causing it, there was no telling *what* they might discover, and how much it would cost to fix.

"Bullshit," Conner said. "He let you rot in prison. There's no way you'd sell your car for him. There's something else. And you must be desperate if you're trying to sell your car to me."

Iggy thought about what Pops had said when he wanted Iggy to sell the deer to Orin, how some people needed to feel like they were getting a deal. And if he wanted Pops's bail money and lawyer money, then Iggy needed to convince Conner G. Harrison to buy his pride and joy. He didn't know anyone with enough money to cover the cost of Armando's bail and legal fees, much less buy Azúcar Prieta, and if he was going to part with his car, he was going to make sure they didn't have to worry about legal bills again. Iggy looked out the window at the trees across the street. The sky behind them was growing dark. But Iggy knew it wouldn't rain.

"My father is coming home as soon as humanly possible, Conner. Azúcar Prieta is the only thing I own that's worth something. Selling her is the quickest way to bail out my old man and pay his lawyers. So the question you need to ask yourself is this: Do you want to buy this car today?"

Conner's eyes narrowed. "That depends. How much you want?"

"You know what that car's worth?" Iggy asked, pointing out the window.

Conner looked out at Azúcar Prieta. "I do," he said.

"Good," Iggy said. "Then make me an offer. In cash."

"Half," Conner said. "I'll pay you half of what it's worth."

Iggy wiped his face. He wanted to backhand the smirk off Conner's face. He stood. "Add five racks to that and she's yours."

"Five what?" Conner asked.

"Five thousand dollars." Iggy held his hand out for Conner to shake. "Add five grand and she's yours. When can you get the cash?"

Conner's eyes lingered on Iggy's hand. "I didn't think you'd take such a lowball offer, especially not that quickly."

"If you're gonna kick me when I'm down, don't kick too hard." Iggy slipped his hand in his pocket to stop it from grabbing Conner by the throat.

"I don't know if I want it that badly," Conner said. "Not anymore. I'm actually looking at another car. One that'll make your car feel like it's driving in slow motion. I'm trying to decide whether or not to buy it. Should be here any minute."

Iggy heard it rumbling down the block before he even saw it. It bellowed when it turned onto the street, accelerating down the straightaway toward the Chop Shop.

An orange 1969 Plymouth Road Runner pulled up next to Azúcar Prieta. The long, tapered back end made the car look like a streaking comet frozen in place. The driver's door swung open and out stepped Seth Baker.

What Iggy remembered as mussed-up blond hair was now combed back, and the sides of his head were faded. A golden mustache formed a triangle between the edges of his lips and the bottom of his nose. The aviator glasses he wore made Seth look like even more of a snake rat snitch.

"What the fuck is this bitch doing here, Conner?" Iggy spit in Seth's direction.

"You know him?" Conner asked. He scratched the cinnamon dusting of stubble on his chin. "This just got interesting."

"That scumbag is a police informant. Turned on me, then chirped like a bird for a shorter sentence." Iggy spat again. "He's got less spine than a worm. Best watch yourself, Conner. He'll sell you out faster than Azúcar Prieta can sprint a quarter mile."

Seth leaned against the Road Runner.

Iggy pushed through the Chop Shop's doors and marched right up to Seth, but Seth got back inside the Road Runner and closed the door. Iggy yelled at him through the window. "Don't fucking *talk* to me, you traitorous, backstabbing, coward-ass degenerate. Don't *look* at me. Don't even *think* about me." Spit sprayed the glass. If that maggot had hidden in any other car, Iggy would have smashed the window and dragged him out by his neck. Iggy backed away from the Plymouth.

"Go easy on him," Conner said, stepping between Iggy and the Road Runner. "He's got another baby on the way." He turned to Seth, who was still in the car. "How many is that now? Four kids? Five? And what, three different baby mamas?" He turned back to Iggy. "He told me all this over the phone. Never met the guy till now. I see what you mean about the chirping. That's why he's selling the car. His police informant jobs dried up and he's got child support to pay."

"I'm not surprised," Iggy said, still eyeing Seth. "He's fucked a lot of people."

"Good one, Iggy," Conner said.

"It's Ignacio."

"Anyways, Iggy. Here's what I'm thinking. I can only afford to buy one of these cars at the moment since my money's tied up in the restaurant. You're both in need of a buyer, I'm in need of a car, so I'll let you two race for it. I called a lot of people looking for a car faster than yours. It seems like you raced and beat a lot of people. I want to see it for myself before I buy either car. Something about launching a nuke, whatever that means—I'm assuming it's a race—so whichever one of you wins gets to sell me their car. Oh, and Seth, Iggy's offered to sell me his car at quite a discount, so you'd better race extra hard."

"Fuck that," Iggy said. "Fuck you both." He stalked toward Azúcar Prieta.

"I thought you wanted to get that jailbird father of yours out from behind bars? Is that any way to treat the only person who can help you get him out?"

Seth cracked the Road Runner's window open about an inch. "What the fuck, Conner? We had a fucking deal, man. If I don't pay those bitches their child support, I'll end up in prison again. I'm still on parole, man, so street racing isn't a good look for me right now."

Iggy stopped before opening the car door. He hated having to rely on Conner for anything, but if putting up with his shit a little longer meant Iggy could get Armando out even a day early, it was worth it. But first, he needed to make sure Seth didn't convince Conner to buy his car flat out. Iggy needed to get in their heads. He slipped Azúcar Prieta's keys in his pocket and walked over to the Road Runner. Seth rolled up the window again.

"Tell you what, you piece of shit. Let's go launch a fucking nuke. You beat me, you can have my car. I'll give you the slip right then and there. But if I beat you, Conner buys my car and you go back to making enough kids to field a baseball team."

No one spoke. Seth and Conner just looked at each other, as if what Iggy had said was too good to be true. Which, of course, it was. But Iggy knew one thing about greedy people: they can't help themselves.

"Good. It's settled," Iggy said, pointing to the Road Runner. "Now pop the hood."

"What?" Seth asked. "Why do you want—"

"Pop it, asshole." Iggy needed to know *exactly* what he was dealing with if he and Seth were going to tangle in the middle of the Everglades.

The hood clanged open, and Iggy lifted it up to examine the engine.

"This ain't the original engine," Iggy said. "How'd you even get your hands on this? You sell a few of your kids?"

Conner stepped over and looked under the hood. "What is it?"

"It's a supercharged Hellcrate," Iggy said.

Iggy had never seen one before. The engine was beautiful. "That's a six-point-two-liter Hemi. Puts out almost eight hundred horsepower." His hate for Seth was momentarily muted by how impressed he was. But only for the briefest of moments. That fleeting semblance of respect was overtaken by concern. Iggy had never raced a car like that. There was no way Iggy could beat Seth on a straightaway, not with the sheer muscle the Road Runner was packing beneath its shiny hood. If Iggy was going to beat him, he'd have to rely on much more than muscle. He was going to have to be the better driver. Thankfully, the race would take place on a course Iggy knew well, someplace where Azúcar Prieta could show off everything that made her beautiful.

"Is this a thing you guys do, check under the hood to see what the other guy has? Like a dick-measuring contest?"

When no one spoke, Conner coughed. "Is that why they said this car was faster than yours?" Conner finally asked. "Because it has that engine?"

"It might be faster on paper," Iggy said, "but the driver makes all the difference, Conner."

"Whatever. I was just curious. Speaking of curious," he said, pointing to the Camaro, "let's see what's under your hood."

"I thought you'd never ask." Iggy turned on the engine and popped the hood. The all-aluminum 427 V8 shivered in place like a demon waiting to be summoned. "All original, all-American muscle."

"You know you can't beat me, Iggy," Seth said as he got out of the Road Runner. He leaned against the orange monster. A Taurus GX4 stuck out of his waistband when he crossed his arms. "You know I'm gonna smoke that ass. And if you ever come at me like that again, I'm gonna shoot you in the fucking face."

"You know where to launch a nuke?" Iggy asked Conner.

Conner looked from Iggy to Seth and back to Iggy as if he were enjoying a show.

"I know where to go," Seth said, hopping back in the Road Runner. "I finally get to launch a nuke against Azúcar Prieta."

"I'm gonna gas up and head over," Iggy said to Conner. "You ride with him." He got into Azúcar Prieta and fired up the engine. "Everglades National Park. Thirty minutes." He closed the door and rolled down the window. "And Conner, I'm holding you to your word. You're buying this car from me when I win."

The road to Nike Hercules nuclear missile base cut through the Everglades in long, languid curves; sharp, angular turns; and flat, severe straightaways. Iggy thought of it as a signature that the engineers who designed the road scrawled into the Everglades in hot tar and asphalt. Iggy had launched a nuke against anyone who'd even *thought* they could beat him in a race. All they had to do for the privilege of racing Azúcar Prieta through the Everglades to the decommissioned missile base was pony up a thousand dollars. The first car to reach the Everglades' Cold War secret nuclear base was the winner.

Iggy had made good money outdriving competitors back in the day, but today he'd have to win a race in order to lose his car. Part of him wanted to bust a U-turn on the narrow two-lane road and drive right back to the shop. The other part of him was sad and worried. He'd worked so hard on this car, sacrificed so much to make her what she was, and now it would all come to an end. The last thing Iggy needed was to lose to Seth the bitch-ass informant. Not only would the rat bastard never let Iggy live it down, but the crown would pass onto another head and Azú-car Prieta would be undefeated no more. And worse, Armando would stay locked up indefinitely.

The clouds over Everglades National Park were pink cotton candy stretched over the baby-blue sky. Out here in the open, Iggy could see to the horizon in every direction. The only thing that cut the miles of mottled green was the narrow two-lane asphalt path on which Azúcar Prieta and the Road Runner now sat. Trees stood still in the distance. The sun reflected brightly off patches of water where the grass wasn't thick enough to ab-sorb it all. The heat coming off the blacktop ahead looked like a shimmering puddle.

Conner paced in front of Azúcar Prieta and the Road Runner, a maniacal toddler who'd taken over a candy shop. "It doesn't matter which of you wins," he said. "In the end, I win." He paused and turned to Iggy with a confused look on his face. "How will I know who wins?" he asked.

"You'll know," Iggy said. He flexed his bandaged hand to work the stiffness from the cut. "Now shut up. Let's do this shit."

Conner stepped off the road. He looked from Seth to Iggy and held out his arms. "You ready?"

Both cars revved their engines.

"OK, here we go! THREE . . . TWO . . . O—"

The Road Runner leaped off the line before Conner had fin-ished speaking. Iggy had been expecting that snake Seth to be a snake, so he popped the clutch and stomped the gas a

split second later. Azúcar Prieta let out a monstrous howl that
tore into the Everglades. When Iggy shifted into second gear,
the Camaro lunged forward in savage splendor. The continued
acceleration drove Iggy into his seat and pressed on his head and
chest as the g-forces grew.

The might of five hundred horses stampeded through the
Everglades with ever-increasing speed. The various shades of
tan and green that created depth and breadth in that vast landscape were reduced to a single blurry streak by Azúcar Prieta's
acceleration. Iggy shifted again. The Road Runner began falling
away, about three lengths behind. At ninety miles per hour, Iggy
barely registered trees as he blazed past them—the shadow they
cast on the road was a solid wall of shade.

The road began curving to the left, but since it was a long,
lazy curve and he was on the inside lane, Iggy made no plans to
slow down. At least not in any way that Seth saw coming. Iggy
was being pulled to the right side of the car as he forced her to
the left, but her ability to accelerate and still grip the road gave
Iggy a chance to mount as big a lead as possible while Azúcar
Prieta had a legitimate advantage. Iggy needed to be ahead of
Seth when they hit the course's main straightaway. Otherwise,
Seth would box him out and open a lead that would make win-
ning nearly impossible.

The road would be nearing a fork soon. Iggy needed to veer
right and enter another swooping stretch of asphalt that eventually bent to the left again. Seth was only three lengths behind
Iggy, but Iggy needed more distance between them. Instead of
downshifting to make the turn, Iggy let Azúcar Prieta stay low
in third gear and plow forward. That was the gear that snarled
with power, the one she used to tell Iggy that she was ready to
run for real. Her hunger surged through the stick shift and into

his hand, and he needed to keep her where she was, dancing on the edge between artless driving and genuine racing.

Iggy saw the fork up ahead and white-knuckled the steering wheel. Iggy cut sharply to the right way before the turn appeared. It was the only way to make that turn and maintain any real speed. Thick white smoke bellowed from Azúcar Prieta's tires as the Camaro fishtailed, becoming perpendicular to the road. This meant that Seth would be forced to nail his brakes, and that loss of momentum meant that he'd have to downshift, slow down, make the turn, and then accelerate, all of which would cost him valuable seconds in this early leg of the race.

Azúcar Prieta screamed for fourth gear. Iggy hit the clutch and gave it to her. Iggy caught a glimpse of Seth's wide-eyed disbelief as he drove past the turn. Azúcar Prieta grabbed hold of the road, turning the sideways momentum into forward motion just as she hit the fork in the road.

More white smoke filled the air from beneath the Road Runner. Iggy didn't even bother looking back when he heard the shriek of rubber clawing asphalt. The main straightaway was coming up fast, and it was a long stretch that Iggy wanted to get to work on. Beyond that was the sharp left turn to the finish line at the old missile base.

Iggy downshifted to make the sharp right onto the straightaway. Azúcar Prieta screeched like a banshee and shuddered violently. "Oh, baby, I'm so sorry," Iggy said to Azúcar Prieta. "Hang in there for me. One last time." After a few aftershock spasms, the Camaro seemed to recover. But the turn was quickly approaching, and Iggy was still going way too fast.

Azúcar Prieta gingerly slipped into second gear and the hum she'd first made a few days back was now a full-blown death rattle. Iggy flinched as they slowed enough to turn the solid line in the road back into individual dashes. Iggy didn't want to risk another downshift at that speed—he couldn't predict what would happen—but was still going too fast to make the turn safely.

He needed to slow down a bit without downshifting if he wanted to make the sharp turn. It was the only way he stood a chance of keeping Azúcar Prieta in one piece and beating Seth. Before reaching the upcoming turn, Iggy kissed the rosary hanging from his neck and yoked the wheel. Azúcar Prieta plowed through the sawgrass, hugged the road, and immediately met resistance. The Camaro hydroplaned, sending a wide spray of water and blades of sawgrass through the air as if the car were a scythe. Iggy hit the clutch, hit the gas, and shifted back into third. He cut the corner through the grass and Azúcar Prieta snarled back to life just as she slid back onto the road, pinning Iggy to the seat.

A loud pop tore through the air. Iggy looked through the rearview. Seth had just made the turn and was leaning out of the window and gaining ground fast. Another pop rang out. Iggy saw the flash from Seth's hand. Seth popped off another shot, sending the bullet whizzing by Iggy. The Road Runner was just a few car lengths behind Azúcar Prieta. Iggy floored the gas and shifted into fourth gear. The world around Azúcar Prieta was a smooth, glimmering tangle at that speed. Mangroves and cypress trees became an undulating smudge against the sky.

The two cars blazed by Camp Everglades, the midpoint of the straightaway, which meant, at this speed, the impending sharp right turn to the finish line was coming up in the distance. The road before them was bathed in heat haze. Iggy had no idea how he was going to make the upcoming turn without downshifting.

Azúcar Prieta was pushing 120 miles per hour, but the bullets flying from Seth's gun were faster. Iggy peeked at his rearview mirror and his back windshield exploded in a shower of tiny glass shards. Another bullet zipped by. The air rushing through Azúcar Prieta's interior was deafening.

The Road Runner pulled up beside Azúcar Prieta on the narrow road. Seth aimed the gun at Iggy. Iggy jerked the wheel and slammed into the Road Runner. Seth swerved and dropped the gun. He shifted gears, and the Plymouth began pulling ahead of Azúcar Prieta. Soon, it was a whole length ahead. Then two.

The turn to the missile base met the road that Azúcar Prieta and the Road Runner were on at a perfect ninety-degree angle. Off on the horizon to the left, Iggy spotted the metal coils of barbed wire that floated over HM-69's perimeter like a spiral fog. Iggy popped the clutch and put Azúcar Prieta in neutral. He coasted toward the turn while Seth's lead widened to six lengths. Iggy eased off the road and into the sawgrass. The blades of grass slapping against the fender fluttered like someone thumbing through the pages of a book at speed.

Up ahead, Seth downshifted. He leaned out of the car and fired two more bullets at Iggy. Azúcar Prieta's purr grew tamer as she slowed without downshifting. The turn was just up ahead. Seth retreated into the car and downshifted again. Iggy was catching up to him in a hurry. Seth slowed down even more and drifted into the right lane in order to open up and make the turn at speed.

A fighter jet from Homestead Air Reserve Base came tearing through the sky. "All right, Azúcar," he said to the Camaro. "One last run, baby. That's all I need." That's when Iggy gunned it. He punched Azúcar Prieta back into third gear and cut the wheel hard to the left. Iggy was going so fast that he caught up to Seth almost immediately. The Camaro burst through the grass and drifted sideways into the turn, broadsiding the Road Runner. The two cars slid through the grass in a swooping curve. Azúcar Prieta eventually found traction and sloshed through the water onto the road, but the Road Runner flipped over on its side and began barrel-rolling through the sawgrass. The car was still rolling as Iggy crossed the finish line.

Iggy put Azúcar Prieta in neutral and coasted to a stop. The steering wheel was smeared with blood and his hand burned as if the cut were being held to an open flame. He slid into first gear and drove back to where the Plymouth had disappeared into the swamp.

Iggy scanned the water for gators and snakes. The water was the color of sweet tea, and Iggy couldn't see much as he waded through the long grass. He found the orange beast on its side. Seeing it like that made him cringe. "Seth! You'd better be alive so I can kill you!"

Iggy reached the Plymouth and pounded on the roof. There was no response. He peeked through the shattered windshield and found Seth unconscious and half submerged in the water. That might be a fitting end for the two-faced fuck, but Iggy didn't want his kids to grow up without an example of what *not* to be. Besides, if Seth's corpse was discovered out here half munched by a gator, it would take only a single chirp from Conner for the authorities to link Iggy to his death, and that would land Iggy in a cell right beside Armando.

Iggy kicked in the windshield and dragged Seth out to prevent him from drowning in the water. He propped him up against the roof and frisked him to make sure he didn't have the gun on him. Seth groaned when Iggy threw him over his shoulders in a fireman carry.

The asphalt was radiating heat when Iggy reached it. He

unceremoniously dumped Seth onto the side of the road and assessed the damage to Azúcar Prieta: both windshields shattered, a bullet hole through the passenger headrest, a long, continuous scraped-up dent all along the right side, and enough dents in the front bumper to make Iggy want to cry.

He turned to Seth and delivered a swift kick to his ribs. Iggy reached into Seth's pocket and pulled out his wallet. Iggy took all the cash he found and tossed the wallet into the swamp. "That's just the beginning!" Iggy screamed at him. "You owe me! And you're gonna pay!"

Iggy got a running start and hit a dead sprint through the water until he plowed his shoulder into the Road Runner's hood. The steering wheel had been turned to the left, so when Iggy pushed himself up against the car, it slowly gave and splashed back onto all four of its wheels. Seth might be an irredeemable piece of shit, but the Road Runner was blameless. Iggy couldn't imagine letting that beautiful machine, banged up as it was, stay on its side and take on water. Hopefully the engine was intact. Iggy reached inside the soggy interior and took the keys out of the ignition. He slipped them into his pocket, then grabbed the car's title and a pen from the glove box.

Seth's gun was on the floorboard of the passenger side. Iggy grabbed it and checked the chamber. There were six rounds left. Iggy cocked it, checked the chamber again, and walked over to where Seth was sitting up, slowly coming to.

Iggy leveled the gun at Seth's head. "Wait, Iggy, man, hold up." Seth's hand was sliced much like Iggy's. His hairline was oozing dark red blood down between his eyes and off the tip of his nose. "I needed that money, man. I wasn't trying to kill you. I just needed to win. Please, Iggy."

Iggy pulled the trigger. The asphalt in front of a gator that was slithering out of the water exploded. It hissed. The sound was so primal, so savage that even the Taurus in Iggy's hand didn't make him feel totally safe. Seth turned, saw the gator, and crawled across the blacktop so fast he might as well have been running. Iggy fired another shot and the gator vanished into the water.

"Your car's mine now, Seth. You heard? I'm claiming it from you instead of claiming you. You know the rules. You came for my head and missed. Not only did I save your ass from drowning and from a gator, but I'm letting you keep your life. All it's costing you is your car. Nod if you understand."

Seth spit up blood but nodded all the same.

Iggy dropped the deed and pen in front of Seth. "Sign it."

Seth scrawled his signature on the back of the title and handed it to Iggy.

"I'm gonna call my homies Al and Manny from Down South Towing. They'll be here soon enough to pick up the Road Runner. You'd better not be anywhere near here when they show up. They'll bury you out here when I tell them what you did, no questions asked." Iggy slipped the title into his back pocket. "And if I *ever* see you again . . ." Iggy walked right up to Seth and fired off the remaining rounds at the grass behind him, letting the bullet casings rain down on Seth's bloodied head.

•   •   •

Iggy pulled up to the Chop Shop with Conner G. Harrison in a mostly intact Azúcar Prieta.

Conner insisted on keeping the passenger side window up even though the windshields were gone. "I wouldn't be buying Butcher's Blade—that's this car's new name, by the way—if it didn't hurt you so much to have to sell it to me. And if I weren't getting it at such a deep discount," he said. "Looks like I'll be spending the money I saved on fixing up all the damage you caused."

"Seth shot up my car, Conner. Save your complaints for him." Iggy coasted to first gear and shut off the engine. On the drive out of the Everglades, Iggy realized that Azúcar Prieta had no problem downshifting from second to first gear. In those gears, all she did was hum. The real trouble happened in the higher gears, but Azúcar Prieta's downshift dilemma was a surprise he'd let Conner discover on his own.

"Did you really just leave him out there?" Conner asked.

"Did you miss the part where he shot at me?" Iggy replied. "He's lucky I didn't feed him to a fucking gator."

"For the record, I was never going to buy Seth's car. Especially not when you offered to sell me Butcher's Blade so cheaply. I'm about to hand you the last of my liquid cash, but I'll be making money hand over fist when I open up the Chop Shop this Saturday, so everything works out."

"Great. Perfect. But don't change my car's name until you've paid me."

"Fine," Conner said. "Give me the keys and I'll come back with the cash."

"Fuck that," Iggy said. He grabbed the Camaro's title from the glove box. "I'll wait inside."

Iggy followed Conner into the Chop Shop. The adrenaline had left his system. His body ached as he slid into a booth. The cut in his hand was open once more. Blood was filling his fist.

"You know," Conner said when he came out of his office, "the best thing about all this is not that I got such a badass car. It's that I got *your* car."

Iggy felt like crying, but he wasn't going to give Conner the satisfaction of seeing his tears. "I don't give a fuck. Let's see that green. And pass me a paper towel."

Conner dropped the stacks of banded bills on the table in front of Iggy. It was more money than Iggy had ever seen, and this guy just had it sitting there in a safe. This money could change Iggy's life, or at least it would greatly improve Armando's. The only good thing about the old man being locked up was that he'd had to dry out, but even that wasn't worth leaving him in there a second longer than he had to.

Iggy took the first stack, broke the band, and counted out the bills one at a time, placing each crisp Benjamin flat on the table. He made it through two stacks before he bled on the table, so he asked Conner for some paper towels again. After patching up his hand, Iggy resumed counting hundred-dollar bills.

When Iggy had finally finished counting the forty-five thousand he'd negotiated, he slid the title and car key across the table.

"You satisfied?" Conner asked. "Is it all there?"

Iggy slid the stacks into the pockets of his La Carnicería Guerra hoodie. "Every last dollar is right here," Iggy said, patting the bulge.

"Good," Conner said. "Now get out of my shop."

Iggy stood. He said, "Fuck you very much," and pushed through the doors. The money pressed against his stomach as he walked into the afternoon sun and back to La Carnicería Guerra. He heard his Camaro roar to life; Conner Harrison wasted no time in playing with his new toy, beat-up as it was. Conner roared down the street in Azúcar Prieta with his arm out the window, whooping like a coked-out bull rider as he blazed by.

Carlos and his crew were admiring their respective murals

when Iggy came up on them. They'd each done one of four walls; the storefront had been painted plain white. Carlos had just finished the neon-green cube floating above his mural. "Where's Azúcar Prieta, Iggy?" Carlos asked. He hopped down from his ladder. "I *hear* her, but I don't *see* her. What have you done?"

"I'm getting Pops out of jail, that's what. Give me ten minutes, then come see me. I'll be in the office." And with that, he went straight into the office and locked the door. He opened the safe, tossed the bills inside, and locked it. Next, he grabbed the phone and called Lowell, Pops's lawyer. He stated, in no uncertain terms, that he wanted Armando bailed out right away.

"We'll see what we can do," Lowell said. "It takes time. You know how it goes."

"I do," Iggy said. "That's why I want him out now. Make it happen." Iggy could still hear Conner tearing down the street in Azúcar Prieta. She was too much car for him. Iggy hoped the maniac wouldn't lose control and crash her into a parked vehicle.

"I can't make any promises," Lowell said.

"Listen, Christopher. I just sold my car to get Pops out now. I don't need to explain the motherfucking significance of that to you. And if you want to remain our lawyer, you'd better come to our party tomorrow and buy a lot of fucking meat." Iggy hung up.

The cold air felt good on his skin as he leaned back on the faux leather office chair. There was a knock on the door. Iggy unlocked it and Carlos poked his head in. "Why is Conner driving Azúcar Prieta?" he asked.

"I sold her."

Carlos looked like he was about to cry. "Iggy, why did you do that? I can't believe you sold your car to Conner, of all people."

"I know, Carlos. I know. But you don't know what Pops is going through right now. Thanks to Azúcar Prieta, we can bail Pops out and hire lawyers and *still* pay some bills."

"Iggy, I get it. But still."

"But nothing. It had to be done." Azúcar Prieta roared down the street again. "Besides, Al and Manny from Down South Towing are dropping a little surprise off at Swanson's for me. We'll have something new to work on."

"Iggy, you're out of your fucking mind. But you're a good son."

"If that were true, Ma would still be alive."

19

MEAT AND GREET

The breeze tugged at the hot air, but not enough to keep sweat from beading on Iggy's skin. He dabbed his forehead. The smell of wild boar and pork cooking in Caja Chinas wafted from the lot for blocks, or so the first few folks who'd joined the party had said. The crowd packed into the rear lot of La Carnicería Guerra reveled in the music pulsing through it. The tents hugging the periphery of the lot formed a rectangle of shade where vendors sold their goods while providing partiers some relief from the afternoon sun.

Fabrice and Miami Mussel's crew had set up a long bank of grills and Caja Chinas in the shade under the oak. They radiated heat, so Iggy had made sure Fabrice and his crew had all the shade and water they needed. The boar, gator, wild turkey—even the otter and python—on their Edible Everglades menu seemed to be a hit with the crowd, and Iggy was confident that their success at this party would carry over to the restaurant itself.

Dro was DJing on a stage beneath the awning near all the electrical outlets. The middle of the lot was dotted with domino tables and clusters of neighborhood folks dancing. The Buy-One-Get-One Anniversary Celebration had been going all afternoon with no signs of slowing down. Best of all, everyone who'd shown up to the shop's cookout had eaten, danced, and, at one point or another, bought meat.

Iggy grabbed his sweaty bottle of Fabrice's CCCV pilsner by the neck, chugged the rest of the beer in it, and listened as it clinked into the garbage can. He motioned to Dro, who handed him the microphone.

"How's everyone out there doing today?" he asked, hopping onto the stage. "My name's Iggy Guerra, and I wanna thank y'all for coming out to celebrate with us! Shout-out to DJ Dro Blaze, spinning on the ones and twos. I need everyone out there to look this way and make some noise." The crowd let out a raw cheer and turned to Iggy. He adjusted his guayabera and held up his phone.

"Now I need all y'all to smile for me. I'm gonna take a picture of all your beautiful faces and post it right quick. Say cheese!"

The crowd roared again. Hundreds of hands went up. Iggy snapped the photo. He looked it over, added a caption and some hashtags, then posted it. "Now," he said, his voice louder than he expected over the speakers, "follow us on social media, and make sure you like this pic! I've been taking photos all day today, so go find yourselves on our feed and like the pics you're in. And while you're at it, tell everyone you know that starting today and for the rest of next week, all the meat in the shop, pound for pound, is buy one, get one free."

The crowd roared again. "That's right! No one celebrates summer like we do down here in the three-o-five! Grab a CCCV lager from Miami Mussel and drink deep! Head into the shop and buy as much meat as you can carry home! Oh, and we're putting everything you buy in a free Styrofoam cooler so it stays fresh. And you get a free limited-edition La Carnicería Guerra

T-shirt designed by my brother, Carlos. How does that sound to y'all?"

The cheers went up higher than their outstretched hands ever could. Iggy popped the top off a new beer and held it up. "Now hold up your drinks right quick for a toast." Bottles, red plastic cups, and cigars floated up over the crowd's heads as they quieted.

"I wanna thank all our vendors and sponsors for making this party happen; DJ Dro Blaze for the music; my insanely talented baby brother, Carlos Guerra, over there for the amazing art; Magic City Cigars for rolling those sticks you're smoking; and the crew of La Carnicería Guerra for hosting this party and for providing us with the meat you're enjoying. And last but not least, my boy F-Breezy from Miami Mussel for preparing this delicious Edible Everglades feast. I hope y'all are enjoying their new Everglades menu as much as I am!" The crowd cheered again.

"The reason I'm here is because of you. It's the people who *love* the three-oh-five, who *live* the three-oh-five, who make this the most unique city on earth. Y'all are our heart and soul. Y'all know what it takes to make our city great, know how important it is to support local businesses. So I want to thank you, from the bottom of my heart, for buying from us, your local butcher shop. For eating at locally owned restaurants." He held up a CCCV. "For drinking our local beer."

The crowd cheered. Iggy looked from face to face and recognized so many of them that he couldn't help but smile.

"You all are the best part of this," he said. "You keep Miami alive by supporting us. We are a reflection of you all. We serve you. We are you!"

Another cheer filled the lot. "Not like these gentrifying motherfuckers we see out here, barging into our neighborhood, acting as if they know you in order to sell y'all shit you don't really want. Trying to put all your favorite shops out of business, spray-painting fucked-up shit on our walls as if that could ever scare us away. I've been to prison, bitch! Ain't much that scares me!"

The crowd erupted into cheers and laughter.

"And just so we're clear, y'all are doing much more than just dancing and smoking and eating. Y'all are thriving. Which means that we, your humble servants, are thriving."

Iggy held up his CCCV. "So cheers to you, familia, for supporting local artists and businesses year after year. Thank you for taking pride in our neighborhoods and keeping them a hundred percent Miami. Now let's have a good time! Make it so that when all this shit's underwater in a hundred years, they'll *still* be talking about this party right here!"

Iggy chugged his beer. The crowd boomed. Iggy screamed, "Yo, Dro Blaze, spin that shit!" He handed the mic back to Dro, who handed Iggy some shirts. Iggy tossed La Carnicería Guerra T-shirts into the crowd. Music filled the air once more.

The crowd was electric chaos. Iggy scanned the faces. He found Abuelo Calixto, who'd spent the day with a cloud of smoke around his head made possible by what seemed to be a single never-ending cigar. Iggy wove through the crowd, shaking hands and high-fiving people as he went. Abuelo Calixto was sitting at a domino table across from his buddy Máximo, schooling the pair of younger guys they were playing against.

"¿Cómo está la cosa por aquí?" Iggy squatted beside the old man.

"Todo bien," Abuelo Calixto said. "We sold out of pork sausages, pero Mauro is making more as we speak."

Iggy looked over the table. Abuelo and Máximo had this game well in hand. "Cuando termines aquí, do me a favor and head inside and help Mauro. I'm gonna chat with people, shake some hands, make sure people are making their way into the shop for meat. Then I'll head in there to keep things smooth."

Abuelo Calixto nodded. "The moment we finish off these muertos, voy a dar una vuelta por este circo then I'll go inside."

Iggy patted the old man's shoulder and made his way toward the back of the lot where Fabrice and his crew were set up. He pressed through a few groups of people and found himself by a bunch of girls with Hialeah Red hair. He clinked beer bottles with them and thanked them for stopping by.

Fabrice sweated as he added charcoal to one of the Caja Chinas. Iggy pulled a bandana with a large green G on it from his guayabera pocket and handed it to him. "How's everything over here?" he asked.

Fabrice took the bandana and wiped his face. "Bro, this shit's nuts. This boar meat with mojo is straight-up magic. People love it. You sure you can get us enough to meet demand? 'Cause Magda called and said there are people at the restaurant buying three or four of these tacos at a time. Oh, and we're gonna need more gator meat too, like as soon as possible."

Iggy mopped his brow with his own bandana. He looked back toward the shop and saw that the line to buy meat had wrapped around the side of the building. It seemed that, for the moment, his plan was working, but all that didn't mean jack shit if they couldn't sustain their momentum. He pulled out his phone and dialed.

"Orin, I need more boar. And more gator. And I got some more of Pops's debt money for you, by the way."

"Not a problem," Orin said. "But I need something from you. Meet me at the Sawgrass Saloon in thirty minutes. I have a surprise."

"I can't, Orin. I'm at the shop's anniversary bash. Can't you hear it in the background?"

"You're going to want to see this. Besides, I have some meat for you right here."

Iggy looked at the party going on around him. There was no way he could just up and leave right now. But he also didn't want to keep Orin waiting, especially if he had meat ready. "Tell you what, Orin. Give me about an hour. Maybe two. When things slow down a bit here, I'll head your way." The exhaustion Iggy had been feeling grew heavier the moment he made the promise, but he couldn't afford to slow down now. "I'll see you later on, okay?"

There was silence on the other end of the phone. "Fine," Orin said. "But don't keep me waiting for too long." He hung up.

"What's up?" Fabrice asked Iggy. "Why's your face look like that?"

"I gotta go meet my supplier. He's got meat. And a surprise." He looked over the crowd. Mami would have loved it. He turned to Fabrice. "I gotta ride in a bit. You need anything else for now?"

"Nah, man, we're all set here."

"¡Dale! Hold this shit down for me. Let Carlos know if you need anything." And with that, Iggy cut through the press toward his brother.

Iggy hadn't taken three steps when he bumped into Sofie. He reached out and took her hand. "Sorry," he said with a huge smile on his face. "I didn't see you there. I'm so glad you came."

She smiled and tucked her curls behind her ear. "Of course I came. You know I had to come show some love. But did you sell your car? I heard you sold Azúcar Prieta?"

"Yeah," Iggy said. "I needed money to bail out Pops."

"I heard about that. It's . . . upsetting." She took his bandaged hand in hers. "What happened to you?"

"I got careless," Iggy said.

Iggy loved every moment he spent in her presence. It was like driving Azúcar Prieta—the world seemed to melt away, leaving nothing but possibilities on the horizon. Iggy took out his phone, snapped a pic of the two of them, and posted it just so that he'd have this moment to look back on when reality smashed his peace. After taking another few pictures with Sofie, Iggy turned to her and said, "Listen—feel free to say no, I won't take it personally—but let's grab a coffee one of these days so that we can really catch up. Or dinner, if you're down. Or maybe we can catch a Marlins' game? I think it'd be really nice."

Sofie thought about it for a second. "I'm technically still on the clock right now. My boss is on a business trip, so things are beyond hectic right now." She checked the time. "I actually have to get going."

"No pressure, no stress," Iggy said. "Whenever works."

Sofie and Iggy exchanged a kiss on the cheek, and she disappeared into the crowd heading toward the front of the shop.

Iggy lost her in the churn of bodies but found Carlos waving at him. Iggy waded through the multitude toward his brother. Orin called Iggy as he was reaching Carlos, but Iggy sent him to voicemail.

Carlos was waiting for Iggy with a bottle of water when he finally got to him. "Good news," Carlos said. "Pops is getting out soon, maybe as soon as next week."

Iggy almost spit out the water he'd been drinking. He threw his arms around Carlos and squeezed him.

"And we've sold a lot of meat, Iggy. Like *a lot*. I don't know how much, but your plan worked. Can you please stop spinning me and put me down now?"

Iggy set Carlos down. "My bad." He slapped Carlos's shoulder. "We did it!"

"For now," Carlos said as he rubbed his shoulder. "But yeah, we can breathe a little."

Iggy knew this victory was temporary, but damn it felt good. He wiped his face with his bandana and slipped it into his back pocket. "So check it: I gotta go see Orin. Something about a surprise. And I need to get some more boar."

"No rest for the wicked, huh? What about all this?" Carlos gestured to the crowd. "Can't Orin wait till tomorrow? Or why not ask him to deliver it here? Save yourself the drive?"

"I'd rather go to Orin than let him near this party. Plus, I got some cash for him. And I promised Fab I'd get him as much Edible Everglades meat as he needed, so I gotta make good on that promise. I'll slip away when things ease up here." Iggy gave Carlos a hug and walked toward the shop. His phone dinged. There were countless notifications popping up, every one of them coming from someone at the party. Their customers were letting everyone who wasn't at the party know just how much fun they were having. Iggy cut through the prep area at a jog—it was so cold it made his nipples hard—then right through the front of the shop and out to the sunblasted afternoon.

The door had just jingled shut when Iggy heard, "What the fuck is all this, Guerra?"

Iggy looked up from his phone. Conner G. Harrison stood across the street with his hands in his pockets. He leaned against a somewhat restored Azúcar Prieta, posing for a photographer he'd clearly hired to piss off Iggy. "You think gathering this rabble is going to save you from my grand opening?" A pool of shade danced beside him as a palm swayed above. Conner's face was red and flushed, like he'd been standing in the sun, waiting.

"You're the one who's gonna need saving, Connie. You don't see it, do you?"

"What does that mean? Are you threatening me again?"

Iggy pointed to the huge BUY ONE, GET ONE FREE sign Carlos had made for the shop. "I'm guessing you didn't take any economics or business classes at that college your legacy status got you in and that you barely graduated from."

A look of bewilderment simmered on Conner's face. He adjusted his shades and buried his hands in his pockets again. "You're having a sale. So what?"

Iggy knew then that Conner had no idea how fucked he was. If Conner had understood what was happening, he would have changed the Chop Shop's opening at all costs, postponed it for at least a month. Iggy wanted to laugh, to say, *Let me do the math for you, Connie. When you have your grand opening tomorrow, every fridge and freezer for miles around will be stocked with weeks' worth of our meat. How many folks do you think are gonna need to visit the Chop Shop? We sell the same product and I just flooded the market with inexpensive, high-quality meat. By the time anyone needs to buy more meat, all the hype you've built up will have faded. You and your shop will be a fucking afterthought.*

Instead, Iggy said, "Stop redlining my car when you shift. Now fuck off. I have a business to run," before going back into the shop.

20

NEVERGLADES

Iggy pulled into the Sawgrass Saloon in Armando's Tahoe and parked beside the half dozen pickups that were haphazardly dotting the gravel. The entire left side of the building's exterior was cordoned off with caution tape. The blast marks and scorch lines from the night Iggy had blown up the pickup during his escape from Orin's office were still visible on the E.C.H.O. offices.

Iggy yawned. It felt weird to be driving around in Armando's Tahoe. He missed Azúcar Prieta bitterly and wasn't sure which was worse: that he'd driven her to pieces or that he'd sold her to Conner, of all people. The music from the shop's party still hummed in his bones, but he'd promised Fabrice more meat, so there he was. He got out of the Tahoe and cleared all the porch steps with a hop.

The front door was locked.

"Some surprise, Orin," he said. He pressed his face to the door, shielding his eyes from the glare to get a better look inside. The door was cold against his forehead, the bar's air conditioner was hard at work against the Miami heat. The place was dead inside, dark except for a few bar signs above the pool table. He focused on the back of the bar, on a few doors tucked in the dim corner past the bathrooms, but the crunch of gravel behind him shook Iggy free from his search.

"You made it," Orin said, his eyebrows arching as he spoke.

"So that's what happened the other night," Iggy said, pointing to the taped-off section of the building. "I hope you don't mind that I got the fuck outta here quick that night. I wasn't gonna wait for the cops to get here." Beyond the shattered windows, the building didn't look too bad from the front. Iggy knew, however, that the back was a whole other story.

Orin shrugged. "Someone blew up some oxygen and acetylene tanks on one of my trucks. Blew off the backside of the building. But we're gonna make him pay."

"So you caught the guy?"

Orin said nothing. He only smiled that crooked smile of his.

"Let's do this, Orin, whatever it is I'm here for."

"Always straight to business. I love it. Put this cooler in your car, then come with me," he said, pointing behind Iggy. "That meat should hold you over."

Iggy picked up the Styrofoam box and put the cooler in the passenger seat of the Tahoe. He handed Orin a stack of hundred-dollar bills.

Orin took the money. "What happened to your hand?"

"A knife." He pointed to the cooler. "And I need more meat," Iggy said. "I hope you and your swamp things feel like hunting, 'cause I'll take as much wild hog as you can send my way. And some gator."

Orin stopped walking and counted the bills.

"It's all there," Iggy said.

"Now that you're in charge of the butcher shop, our future is bright. Tell me, how is your father?"

Iggy had tried organizing a visiting schedule for the crew so that Pops would have a daily visitor and wouldn't feel so isolated, but Pops had told him that under no circumstances would he accept any visitors. "Ni a jodida" had been his exact words. Iggy hadn't fought him on that; he knew the exact mix of shame and pride that made Pops sink deeper behind the cold concrete walls of the jail. "He'll be home soon. There's not a whole lot of evidence against him."

Orin nodded and put the cash in his pocket. "Any idea as to who tipped off the cops?"

"Anonymous call. But there's only one person I know who snoops around our dumpsters and dive bars."

Orin picked up the pace again. He pushed through some shrubs. "You up for an airboat ride?"

Iggy followed Orin down a narrow trail through the mangrove stand behind the bar. After rustling through the brush for a bit, Orin's airboat came into view. The boat was steady in the water, barely moving as Iggy stepped on board. Orin climbed up into his chair and started the engine. It was deafening. The boat glided slideways over some long, thin grass and then straightened out over the champagne water.

Iggy watched the sun tuck itself into a mass of low-lying clouds on the horizon. A few stars speckled the purpling sky above. Iggy leaned into the front of the airboat, taking it all in despite the engine's roar. Orin made a few turns, adjusting their trajectory so subtly that Iggy lost track of how long they'd been speeding over the grassy water—it felt like one long moment that changed gradually but completely. Dense hummocks gave way to open, endless green. What seemed like shrubs in the distance soon grew into sprawling mangroves that clamored around towering sable palms. The continuous contraction and expansion of the landscape felt like breathing, and Iggy wondered if this was what a clean conscience felt like.

Iggy wasn't used to moving through the Everglades at such speed. "How do you not get lost out here?" Iggy shouted at Orin through cupped hands.

The engine quieted, and the airboat slowed. Water rushed and lapped as the boat settled into the silence. Orin pointed out into the vastness, the last of the sun's light reflecting off his shades as a red line. "Watch how the land lays. You got mangroves to the south, the marsh here is in the middle, and to the north there's cypresses. As long as you know that, you won't get lost."

Iggy looked around and situated himself. In his mind's eye, he mapped out where he was in all this water and grass. In the process, he realized that it wasn't actually quiet, that the engine never stopped rumbling even as the massive aluminum blades that drove the craft lay motionless behind Orin. "You any good out here when it's dark? Hunting, I mean."

"You think I need the sun to hunt?" Orin asked. "Ever since the Big Cypress Preserve took over all of this in '93—and I'm talking almost a million acres—we haven't been allowed to run our airboats, swamp buggies, four-wheelers, and ATVs out here. Not legally, anyways. I know my way through all this better than most people know their own minds. Spent more time out here at night than during the day. This is *my* land."

Orin leaned forward and flicked a switch. The engine roared and the blades began spinning. "But we're almost on my ranch now," he said, raising his voice over the engine, "and we've got these." Banks of spotlights glowed across the front and sides of the boat, illuminating the water around them as though they'd turned on a small sun. Two larger lights to either side of Orin lit the space way ahead of the boat, allowing them to see well into the night.

They lit up the grass and water as they sped over it. Iggy spotted clusters of gator eyes reflecting like glowing embers. Birds and bats flocked around the constellation of trees toward where Orin had aimed the front of the boat. Just as the night became absolute, Orin cut the engine. They coasted into a tangle of mangroves, sliding silently through the water until they came to rest on land that Iggy hadn't known was there.

Orin led Iggy through a trail of his own making, but after a while, it was clear that Orin knew exactly where he was going. His steps were deliberate, flashlight leading the way like a bright divining rod.

Live oak reached down with gnarled branches so thick with Spanish moss that visibility was limited to a few feet. It was cool in this place, so much so that Iggy shuddered as the sweat of the day dried on his skin. Leaves and roots crackled beneath his feet, but he noticed that Orin made almost no noise as he stepped through the night. Iggy looked up, and the thick canopy above pressed down.

"We're here," Orin finally said as they stepped into a clearing. "Look," he said, pointing to a faint glow in the distance.

Iggy squinted. A tiny red blaze winked from beyond a stand of skeletal cypress trees.

They walked for a few more minutes, past palm trees whose trunks and fronds looked like dinosaur teeth. A clearing in the dense press of trees eventually emerged.

"After you," Orin said, holding back some fronds.

Iggy stepped through.

Lew knelt on the porch of a shack, his knife slicing through the belly of a raccoon. He made no move to acknowledge Iggy's presence.

Iggy shone his flashlight on the shack. It was one room, and judging by the weathered wood, it had been there for quite some time. Moss hung from the edge of the porch. Iggy knew then that this was one of the three buildings he'd seen on the map in Orin's office.

Lew cocked his head to the side. The lantern light flickered, casting wide shadows on the wall behind him. His face was buried beneath his hair. When he finally made a sound, it seemed as if his laughter came from the trees.

"Show us what you got," Orin said, thumping up the steps that led to the shack's front door. He pulled the door open and stepped into the yawning void within.

Lew sank his blade into the raccoon's guts and stood. He gave Iggy a once-over and held the door open. "After you."

Iggy aimed his flashlight at Lew's face. The fat man's chest was covered in blood. "Nah. You first."

Lew said nothing and disappeared into the dark with his lantern.

Iggy took the steps one at a time, and somewhere in the distance, he thought he heard a horse whinny.

A shirtless Pico was strapped to a chair against the back wall of the shack, bleeding from various X-shaped cuts. Each one was deep and oozed blood into the ones below it. The gag they'd tied over his mouth was red with blood, as were the ropes that held his hands behind his back. At Pico's feet was a tangled brown wig, and beneath him lay a pool of piss that filled the room with a stench so thick Iggy felt it on his tongue. The top half of a ghillie suit lay shredded beneath the seat.

Lew smacked the back of his head and the bald man groaned. He looked small in that chair. And weak. Whatever spunk and scrappiness that Pico had possessed when he confronted Iggy at the shop had been beaten out of him.

Iggy scanned the room with his flashlight. It was empty

except for a table covered in knives and cameras and a pile of sheets in one corner. "Why's he here like this?" Iggy covered his nose. "The fucking guy looks like he was in a car accident. You find him on the side of the road like this?"

"Lew caught him coming through the grass right where you said he'd be," Orin said, spitting. "He was planning on setting my horses free and videotaping the whole thing."

Pico groaned.

Iggy turned his flashlight on the beat-up cowboy. "How long you been carving him up?"

The more Orin and Lew laughed, the guiltier Iggy felt. "Listen, Orin. I know you hate the guy, but ain't this a bit much?"

Orin and Lew turned on Iggy at the same time. Iggy focused his gaze on Pico. He instantly realized that he'd been brought here with the understanding that he hated Pico just as much as they did. They thought he'd be happy to see the man who'd sent his father to jail in such agony. Iggy was there to share in their twisted joy, not to question it. "Kill him and be done with it," Iggy added. "All this seems like extra work."

Orin pointed at Pico. "This man has been threatening my land for over a year. Destroying my farms and putting it on the Internet to mock me. He put your father in jail. He's put us through way too much trouble for us not to return the favor. I don't think we've done nearly enough."

Pico started to say something, but Lew backhanded him into silence.

Iggy said nothing. He kept his flashlight on Pico. Even though the little man looked like he'd been chewed up by a bear, Iggy wasn't sure what he felt. He thought about how he'd had to rebag all the animal leftovers after Pico had sliced up the bags in the shop's dumpster. He remembered the rage he'd felt when Pico had tucked Pops's knife back into his bag instead of returning it. Then he remembered that Armando was sitting in a jail cell right now, and that Conner was probably joyriding in Azúcar Prieta at that very moment. Those things were Pico's fault. A wisp of anger flared up inside him. "Maybe we haven't done enough," he finally said.

Iggy turned to Pico and leaned forward, stopping inches from his face. "Why the fuck didn't you listen to me when I told you to stay the fuck out of here? Do I look like someone who lies?" Iggy looked Pico in his one open, unflinching eye. "I told you to stay the fuck out of the 'Glades."

Pico said nothing.

Iggy stood and turned to Orin. "Dangerous as it is beautiful. That's what I told him."

Orin and Lew both nodded.

Somewhere in his heart, Iggy didn't like where this was going, but at that moment, it looked like the solution to his problems. This man's death wouldn't grant him any relief, but the shop would be safe. Which meant the family would be safe. Iggy turned his flashlight on Pico and pushed his head back to get a good look at him. His face was a ruin, only that one eye open, but Pico gazed defiantly at Iggy. "Why didn't you fucking listen to me, mini cowboy? It didn't have to be this way." Pico jolted upright and strained against the ropes. Iggy leaned even closer. "There's nothing you can do about it now. You came into the Everglades and chose danger over beauty. You got what you asked for."

Pico's muffled yells grew louder, and Iggy turned away. He edged over to the table of knives. Many of the sharpened tools were bloodstained. He recognized his father's blade. Iggy reached for it, but not before looking over the smashed cameras and cracked GPS resting next to a pair of Glocks on the table.

Iggy picked up the knife, walked over to Pico, and wiped it on a small dry patch he found on his pants.

"Thanks for getting this back," he said to Orin. He slipped the knife into his waistband. Iggy stepped back, keeping Orin and Lew in front of him and the door out to his back. "So now what?"

"Now we feed him to the gators," Orin said.

Pico yelled at them at the top of his lungs. Iggy could somewhat make out the curse words spewing through the bloody gag jammed in Pico's mouth.

Pops's blade was cold against the small of his back. Iggy remembered how standing up to Pops had felt wrong even though he knew it was the right thing to do. How was this any different? Iggy then realized that he'd inadvertently prolonged Pico's torture by staying at the party instead of coming over when Orin had asked him to. "How's this going down?" Iggy asked, over Pico's muffled screams.

Orin punched Pico square in the face until there was silence. "When we're done turning every bone in his body to dust," he said, massaging his fist, "we'll dump him in the gator pit. Toss his gear in the wood chipper. The usual."

Pico came to, winced, and looked Iggy dead in the eye. There was no plea in that look. No fear or doubt or hesitation. Pico just *was*. He embodied what he believed in at that moment, and Iggy respected him for it. Then pain set in and Pico's eye watered.

But there was nothing to be done now. All Iggy could do was go with the flow, get out of the Everglades in one piece, and get Pops out of jail.

"All right then," Iggy said. "Let's go."

"This guy never beats around the bush," Orin said to Lew. "You see now why I love him?"

Iggy pulled the butcher knife from his waistband. He cut Pico's feet loose, then worked the blade through the rope that held Pico's neck and chest to the chair. Pico slumped forward, then collapsed at Iggy's feet, his hands still tied behind his back.

Orin's phone rang. Silence filled the room until the phone rang again. Iggy, Orin, and Lew looked at each other.

"What?" Orin yelled into the phone. He was silent for a moment, and Iggy heard panic in the voice on the other end of the line. "Don't say a word," Orin said calmly. "Nothing, you hear me? Nothing. We'll be right there."

Iggy and Lew waited as Orin slid his phone into his pocket. "That was Rana," Orin said to Lew. "Cops are at the Sawgrass. They're looking for him," he said, gesturing to Pico with his chin. "They want to speak to us. Asked for us by name." He turned to Iggy and held out a set of keys. "They did not ask for *you*, so *you're* in charge of feeding the gators." He tossed the keys into Iggy's chest. "I trust you know that nothing good will come from the law discovering what's going on here. That's bad news for all of us. And we don't want to give the cops any reason to search farther than the bar, so Lew and I will be going." He turned and kicked Pico so hard in the head that Iggy was sure Pico was dead.

Orin turned toward Iggy. "And just so we're clear: I don't *like* that I have to trust you with so much this early in our relationship. But you've got as much to lose as I do, so I know you'll make this problem go away." He turned his flashlight on Pico, who lay in a puddle of piss and blood. "But if you try fucking me, the things I'll do to you will make this look like a therapeutic, restorative spa treatment. I'll bring down lightning strike after lightning strike on your head. But I don't think it'll come to any of that. I think the idea of sinking yet another of your family's businesses will help guide your hand. Can you imagine Carlos having to give up his college dreams *and* becoming homeless on the same day?"

Iggy tightened his belt and slid Pops's knife back into the space between his underwear and shorts. The blade lay flat against his right hip. "I don't like this any more than you do. Let's just get it done."

Orin paced the room silently, as if staying in motion would help him work everything out. "Someone knows he's out here, so we have to make it look like we know nothing and that he vanished on his own. I keep a truck out on this island. It's out back. Take the truck and load it with our friend here and all his gear. Drive southeast and dump him in the pit at the end of the road. It's just like the pit you and I walked to the other day. When you're done, take an airboat back. I'll call you later."

The floor creaked as the two men thumped from the room. "And Ignacio, now that you've seen how we deal with our enemies, I trust you won't do anything to become one." He walked back to the table and tucked the two Glocks into his waistband. He stopped over Pico and spit on his head. "See you in hell," he said, driving the heel of his foot down between his shoulder blades.

21

AGUACERO

The floodlights mounted on the truck's roof were all trained on a single spot, lighting up the road like a beam of sunlight through a magnifying glass. One moment the rocky dirt road was visible, the next it was gone, and the canopy overhead was illuminated. The cigarette stink that emanated from the seats tainted the otherwise crisp, luscious night air. The truck's well-worn suspension squealed like a stuck pig, doing little to steady the cab as it bobbed and crunched over rocks and potholes. Empty beer cans and bottles clattered each time they hit a bump, adding to the croaks and chirps that sang in the darkness. Iggy hit a bump and cigarette butts rained onto the floor from the old truck's overstuffed ashtray.

The night out here was darker than nights in the city, and since the circle of light provided the only visual stimulus outside the cab, Iggy had no choice but to keep his eyes trained on the bouncing beam for fear of running off the road and getting stuck. He considered driving slower to make the drive less nauseating, but that meant disposing of Pico would take longer, and that was something he wanted to get over with as soon as possible. He pressed down on the accelerator.

Pico slipped in and out of consciousness in the passenger seat. He smelled like three-day-old roadkill. Iggy had strapped him into the seat before remembering that his safety and comfort weren't important. The screens on Pico's smashed gear flickered every once in a while, lighting his battered face in such a way that cuts and welts seemed like the work of an amateur special effects artist. Another cracked screen flashed. Orin and Lew hadn't even bothered to turn them all off, and they clearly hadn't destroyed all the gear Pico had on him. Iggy was pissed to have yet another thing to worry about.

Pico groaned. "You look like shit," Iggy said, half expecting an answer. "I told you to stay the fuck out of our business. Didn't I tell you those swamp-asses were bad news? And now I'm caught up in this bullshit? I hope you understand just how fucked we both are. You more than me, obviously, but still." Another groan filled the cab. Iggy wasn't sure if it had come from Pico or the pickup's worn shock absorbers.

Iggy slowed down to take an oncoming curve. The floodlights flashed across a log on the road. Iggy pressed down on the brakes, sending the pickup into a skid that left it halfway off the path. Iggy threw the truck in reverse and eased his way back onto the barely visible trail, making sure to light the log.

In the steady light of the stationary truck, Iggy watched the log turn and open its mouth, growling as its snaggletoothed jaws snapped shut. The sound crawled over Iggy, leaving goosebumps on his skin. He looked from the hair rising on his arms to the peaks lining the reptile's armored back.

The gator snarled and snapped its jaws. Iggy opened the door and stepped out. He made sure to keep the truck between him and the beast sprawled out in front of him.

"Yo, asshole!" he yelled into the night. "Move your shit outta the way!"

The gator thrashed its tail and sent rocks flying at Iggy. He jumped back as the loose gravel pelted the front of the truck. He picked up a pair of green bottles from the cab's floor and clinked them together, hoping the sound would spook the beast. More cigarette butts littered the cab floor. The gator hissed. Iggy threw the bottles at the open jaws with all his might. One hit the gator's maw and it slithered off into the brush.

Iggy hopped back into the truck and closed the door, but the dome light in the cab stayed lit. On the dashboard, the words DOOR AJAR were illuminated. He looked at the passenger side and there was in fact a door ajar. Pico's seat was empty, a streak of blood sliding across the backrest.

"Mother*fucker*!" Iggy yelled into the night as he pushed open his door. He hopped out of the cab as it began to sprinkle. He ran across the front of the truck and found Pico crawling along the edge of the floodlights, raindrops pattering around him.

"Are you for real, bro?" Iggy grabbed Pico by the shoulder and the battered man curled up in the fetal position.

"Stop! Get back!" he screamed. "Don't cut me again." He was breathing hard. "Please."

Iggy understood the terror it took to make a person ball themselves up like that. He vividly remembered how he'd felt when Armando had beaten an eight-year-old version of himself while he was balled up like that. He looked down at his hand, and even though he knew it had been his fault, he partly blamed Armando for the cut that burned across his palm.

Iggy pulled back his hand and watched Pico tremble. "Yo, I'm not gonna hurt you," he said. "Not yet, anyways." Pico shielded his head with his lacerated arms and balled up even tighter. Iggy brought his hands to his face to wipe the drizzle and sweat that had gotten in his eyes. He pressed his bandaged hand to his eyebrow. The pain made him angry.

"All right," Pico mumbled. "I'm ready. Do it. Let's go. Kill me already."

Iggy opened his mouth, but nothing came out. What was he doing out here, taking care of Orin's dirty work? Wasn't that the same thing he'd asked Pops *not* to do? Back at that isolated torture shack, in a moment of surprise and confusion, he'd decided to go with the flow instead of thinking things through, and now he was here, in the middle of nowhere, in charge of making sure Pico never saw tomorrow. But if butchering horses and killing trespassers were things that Orin was into, why the hell was that any of Iggy's business? And why the hell was Iggy in business with him? This wasn't resolviendo. This was digging himself to rock bottom.

But if the shop was going to survive, Pico *had* to go. He knew too much. He'd gotten Pops locked up. He was looking to shut down the shop. Even if Iggy stopped butchering horses for Orin, there was no guarantee that Pico would back off and leave the shop alone.

What the fuck had he gotten himself into? Iggy screamed into the night. When he was out of breath, he filled his lungs and screamed again, kicking the front of the truck until cracks spidered one of the headlights.

Iggy looked up, hoping the sky had some answers. Rain sprinkled in his face. He'd hoped to see some stars, but they were tucked behind the clouds. He thought of his mother, then remembered the cigarette butts he'd found in the truck. He slid into the cab and studied the cigarette butts. They matched the ones he had found at the corner where Mami had been hit. But

El Loquito had said that the truck that killed Mami was white. This one was black. But still, he couldn't shake the feeling that the butts in that cab and the cluster of butts he'd found on the grass across from Sedano's were connected.

Iggy's eyes burned. He screamed once more and kicked the truck until the headlight went dim. "Don't tell me these fuckers killed my mom!" he yelled. He reached for his bandana and wiped his face. He studied the bandage on his hand, then the dirt wedged between the creases on his fingers, under his nails. A mosquito buzzed in his ear and he swatted at it. The rosary around his neck clinked. The rain grew louder.

Pico still cowered in the dirt on the floodlights' fringe when Iggy turned toward him. A cloud of mosquitos hovered over him, covering his skin. Iggy waved them off with his bandana and Pico flinched. "Get your ass up!" Iggy screamed. The bloodsuckers circled back and landed on Pico once more.

A breeze pushed through the night and the leaves whispered. Rain pecked harder at the grass around them. Before long the soft sizzle became an all-out downpour. Iggy jumped into the truck and put it in reverse. Where would he go? Home? To confront Orin about the cigarettes? Iggy couldn't just leave Pico out here, could he? He'd die on that road and get eaten by who-knows-what. That was a good thing, wasn't it? He punched the brakes and watched the rain wash blood and mosquitos off Pico's back.

Pico tried getting to his feet, but his left leg trembled when it tried to hold his weight. He fell forward, crying out as he hit the muddy gravel. The rain seemed to have returned a bit of his energy to him. He crawled for a bit and rolled over onto his back and squirmed in the floodlights. Heavy rain fell sideways through the beam, and the wind pulled on the leaves and fronds. The night was alive, shaking and shivering, just like Pico.

Iggy flipped on the windshield wipers, but they weren't powerful enough to wipe Pico off the road and out of his life. What if he ran him over and just left him there? The cops would find him if they searched for him. That was no good. If Iggy wanted to save the shop, he had to make Pico vanish forever.

Any alternative wasn't an option. If Pico lived, Iggy and his family were finished. Everything that Iggy had worked for would be undone the moment Pico spoke to the cops. Armando would stay in jail, Iggy would return to prison, and Carlos would have to drop out of school. The rest of the crew would be jobless and the shop would go under. Conner would buy La Carnicería, burn it down, and piss on the ashes. Mami's rosary clinked. He pressed the beads into the cut in his hand. In a moment of clarity, he knew what to do. He kissed his rosary, opened the door, and stepped into the downpour.

Pico sat up at the sound of Iggy's approaching footsteps. He shielded his eye from the floodlights with his hand. "Is that you, Guerra?" he asked in a low voice.

"It's been me this whole time."

"I'm not afraid to die, Guerra. If you knew how much evidence I've already uploaded to my cloud servers, you'd have killed me a long time ago." He spit. "Even if they never find my body, the cops will know exactly where I disappeared the moment the footage shows up in their inboxes."

Iggy stepped farther into the light and knelt beside Pico, his shadow spreading over him in sharp long lines.

"I don't care about any of that," Iggy said softly. "I'm not gonna kill you, even if you did get my old man locked up." He cupped his hand over his brow to shield his eyes from the rain.

Pico sat up, reinvigorated by Iggy's words. "Prove it. Prove you're not here to do what I think you're here to do."

"I was here to do just that." Iggy tossed his phone in Pico's lap. "Call the cops."

Pico lowered his hand.

The sight of his face made Iggy's head hurt. "The passcode is 6264," Iggy said.

Pico's eyes shifted to the phone on his lap, then back at Iggy. He picked up the phone and tried the code, his eye widening when it worked.

"I'm done with all this bullshit," Iggy said. "I ain't killing you. I don't know *what* I'm doing, but killing you ain't it." He stood over Pico. "C'mon, let's get you some help. If Orin comes back, you'll never get out of here." Iggy held his hand out, his shadow widening as he stood.

"Wait," Pico said. He dialed a number and held the phone to his ear. "Hey, it's me," he said without taking his eye off Iggy. "Don't worry about why I'm calling you from this phone. Yeah, I'm OK. Now listen carefully. Download and back up everything on the servers. All of it. And don't upload the new footage to the site just yet, but definitely back it up. I'm guessing you saw what happened to me?"

Pico winced as he shifted his weight forward. "Yeah," he said, "I'd be dead if you hadn't sent the police to the Sawgrass Saloon. Was that the last place the GPS said I was? No kidding? That's a bad lag then. But yeah, I found some horses. And more. The coordinates are on the GPS maps. I have video. . . . Yeah, I'm in the rain. . . . No, not all the evidence, but after what I've seen here— No, I'm not OK." He gave Iggy a once-over. "Yes. I need medical help. But I'll be all right. I won't be heading back to the office for a while, change of plans. But you know what to do if you don't hear from me. By the way, you were right about Guerra." He hung up and closed his eye, flopping down in the puddle that had formed beneath him.

"Who were you talking to? How do they know me? And what were they right about?"

"You'll see. You're not the only one who can gather information quickly. I know more about you than you think. And now that I know you're not a killer, I want you to help me bring these horse killers down. In fact, I know you desperately want to help."

"Is that a fact? How do you know that?"

"Because it's in your best interest. And your father's."

"So what do you need from me? Evidence? Look right there on my phone. Go on. Check the pictures."

Pico arched the eyebrow over his only good eye, but he did as Iggy asked. He swiped through some images. "What am I looking at?"

"See that map there?" Iggy asked. "That's where he keeps the horses you're looking for. At least I think it is. And if you swipe to the end, I'm pretty sure that's where he got the horses from. All you need to do is confirm what my brother found. He thinks those are the places from where Orin has stolen horses for his meat market."

Pico's eye widened. "Where'd you get this from? And what about these names and numbers in the middle?"

"I got it from Orin, from his office. I had to know what his role in all this was. I saw an opportunity to snoop around the other night, so I took it."

"Was that the same night the side of his building blew up?"

"Maybe," Iggy said. He pointed to the phone. "My guess is

that the names you see there are people he's sold horse meat to. The number on the edge of the page is how many pounds of meat they bought."

Pico studied Iggy, his eye searching his face. "She was right," he whispered. Iggy wasn't sure he'd heard it.

"Who was right?" Iggy asked.

Pico returned his eye to his phone.

Iggy thought about Armando sitting in some cold jail cell. "You know my old man wasn't torturing or killing horses, right?"

"I know," Pico said, eye still on the phone. "But fuck your father. He was laundering horse meat for Orin Cypress so that there wouldn't be any evidence for me to take to the cops. No one ever thinks to look for illegal animal parts in a butcher's garbage, especially not your father's, since he sells all sorts of meat. And he did a good job of hiding horses' carcasses after he'd cut the meat off. There weren't any horse remains at your shop. I just sent myself all these images, by the way. And I erased the numbers I called and texted so you can't trace the number."

"You know I'll find it on my phone bill if I want?"

"That won't be until the end of the month. I'll be more than safe by then, assuming I make it out of here."

Iggy studied Pico, piecing together everything he'd just learned with what he already knew. There was a new light in the cowboy's eyes despite the severity of his injuries, as if he'd gotten his second wind. Or like he'd been playing possum.

"You played dead back there, with Lew and Orin. Didn't you."

"I didn't have to play too much. Lew fucked me up, obviously. And I might have laid low as best I could so that sociopath would quit beating me, but if you're not gonna kill me, that means we have work to do, no matter how badly I'm hurt."

"Why are you so sure I still won't kill you?" Iggy asked. "And why didn't you call the cops just now?"

"My gut tells me you won't kill me. If you wanted me dead, I'd be dead. I think that me and you want the same thing."

He looked Iggy up and down, but Iggy said nothing. Iggy could see the wheels spinning in Pico's head, beat-up as he was.

Pico pressed on. "And we can't go to the cops until we've made their case for them, meaning we need all the proof we can possibly get because they don't give a shit about any of this. Not about horses, not about the Everglades, and especially not me." Pico groaned as he sat up a bit taller. "But you, you can get what we need. You have access to everything I could never get to. The cops will listen to me now when I show up at the station with the evidence you're going to gather for us. No matter what happens, it's only levels of victory for me from now on." He sat up slowly, grimacing with the effort.

The rain fell harder and louder. "Why would I help you bring down my old man, especially since you called the cops on him knowing there was no evidence?"

"I had nothing to do with that. I didn't get anyone arrested. At least not yet. If I had that kind of power, I wouldn't be slogging through the Everglades at night."

"Then who called the cops on my old man?"

Lightning struck nearby. Deafening thunder roared over them. Pico's sloppy smile made his face look even more contorted. "My guess is that Orin Cypress wanted your father out of the way for the same reason he wanted your mother gone."

"What?" Iggy asked, certain he'd misheard Pico. "Why would you say that? Orin needs Pops in order to—" And here he paused briefly, adjusting what he was going to say. "Pops buys whatever he's hunting, no matter the season. And what's that got to do with Mami?"

"You'd be surprised at the things people admit when they think no one's looking. Or in front of a dead man." He held his hand out to Iggy. "Help me to the truck and I'll show you."

•　　•　　•

Rain clapped against the truck like a crowd demanding an encore. The cab was humid and musty with the sweat of the two men huddled around the shattered screen of a digital video camera.

"I thought they destroyed all your gear," Iggy said, wiping rain off his face.

"They did," Pico said. "Most of it, anyway. But this camera has a nearly indestructible shell around it. It might still work."

The camera was no bigger than Iggy's cell phone, and had a harness that Pico would have worn in order to mount it on his chest. Iggy rummaged through the pack full of gear, looking for whatever was blinking inside. He found the dim light of the GPS system and pulled it out. "You did all this for some animals?"

"I believe in this with every ounce of my being," Pico said, taking the GPS from Iggy. "It's bigger than I am, more important than my life."

"You have serious issues. Have you seen yourself?"

"Give me your phone. I need to access my cloud. There's something I want you to see."

Iggy handed it to Pico.

Pico tapped on the screen as rain continued to cascade down the windshield.

He returned the phone to Iggy. "Press play."

"Why are you showing me this?"

"If I were in your shoes, I'd want to see this."

The video was shot on a chest-mounted camera, and for the first few seconds, the lens struggled to focus on the blades of grass in the frame. A breeze muffled a pair of voices off-screen. "What is this?" Iggy asked.

"It's a surveillance video I took earlier. Watch."

The camera jostled as Pico stepped into a small clearing. In the frame, his arm reached out and brushed aside long stalks of sawgrass. He was in waist-high water, but the camera on his chest captured most of a burned white pickup truck with a smashed windshield.

"What am I looking at?" Iggy asked, afraid of what he'd see next.

"Just watch," Pico replied.

The truck was half submerged in the grassy water, but it was clear that it had been driven out here and abandoned. The camera swept across the front of the truck, taking in the crumpled hood and steepled roof.

Tears blurred Iggy's vision.

"Someone ditched that truck and set it on fire," Pico said as he picked up the phone, "but it didn't burn all the way. If I had to guess—and it looks like you think the same thing—that's the truck that killed your mother." He tapped on the screen for a few minutes, giving Iggy a moment to gather himself.

"I took this footage a few days ago. Here's why I think that's the truck," he said, handing the phone to Iggy when his breathing had slowed down a bit.

The camera focused on a man leaning against a different pickup truck, a black one. There was barely any sunlight left in the sky behind him. "Whose truck is that?" Iggy asked, recognizing the black F-150.

"Just watch the video," Pico said.

Iggy recognized Orin Cypress puffing on a cigarette, exhaling a white stream upward before dropping the butt at his feet. He said something that the camera didn't record clearly, and Lew entered the frame with a dead hog on his shoulder. The wind died down and their voices became clear.

"I don't like him," Lew said, dumping the hog into the truck bed.

"He's easier to control than Armando," Orin said. "Can you imagine the balls on that man, not wanting to butcher horses anymore? At the price I was giving him, he needed to be butchering twice as many."

"You should have run over daddy dearest too."

Lew's words broke something in Ignacio Guerra, who stopped breathing but dared not look away from the screen.

"No, this works out better," Orin said. "She needed to go. Almost convinced Armando to stop butchering horses for me. But now Iggy thinks he can save his old man *and* the butcher shop, and we're going to provide him the means to do so. He's already ordering more boar. Now imagine how much more indispensable we are now that the shop isn't the only thing at stake?" Orin tucked loose strands of hair behind his ear and lit another cigarette. "Now that Armando is locked up and needs help, Iggy will see the business we bring as a godsend, and us as his saviors. And he's going to need more money. Soon enough, he'll be begging me for horses to butcher the same way his father was early on."

The wind muffled the microphone and blew long strands of sawgrass over the lens.

Iggy looked up from the screen, tears streaming down his face. Pico took the phone and queued up another clip.

"I haven't had a chance to see this," Pico whispered, his eye on the screen. "I took this next bit before they found me."

In this video, it was twilight. Lew was alone in the frame, stalking through the grass, chasing Pico as he tried backing away. The wind was blowing savagely, but the night vision was crisp. When the grass finally shifted, a terrified shriek overwhelmed the microphone and Lew's face filled the screen. The camera rolled in the grass and lay on its side while Pico's cries filled the twilight air. The lens refocused on long strands of sawgrass tussled by the heavy wind. The screen went blank and each man turned away to let the other weep silently into his hands.

22

THE BUTCHER'S CUT

Sofie gave Pico some serious side-eye as she finished bandaging the gash above his eye. She flashed Iggy a quick glance and returned to dabbing the bald cowboy's wounds, searching for another one to attend to. "Why are you so hardheaded?" she asked Pico. "I can't believe you didn't go straight to the emergency room like I told you to."

"We're not done yet," Pico said. "Now's when it actually starts."

The three of them stood together in a tight cluster: Sofie cleaned Pico's wounds; Pico prepped surveillance equipment and strapped it to Iggy's body; Iggy stared at Sofie, trying to wrap his mind around the fact that she had been working for Pico this whole time.

The undeveloped land behind the almost-finished apartment complex they met at was dimly lit. The headlights from Sofie's Jeep cast long, wild shadows onto the swaying sawgrass. Pico had said little on the airboat ride back to the mainland—he just stared off into the distance with his good eye—but he was a bit chattier now. And no matter how hard Sofie pressed and scraped his wounds while cleaning them, he never winced.

It was that defiant look that had made Iggy root for Pico, even when Iggy had wanted him dead. Even when there was zero evidence to suggest that Iggy wouldn't kill him and feed his fresh corpse to a swarm of gators, Pico had kicked and yelped and dragged himself because there simply wasn't any quit in his blood. That never-say-die look had changed the way Iggy perceived him, so much so that the name Pico, a mispronunciation of his last name that he simply ran with on his online posts— the name Orin and his swamp-asses had given the Everglades vigilante—no longer made sense to Iggy. Iggy now saw him for who he'd always been. He saw him as Sam Picoult.

But now Iggy wasn't so sure who Sofie was. He couldn't get over the fact that she and Picoult had known each other for quite some time.

"So when you opened the door that night at your house, when you came to the shop to buy meat and hang out"—Iggy pointed at Picoult—"you were really just working for *him* the whole time?"

Sofie looked pained, but Picoult spoke before she could. "I put her up to it, Iggy. She *really* is my personal secretary. And I *really* do run a real estate development company."

"And you *really* are a fucking maniac animal rights activist who got my ex to spy on me." Iggy turned to Sofie. "That night at your front door. You told him about it, didn't you?" Iggy took a step away from Picoult. "How long have you been watching Armando and the shop?"

"It's not like that at all, Iggy," Sofie said. "I was worried. You were talking about keeping your knives sharp. Besides," she said, slipping a strand of hair behind her ear, "I wanted to help. And just so you know, I spent time with you because I wanted to. Do you really think I'm going to do anything I don't *want* to do?"

"So you're telling me that it's a coincidence that you work for him and *then* you start coming around the shop? While he was *actively* trying to bring us down?"

Picoult returned the camera he was tweaking to the box that Sofie had brought him from the office. It overflowed with wires and gadgets. "Look, I hired her because she applied for the job. That was almost a year ago. But yes, I did try to persuade her to gather information for me once I knew about her connection to your family. But you know her. She defended you. All she said was that I was wasting my time by snooping around the shop."

Sofie looked down at her feet. "But I didn't know your dad was butchering horses. I didn't think Armando had it in him."

Iggy looked at his injured hand. "People do horrible shit when they're desperate."

Picoult put a hand on Iggy's shoulder. "And just so we're clear: I'm not turning in any of the footage that incriminates your father. I still think he's a piece of shit, but since you saved my life *and* you're helping me take down Orin, it's something I can give in return." He looked over at Sofie. "Also, she threatened to quit if I brought down your old man."

Iggy looked at Picoult's hand, then into his eyes.

Picoult pulled his hand back.

Sofie returned to patching up Picoult. "I've always stood up for you, Iggy. Even after you broke my heart."

That stung Iggy. He knew it was true. And even if they never went back to being a couple, Iggy was certain he was better off with her in his life, in any capacity, than not at all. "This whole thing is fucked."

Sofie wrapped Picoult's head to keep all the gauze she'd stuck there in place. She looked Picoult in the eye. "If you die, I'll be unemployed, and I can't afford that. You are *not* allowed to die." She double-checked the wounds she'd patched up earlier; some were already bleeding through the gauze. "Did you really toss all your clothes and gear into a gator pit? And *then* get on an airboat naked?"

"We had to," Iggy said. "Orin needs to think Picoult's dead. Otherwise, this little plan won't work." Having tossed everything Picoult was wearing into the gator pit meant that Iggy had brought him to Sofie's place naked and blood-soaked. He was now much cleaner, but Iggy couldn't take him seriously in the Victoria's Secret shorts and tank top combo that Sofie had lent him.

"What exactly is this plan that you two concocted?" she asked. "From what I've gathered, it sounds, you know, risky."

She was right. This was a risky plan. But it was the best chance he'd have to take Orin down. "It's pretty straightforward," Iggy said. "I tell Orin I need to make more money for Pops's legal bills and that I wanna butcher as many horses as I can. We know that Orin wants this, even expects this, so he won't say no to that. All I gotta do is let the camera record and upload anything I find. That way y'all can show it to the cops and they'll have all the evidence they need to send officers into the Everglades to finally take Orin down. Did I miss anything?"

"Yeah," Picoult said. "Keep your hands off Orin."

Iggy looked for the camera Picoult had hidden in his shirt pocket and could barely tell it was there.

Picoult confirmed that all Iggy's wires worked, that the camera hidden in his guayabera had a clear view of everything Iggy saw. He then confirmed that the audio and video were streaming directly to his cloud servers. "You're all set, Iggy."

Sofie turned to Picoult. "Now that you won't bleed to death, let's get you to the E.R. You can call the chief on the way."

The Jeep's dome light shone on a thick patch of tall grass that caught Iggy's clothes every time the wind blew. He closed the back door of the Jeep while Picoult slid gingerly into the passenger seat. "Just make sure you don't block the camera," Picoult said. "And *do not* lose your cool." His good eye searched Iggy's face. "Let's get the law out here so they can see the full extent of what this monster's done."

"He killed my mother. Don't you think that's more important than any fucking horse?" Iggy asked.

"Help me shut down these slaughterhouses and I swear to you I won't stop scouring the Everglades until I have all the evidence we need to prove he killed your mother. He'll go down for it all," Picoult said, with the calm of a man who hadn't been badly beaten hours before. "We're working *together*, remember? Helping each other out. How's it going to look if you go to the police accusing the man who turned your father in for butchering horses of killing your mother? Don't fuck it all up now."

"Fuck it up? Now? Shit, I fucked it up the moment I decided not to feed you to them gators. I'm going to prison again the moment you talk to the cops. The only reason I'm helping you is because you're gonna help my old man stay out of prison."

"You're not going to prison. And neither is your old man, though he deserves to. Now focus. You spared my life and it's going to work out for you. Killing Orin will only land you in prison for a long, long time. And we both know you don't want that."

Iggy looked to Sofie.

She toweled her hands off carefully, cleaning each of her elegant fingers with the same attention she'd cleaned Picoult's cuts. "Stick to the plan, Iggy. It sounds like a good one."

Iggy knew she and Picoult were right. He wanted sweet vengeance, to beat Orin to death with his fists, but he knew this was better. Prison offered a unique hell to a man like Orin, who loved the outdoors. It was also the only way to get Pops out of trouble.

Iggy's phone rang, and he looked up at Picoult.

"Answer it," Picoult said.

Iggy patted his pockets, fumbling through the objects tucked into his various openings, unsure where he'd placed his phone.

"No," Picoult said. "Tap your earpiece. The one we *just* connected to your phone."

Iggy tapped the tiny earbud. "What's good?" he asked.

"Where are you?" Orin's voice was as sharp as it was low.

"I'm around," Iggy said instinctively. "We need to talk."

"We do. Meet me at the ranch in twenty minutes."

"I'm on my way," Iggy said before tapping the earpiece again. Iggy turned to Picoult. "He's headed to the ranch. Wants me to meet him in twenty."

"Good. Let's hope he's convinced the gators ate me." He shifted in his seat. "And remember to act like you killed me."

"It won't be that hard," Iggy said. "I nearly did."

Sofie slid into the driver's seat of the Jeep. She turned on the engine and silently backed out of the grass. *Why would a woman like her want anything to do with me?* Iggy thought. *Maybe she believes in the man I'm trying to be.*

Picoult grimaced as he leaned out the window. "I'm going to call my lawyers and have them meet me in the E.R., but I'll be keeping an eye on you."

Iggy shook Picoult's hand, careful not to squeeze too hard. Picoult's hand felt like a dead rabbit in Iggy's. "I can't take you seriously when you're wearing pink booty shorts," he said.

Iggy tapped the side of the car and Sofie drove off into the night.

"Sofie, wait," Iggy called after the Jeep. "I'm sorry! For breaking your heart!"

After a while, Iggy lost her car in the sawgrass.

•   •   •

When the Tahoe's headlights panned over Orin Cypress, Iggy's first thought was to stomp on the gas and run him down. Instead, he squeezed the steering wheel until the cut in his hand screamed. Iggy felt it fill with blood.

Orin shielded his eyes from the headlights. The truck crunched to a stop on the gravel as Iggy drove right up to him. Iggy threw the truck in park and stepped out.

The night thumped with the music of various radios blaring from other parked cars. People Iggy had never seen before were hanging out at the front of the ranch alongside Orin's ranch hands. The spotlights on the perimeter along the fences lit the scene so that the crowd cast long, dark shadows onto the ranch's front.

"What is all this?" Iggy asked as he took Orin's outstretched hand.

Orin shook Iggy's hand and pulled him in for a hug. "We're celebrating, young Guerra. Pico is dead, my hunters are happy, my farmers are safe, and the future is bright. Come, we have lots to discuss."

Orin led Iggy past a smoking barbecue pit. Folks crowded around a makeshift cinder block bar snorting rails off a broken mirror. *Tremendo periqueo*, Iggy thought. He spotted a group of young women by a raging bonfire, embers landing at their feet as they stared at their phones. Orin turned a corner and entered the backyard of a house.

Rana and Lew looked up from the coolers they were packing with meat. They stared at Iggy.

"Carry on," Orin said, waving them off with his hand. Ice clattered into the white plastic boxes when they continued their work.

"What's that?" Iggy asked, pointing at the slabs of meat.

"Meat orders. They're delivering orders we couldn't make while Pico was around. Lots of folks came out when they heard he was missing, and some still want the meat delivered."

"News travels fast, huh? Even at this time of night?" Iggy asked, looking at his wristwatch. He remembered the camera in his shirt and stood up straight.

"There's money to be made," Orin said. "No better time than under the cover of night." He led Iggy to an open cooler. "We pack the horse meat under pounds and pounds of legal meat, possum, raccoons, ducks, so that if we are pulled over and anyone looks into the freezers, that's all they'll see."

"Who buys all this shit?" Iggy asked.

"Who doesn't? We sell to restaurants, markets, individual buyers." Orin was getting carried away by his good mood, saying more than he normally would.

Iggy forced himself to smile. "So does that mean you don't need me anymore?"

"Far from it," Orin said. He began walking toward a path that led into the shadows. "I need you now more than ever. I come across all these horses, and there's always people who'll buy that meat. The demand is always there, and I plan on supplying it as quickly as possible. But until the police stop looking for Picoult, I need to proceed with caution, though not as much as before. Thanks to you."

"Good," Iggy said. "Because I need to make some extra money. The legal shit we're providing to Miami Mussel sells good, but I need more money. And fast. I gotta look after Pops, you know?"

"I understand," Orin said. He motioned for Iggy to follow him and walked back into the night.

The path grew dark, yet Orin moved through the brush and low-lying branches as easily as if the sun were out. In the distance, Iggy heard a rumble: the truck Lew and Rana had loaded with horse meat pulled out to make its deliveries. The music in their truck trailed after them, leaving only the faint hum of the party to disturb the otherwise perfect silence. They reached the water, and they both boarded an airboat. Orin fired up the engine and they glided off into the dark grass.

After a few minutes, Iggy turned to Orin. "Where are we going?" Iggy asked. Armando's knife jabbed Iggy's thigh. Iggy could end him now, out here in the middle of nowhere. It would be messy and satisfying as fuck to slit open the throat of the man who killed his mother. If he threw the camera Picoult had hidden on his shirt into the water, it would work. No one would be able to prove what happened because by the time Iggy was done, there'd be no body to find.

"We're headed to my *other* stables," Orin said. "The ones Pico never found. I figured you'd want to take over your father's role, so I want you to see where you'll be working."

Iggy wanted to smash the smile off his face.

"But I'll be straight with you," Orin wheezed. "I paid Armando what I did because I needed his shop to launder the meat. I don't need that anymore. I just need to dispose of the equine leftovers carefully. But since you helped rid me of that piece-of-shit

Pico, I'll pay you five hundred dollars to butcher each horse. Just handle the prime cuts, then fillet them into steaks. About a pound each."

Iggy remained silent for the rest of the ride. The Everglades was as beautiful at night as it was during the day. There were so many stars peppering the sky above that it looked like someone had spilled salt on a black tablecloth.

Orin killed the engine. Crickets and frogs filled the night with chirps and croaks now that the airboat was silent. They floated through some brush to a short dock that appeared from within the serrated blades of grass. The smells of wet earth and horses were in Iggy's nose as Orin tied off the boat and stalked through some deep mangroves and down a path Iggy hadn't noticed.

Iggy followed close behind. "How do you get these horses out here?"

"This dock's for a quick in and out." Orin pointed out into the darkness. "There's a larger dock out on the west side of this hummock—that's where we unload the horses. From there we walk them to the paddock until they're processed. Then we bring them out in coolers."

The path wound through the darkness. Eventually, it opened into a small clearing. Iggy looked up. The once clear moon was now shrouded by gathering thunderheads. He rushed to catch up to Orin, who led them into a circular clearing with a heavy canopy overhead. The air was cool beneath the trees. The thick underbrush crunched and crackled beneath their footfalls. An owl hooted from somewhere in the darkness overhead. A soft breeze whispered by, raising goosebumps all over Iggy's skin. The path narrowed on the far side of the clearing and wound through some dense foliage, forcing Iggy to crouch as he pushed through the leaves and branches of a tree he couldn't identify in the dark.

Just as the map in Orin's office had predicted, a small shack with a horse pen appeared.

Iggy counted twelve horses standing inside the pen.

Orin pointed to a table in one of the stalls. "Now let's go. I've got a lot of orders to fill and money to make. All the tools you'll need to get the job done are there. I only need two horses right now, so feel free to get started. I'll be back with some beers and you can tell me all about Pico's final swim." He flicked a switch and a spotlight flooded the pen in a thin, sterile white light. It gave Iggy the impression that this was all a lucid dream.

"Wait. Hold up," Iggy said. "Look at this hand. I can't butcher any horses." He turned his rust-colored palm up to Orin. "When I said *right now*, I meant soon. Not like this very instant."

Orin ignored Iggy's outstretched palm. "Done enough killing for one night? No problem." He stepped into the pen, pulled a gun from his waist, and aimed it at the nearest horse's head.

As Orin pulled the trigger, Iggy instinctively reached out and slapped the gun down. The bullet hit the ground between the horse's hooves. It reared up and whinnied, nostrils flaring, and bolted away from Orin.

The other horses scattered, retreating to the corners farthest from the sound. Iggy's hand burned. He cradled it to his chest, hoping to calm the pulsing waves that filled it with fresh hot blood. He didn't have to look at it to know he'd torn it farther and made the cut deeper and longer.

Orin looked at Iggy with confused disbelief, as if Iggy had begun to levitate ten feet off the ground. "What on God's green earth is wrong with you? Have you lost your fucking mind?"

Iggy felt Armando's knife at his hip. He wanted to pull it out and drive it into Orin's eye. It wouldn't take long to drag his body into the grass for the various nocturnal creatures to find. The

pain in his hand helped him stay focused. That, and he remembered the camera strapped to his shirt. Iggy composed himself
and rose to his full height. "I'm not sure you heard me. My hand
is sliced open. I can't butcher anything with one hand. If you'd
shot that horse, it'd sit there till my hand healed." He leaned
toward Orin. "Don't kill any horses until I can heal up."

Orin grabbed Iggy by the collar, his gun sprouting from
one fist. The barrel was hot against the stubble on Iggy's neck.
"Butcher that animal right now or I'll leave you lying here next
to it."

Iggy bent forward to get in Orin's face. The gun singed
Iggy's skin. "My hand's destroyed. I'm fucking exhausted. I
haven't been home in forever, I'm covered in blood, and I smell
like death." Iggy pushed Orin. "I'm starving and I need to take
a shit and in case you haven't heard, my hand is sliced the fuck
open." Iggy tore the bandaging off and held his hand up. The cut
was raw and in various states of drying, dripping, and oozing.

"If you want me to do a good job, at least give me a few days.
Now back the fuck up and get out of my way." He leaned closer
to Orin. "Otherwise, you shoot me with every bullet in that gun
of yours or I will break your motherfucking neck and feed you
to your gators. It's your call."

When Orin didn't budge, Iggy shoved him with all his might.
His hand screamed almost as loudly as Orin. The old man tumbled through the leaves and gravel and slid to a stop.

Iggy pulled Armando's knife from his hip. It was a reaction,
an instinct, like slapping the gun down. Iggy moved toward
Orin. He'd be on the old man in five steps, way before Orin re-
gained his footing. Even with one hand, Iggy could make quick
work of him, just one flick of the blade. Then he'd stick the knife
into Orin's chest, push down through the breastplate until it

cracked, and bury it into his black heart. He'd kick the gun from his hand and just let the bastard bleed to death. His fat corpse would feed the moonlit pit.

Instead, Iggy flipped the knife around and palmed the hilt so that the blade was hidden behind his forearm. Sofie's voice echoed in his head: *Stick to the plan, Iggy*.

"I'm not doing this shit, Orin. Enough!"

Orin coughed. He rocked back and forth like a turtle on its shell as he attempted to sit up. He eventually gave up and rolled over onto his stomach. Orin slowly rose to a knee, but not before drawing his gun.

Iggy put his bloodied hand up, stretching his sliced palm. It bled profusely.

Orin raised the gun. He stalked over to Iggy and pressed the barrel into Iggy's bleeding palm. It burned as if exposed to an open flame. Iggy didn't flinch.

"Back off, Orin. Don't ruin our celebration."

Iggy kept his hand pressed to the barrel as Orin moved the gun to Iggy's chest. He felt Mami's rosary against the back of his hand.

A horse neighed.

Iggy flipped his father's butcher blade around and quietly held it to Orin's belly button. He lightly pressed the tip into Orin's flesh. Orin's eyes flicked down to the blade.

"You pull that trigger and I'll spill your guts all over our feet," Iggy said. "I already fed a man to the Everglades tonight. Let that be enough."

Orin did not take his eyes off Iggy's face for a long time.

"Back off, Orin," Iggy said calmly. "Get that thing out of my face. Stand down."

Iggy expected a bullet to tear through his heart.

When it didn't come, he curled his fingers around the barrel and lowered the gun to the side.

Orin spat at Iggy's feet and yanked the gun free from Iggy's grip. "If you *ever* even think of touching me again, I'll fucking kill you. Let this be the last time you try any of this bullshit."

Orin raised the gun again. Iggy snatched it out of his hand. "I told you to get that thing out of my face," Iggy growled. He slid the magazine out and threw it as far as he could into the dark grass behind him. The horse that Orin had almost shot, a short brindle filly, spooked again at Iggy's sudden movement. Iggy tried to unchamber the remaining round, but with a knife in one hand and a bloody cut in the other, he was too slow.

Orin wrestled the gun out of Iggy's grasp and smashed Iggy across the face with it, sending him sprawling. Iggy immediately felt heat over his right eyebrow, followed by a steady stream of blood that dripped down his face. Orin aimed the gun at Iggy's face.

"And I told *you* to never touch me, motherfucker." Orin stomped on Iggy's chest as he tried to stand. Orin reached for Armando's knife, but Iggy grabbed it and shot to his feet. He held it out and circled to Orin's right.

Orin's face lit up with a smile so quickly that Iggy thought he was imagining it. Orin opened his arms and the smile grew. It unsettled Iggy so much that he kept backing away, knife at the ready. He circled and kept moving away, even as Orin spoke, even as it put him at a tactical disadvantage and in even greater danger.

"What are we doing here, young Guerra?" Orin's face was serene, as if he hadn't just smashed Iggy's face with a gun. "Look at you. Knife. Gunfight." He laughed. "That gash on your head looks bad. I bet that burns." And with that, Orin tucked the gun into the small of his back. Lightning flickered behind Orin. Thunder soon followed. Orin's face clouded over again and darkened. He walked right up to Iggy, stopping only three feet from him.

Iggy fought hard to not drive the blade into Orin's neck. His hand trembled as he squeezed the blade and took another step back.

"Here's how this is going to work," Orin said, pointing a finger in Iggy's face. "Be here tomorrow morning. Early, before sunrise. And be ready to butcher that horse. If I come out here and you're not working on that horse, I *will* show up to your shop with Rana and Lew and do to everyone there what I should have done to you here, just now." He jerked the finger back as if it were a gun he'd just fired and vanished through a path in the mangroves.

The threat hung in the air like a cloud of noxious exhaust. Iggy stood and assessed his injuries. He had no idea how bad the gash over his eye was, but he could already feel it swelling. And his hand was even worse now that Orin had ripped the gun from it as he'd tried to unchamber that last round.

One last round.

The thought went off in Iggy's mind. That's all Orin had in his gun. A single bullet. The man who'd killed his mother was out here, alone in the Everglades, with only one round in his gun.

Iggy slipped into the mangroves in the same place Orin had. He might not know this stretch of land as well as Orin did, but that didn't matter. Iggy knew where Orin was going. As far as Iggy knew, the airboat was the only way off this patch of land, and Iggy wasn't about to let Orin threaten his cousins, grandfather, and brother and walk away. He knew Orin wasn't lying about killing what was left of his family. Orin had killed Mami for less. That made Iggy's current path a very simple one to walk.

So what if he went to prison? At least his family would be alive. And if Iggy had to choose who lived, he'd choose the Guerra clan without hesitation.

Just as Iggy heard Orin moving through the brush ahead, his phone rang. He started smashing his pocket, desperate not to let Orin know that he was being stalked, then realized that it was only ringing in his ear, thanks to the earbud Picoult had given him.

"I know what you're thinking, Iggy," Picoult said right away. "But stop moving. Let him go."

"Not a chance," Iggy said, his eyes still on the path ahead. "You heard him. There's no way you'll be able to get all the evidence you have to the cops in time to stop him from showing up at my shop." It felt odd saying that—my shop—but it felt right. Accurate. Earned.

Rain began pattering on the leaves over Iggy's head. "You hear that rain?" Iggy asked. "Even the Everglades wants me to catch up to Orin." He hung up.

Up ahead, the old man trudged through the dense brush about thirty yards away. As Orin reached the clearing, Iggy picked up a baseball-size rock and lobbed it high into the air. With the rain masking his steps, Iggy sprinted along the brush to the edge of the clearing on Orin's right, all the while keeping the old hunter in sight. Iggy needed to keep his distance from Orin but wanted to get close enough to strike. So long as he had that one bullet, Orin was a threat. But not as big a threat as Iggy.

The rock came crashing down through the canopy and splashed into a puddle just behind Orin like a meteorite. Orin yelped and tensed up as if an electric current were running through his old bones. He spun around and drew the gun from his waistband. Iggy could see the pistol trembling, the solitary

bullet in the chamber becoming less of a threat with each passing moment. Orin sunk into a practiced crouch and scanned the
tree line from where Iggy had launched the limestone chunk.

"Iggy? Is that you?" Orin's voice was firm, but to Iggy, the upward lilt at the end of each phrase might as well have been a neon
arrow pointing to his uncertainty, which was fringed with fear.

Iggy's phone rang in his ear. He ignored it. Then he remembered that Picoult could see and hear everything he did. Picoult
was recording it all. Iggy reached down and pulled the camera
from his pocket. He tossed it onto the puddle at his feet. He had
his mother's killer in his sights, right where he wanted him. Iggy
needed to get closer before he made his move. And if he could
spook Orin into making a dash for the path that led to the airboat, Iggy could glide stealthily through the grass, blade in hand,
and cut him off.

Orin remained silent, eyes and gun scanning the circle of
bushes and trees that surrounded him. The phone rang once
more in Iggy's ear. "What?" he whispered. The rain came down
harder. Iggy didn't want Orin to catch any movements he made,
so he sank back into the dark brush. His eyes, however, never left
Orin's nervous face.

"You're fucking this up, Iggy." Picoult's voice was flat. "Let
him go."

The rain was softer in the dense shrubbery. Iggy could hear
Picoult better, but he'd make more noise if he moved too quickly.
"I *am* gonna let him go," Iggy said calmly, quietly. "To hell. Don't
call me again."

Iggy hung up once more. The earth was releasing its heat.
The air smelled primal, like wet wood and dirt. Iggy could even
smell Orin. His scent carried across the clearing on the breeze
when the rain pushed down harder in windy bursts. Iggy

inhaled the chemicals released by Orin's endocrine system and sweat glands. All he smelled was fear.

From his shaded nook, Iggy picked up another rock. This one was smaller, but no less porous or jagged than the last one. He edged forward out of his hiding spot. With Armando's knife held gingerly in his left hand, Iggy took a step forward and sent the limestone sphere flying toward Orin.

As he released the rock, Iggy watched a stream of water droplets leave his fingertips and trail it. He immediately took off toward his right, to the opening in the clearing that led to the airboat. If the rock didn't knock the old hunter out cold, at least it would disorient him while Iggy moved to the spot from which he'd eventually pounce.

The rock caught Orin just above his left eye. It staggered him. He put his right hand out to catch himself, but he fell over onto his back. Part of Iggy wanted to rush out there right now and plunge the knife into his temple, but he couldn't risk Orin getting a shot off.

So he waited.

Orin rolled onto his belly, then got to a knee. "Fuck. You. Guerra," he groaned. He waved the gun around as if it were a torch keeping the night at bay. At one point, after he'd gotten back to his knees, he spun around in a circle, gun held out in front of him with both hands and screamed until he ran out of breath and fell over again. The gash on his head gushed blood, so much so that half of Orin's face was a gritty red streak so grumose that not even the rain could wash it off.

Iggy realized then that his phone was ringing in his ear again. He ignored the call and settled into a spot behind a thick cluster of young Paurotis palms just off to the right of the trail that Orin would eventually need to take back to the airboat. Orin might be dazed and out of breath, but he was still too far away for Iggy to lunge at. And even then, Iggy had to be careful—he was hunting a hunter.

The phone rang again. Iggy reached up to ignore it but answered it by mistake instead.

"Iggy?"

Sofie's voice cut through the steady patter of rain on leaves. It caught Iggy off guard. He squeezed Armando's knife as he watched Orin.

"Yeah?" he asked. "What's up? You okay?"

"I'm fine, Iggy. But I'm afraid for you. Because you're not okay. You're about to do something rash right now, something you can't undo, and if you do it, you *won't* be fine. You think you messed up by selling those stolen pills all those years ago? What you're about to do is much, much worse than that, Iggy."

He said nothing. Orin was regaining his bearings. He was already back on his feet.

Picoult's voice filled Iggy's ear. "Guerra, listen. Fade into the sawgrass. Let Orin go, okay?"

"Stick to the plan," Sofie said suddenly. "You're almost there, Iggy. Trust me. Tú sabes que yo tengo buen ashé." She breathed hard into the phone. "Fresh start, remember?"

Iggy sank deeper into his crouch.

"Please, Iggy," Sofie said. "You don't want to go back to prison. What'll happen to the shop? You'd be kept away from Carlos and the rest of your family for who knows how long. This isn't you, Iggy."

Orin was moving toward the opening in the path. The gun was at his side. His other hand was patting the side of his face. Orin seemed shocked by the amount of blood on his hand, his neck, his chest.

Maybe Sofie was onto something. If he killed Orin, he'd definitely do some jail time. Even if he disposed of the body, there were enough people who'd seen him and Orin take off into the night on an airboat. And Iggy didn't want to make Sofie and Picoult accessories to murder. They might even be forced to testify against him, and that wouldn't bode well for Armando. And a trial like that would be costly, even if Iggy *did* get away with it.

Which he knew he would. There were no witnesses. Not really. Who'd contradict his version of the events?

"Say something, Iggy."

Orin staggered closer.

"What would your mother say if she saw you right now, Iggy? You think she wants you throwing away your second chance?" Sofie's voice was smooth but urgent. Exasperated, even. He knew that feeling well. But she didn't understand what was coursing through him just then. Iggy wanted to visit onto Orin the same pain that the old hunter had caused his family. He wanted to leave him there dying, alone and confused, the same way he'd left Mami on the street that night.

Mami. He missed her. If nothing else, she was—Iggy balked at thinking of her in the past tense—positive and optimistic. Then he thought about Carlos, how happy his brother would look at his college graduation. How good it would feel to go pick up Armando as soon as he was released from prison. Restoring his new car would be bittersweet, but doing it with Dro and Mauro would make it exciting. And Sofie's smile. What if he never saw it again?

Orin staggered forward. His hand was as red as Iggy's.

Iggy looked down at his own palm. The cut was raw and full of hot blood. He brought the knife up slowly, the blade tucked behind his forearm to prevent it from gleaming. His fist brushed up against the rosary hanging around his neck.

"Damn it, Iggy! *Think!* Who do you want to be?"

Orin's mouth hung open as he gasped for breath. He stumbled, caught himself, and stumbled again, dropping the gun right in front of where Iggy lay waiting. Orin's blood mixed with the mud and water as he frantically crawled around the puddle searching for the gun.

Iggy whispered, "We're about to find out," and he exploded out from his crouch. He reared back and kicked Orin full in the face as if he were attempting a sixty-yard field goal. Iggy felt the bones in Orin's face give way as they crackled like lightning against Iggy's foot. A spray of blood arched from the old man's head as it snapped back.

Orin was limp by the time he dropped into the puddle, arms flailing out like a rag doll.

Iggy stood over Orin and stomped down on his chest with all the force he could muster.

"What was that sound, Iggy?" Sofie asked. Her voice was an octave higher than Iggy had ever heard it. "What's happening?"

Iggy was about to stomp Orin once more when the old man let out a low groan. Iggy knelt on his bloodied chest and Orin's breath left his body in a rush. Iggy held Armando's knife to Orin's throat. The blade scraped the gray stubble on his neck and a paper-thin horizon of blood spread across Orin's Adam's apple. His eyelids flickered open, but his pupils were rolled up into his head. Orin made no attempt to defend himself.

"That was for my mother," Iggy said to Orin. He snatched the necklace of teeth from Orin's neck and tossed it into the sawgrass. "And that's for threatening to show up at my shop."

"Ask him if Orin's alive?" Iggy heard Picoult's voice in his ear, though it was clear Sofie wasn't giving up the phone.

A bloody snot bubble formed in the crater that was Orin's nose. Iggy wanted to crack his skull some more with the butt of his knife as if it were an egg, but the old hunter wouldn't make it if he did. His face was an absolute ruin as it was, and Iggy realized he wasn't breathing. He got off Orin's chest and the old man immediately began gasping for breath. Iggy cleaned his blade on Orin's pants and tucked the knife into his waistband.

"He's alive," Iggy said, kicking Orin onto his side so that he wouldn't drown in his own blood. "But you might wanna send some paramedics if you want him to stay that way."

"Why?" Sofie asked with a touch of fear in her voice. "What happened?"

Iggy found the gun. He unchambered the round and tossed the gun into the night before putting the final bullet in Orin's shirt pocket. "He fucked with the wrong one. That's what happened."

Iggy wiped the rain and sweat from his face and checked his surroundings. The long grass that skirted the clearing bobbed with the rhythmic patter of rainfall. The air smelled different as it cooled. More like grass, less like earth.

Orin's ragged breathing faded as Iggy pushed through the trees and into a smaller clearing. Now that Iggy was alone with the stars, he closed his eyes and breathed. His arms tingled all the way down to his hands. He opened and closed his fists, and the pain was so bad in his left hand that he winced. Someone was saying something in his ear, that the ambulance was coming and maybe he should get out of there, but the weight of all that had gone down in the last week landed on him, sudden and heavy as a panther. He felt like taking a knee and crying. But he knew better than to let his guard down out here.

Iggy looked up. The rain was now a soft sprinkle. The clouds were moving quickly across the sky. He searched for the moon. Only a small slice of its silver light was visible through the passing storm.

Now what? Iggy thought. He looked across the clearing in the direction of Orin's airboat. The path ahead was dark, but Iggy knew where he was going. There was no way but forward.

ACKNOWLEDGMENTS

I've always been a firm believer that if you weren't here when things were difficult, you don't get to be around when things are good. Luckily for me, I'm surrounded by people who deserve much more than I'm able to offer them for their support and kindness. Writing may be a solitary endeavor, but the imagining, sketching, editing, and revising often involve many people, some of whom have no clue that they sparked something that led to writing. The gratitude I feel for the following people makes me an optimistic human:

Ian Bonaparte: Thank you for believing in me, for championing my work, and for being a patient and dedicated agent. You gave me a shot, I took it, and here we are. I'm excited to see what's next on the horizon. Mil gracias, homie.

Christine Kopprasch: Thank you for seeing and loving this book for what it was, understanding what it could be, and editing it into the novel we published. Your extraordinary vision and grace on the page inspire me to think more clearly, deeply, and richly about my work, and about writing in general. I can't thank you enough, but I'll never stop trying.

Marlena Bittner: Thank you for managing a million moving parts on behalf of us writers and for helping us put our best selves into the world. Your energy is bright, encouraging, and contagious. Muchas gracias, friend.

The entire Flatiron team, including but not limited to: Bob Miller, Megan Lynch, Christine Kopprasch, Maxine Charles, Marlena Bittner, Omar Chapa, Emily Walters, Katherine Turro, Christopher Smith, Eva Diaz, Morgan Mitchell, Nancy Trypuc, Cecilia Molinari, and Malati Chavali. Thank you all for all that you do, especially for the things no one sees or knows about. I appreciate you. Thank you to the entire team at Janklow & Nesbit, especially Khadijah Ebrahim.

The creative writing department at the University of Miami: especially M. Evelina Galang, for mentoring me; the late Lester Goran, for his encouragement; and Chantel Acevedo, for being a kind and thoughtful literary big sister. Thank you for taking in an unpolished guy from Miami and helping him smooth out the rough edges. Thank you to Maureen Seaton, for her beautiful poetry and for sharing her love of Uncle Fun's with us. Her energy and spirit are with us always.

To my MFA friends at the University of Miami, especially Justin Engels, Benji Kaplan, Chris Joyner, Daisy Hernandez, Christina Frigo, Megan Roth, Dana De Greff, and Lindsey Griffin, for reading my early work and for giving generous feedback.

David Tulloch: for being an exceptional friend and mentor. You ensured that I had time to write and that I applied to MFA programs, and helped me become a better editor of my own work.

To my former colleagues at the University of Nebraska, especially Joy Castro, Marco Abel, Eyde Olson, Ingrid Robyn, Hope Wabuke, and Stacey Waite: thank you for the opportunity to learn from you all.

Steve Dishman: Thank you for feeding me and for being a smart, enthusiastic, and incredibly motivating workout buddy.

You helped keep me physically fit and emotionally sound. Most important, you are a kind and supportive friend. Shout-out to Poppy and Amy for being awesome.

Gama and Kara Viesca: thank you for sharing your beer, your academic endeavors, your food, your music, and your puppies, and for having my back when I needed it.

Raúl Palma: Thank you for being a fellow writer and Miamian who was at the right place (Nebraska) at the right time (when I was there). Gracias por el dominó, los cigarros, y las cervezas. Write on.

Luis Othoniel Rosa Rodriguez: Thank you for reading early versions of this novel and for sharing your work with me at Jake's over beers and cigars. You stood up for me, you had my back, y aunque me porté mal contigo, has sido un mejor amigo de lo que merezco. Te aprecio, hermano. To Ted Genoways and Mary Anne Andrei for sharing their food, friendship, and tequila.

The staff at Jake's in Lincoln, Nebraska, especially Myles, Morgan, and Toni, who kept the beers coming and the cigars lit while I wrote.

To Pepe Fierro: thank you for bringing me into the Pepe's Bistro family and feeding me (and countless other artists and bikers).

To my sister, Victoria Nodarse-Wood, for letting me tag along with her to butcher shops and meat-processing facilities.

To the late Captain Leonard Zamonis, for being a true friend, a laid-back mentor, and a stand-up guy. I miss you, Len.

To Ms. Carol Díaz-Zubieta, my seventh-grade English teacher, who encouraged me to keep writing.

To Marco Ramírez, one of my favorite writers in any genre, for always opening his home to me and for being my ideal audience.

To Danny Pino, for giving all of us from Westchester someone to look up to and, most important, for his generosity and support.

To the entire Las Dos Brujas community for their energy, power, and support, and once again to Cristina García for making dreams come true. Special thanks to Kristabelle Munson, Carolina de Robertis, Denise Chavez, Chris Abani, Claire Calderón, Gary Aguilar, and Pilar García-Brown.

To the VONA community, for your grace, elegance, and unstoppable spirit. Y'all showed me how to believe in myself when I didn't know how.

Special thanks to Cristina García, M. Evelina Galang, Mat Johnson, Tananarive Due, Vanessa Mártir, Gabino Iglesias, Mary Volmer, Alex Segura, Alice Feeney, S. A. Cosby, Kellye Garrett, Laura McHugh, Roxane Gay, and Jesmyn Ward for being stand-up humans and giving me writers to look up to.

To the entire ForYouCanSee Artist Collective, especially Alex Fumero, Marco Ramírez, and Elena Santayana, for creating a space for Miami artists to come together and create.

To the Grind and all the writers that ground through drafts of their work alongside me for many, many months and years. Special thanks to Ross White and the Grind Council for doing what they do.

To Bryn Chancellor, Marjorie Sa'adah, and Stephanie and Al Pruitt for being true friends, saviors, and allies. Thank you for your writing, your poetry, and your friendship.

To Los Neighbors: Roberto, Lora, Kiko, Loraine, Kelly, and co. for putting up with me in my youth. For their hospitality, I'd like to thank Jessi Crowly, Scott Ferguson, Lynn McCann, Matt Berkowitz, the entire D'Amour family, Marco Ramírez, Chris Koelling and Laura Lampton-Scott, Adriana E. Ramírez and Jesse Welch, the Nasseri Family (Lourdes, Massud, Bijan, and Giselle),

Tía Flora and Randy, El Chino de Tampa, Sergio and Gilbert Pérez (and their families).

To the Members of the Board: Luis Cardona, Rodrigo Ortiz-Meoz, Chi Wong, Jason Lowell, and Christopher Pardo. Thank you for urging me to keep writing and for being my brothers despite the fact that I'm me.

To Laz Dominguez, Manny Ramírez, and Paco Pino: I've got the dominoes and cigars ready. Y'all bring the beer.

To Arlo Haskell and the entire Key West Literary Seminar team for allowing me to complete a draft of this novel in Key West.

To P. Scott Cunningham and the entire O, Miami crew for all the amazing work you do in Miami.

To Dr. Crystal Alberts, for including me in all the amazing activities that take place at the University of North Dakota Writers Conference.

To the staff at the Desert Nights, Rising Stars Writers Conference, and my cohort of fellows there, especially Bruce Owens Grimm, Gionni Ponce, Reyes Ramirez, Peggy Robles-Alvarado, and Brian Lin.

To Mitchell Kaplan, Cristina Nosti, and everyone at Books & Books. To all the independent bookstores who've welcomed me. I know that heaven exists because I've spent afternoons wandering your stacks. And to all my fellow booksellers: You dabble in magic, make homes, create communities, and foster curiosity. You just might save the world.

To all the students at Homestead Senior High: You are so smart, so curious, so kind, and so humble; you amaze me with your brilliance and unbreakable sense of humor. Thank you for entrusting me with your time and attention, two things I hold sacred, and for letting me be a small part of your lives. You are the future, and that gives me hope.

Finally, I'd like to thank Sandra. Tú sabes por qué te aprecio, ahora y siempre. You inspire me each day with your hard work and dedication to us, to your profession, and to our family and friends. I am awed by your ability to remain unflappable even when life lands haymakers that would obliterate most people. I appreciate your love and support in ways I can't fully express, and I admire your ability to make things happen and to shape the world around you. From your lips to the universe's ears. Now and always. Te amo. Gracias por todo.

If I've forgotten anyone, please know it might have slipped my mind but you're in my heart.

And thank you to anyone who read this book. There's no magic without you.

ABOUT THE AUTHOR

Alejandro Nodarse holds an MFA from the University of Miami and a master's degree in English literature from Florida State University. A former independent bookseller, he is an alum of Las Dos Brujas Writers' Workshop and staff member of the VONA Writers Conference. *Blood in the Cut* is his debut novel.